WHEN

THE

CUCKOO

CALLS

By

JO HAMILTON

Sign up to our newsletter to receive emails about special discounts on my books, news and stories.

www.hazelwoodpress.weebly.com

Prologue

Two bags of clothing, a beat-up old car and a key.

Sian glanced in the rear view mirror expecting to see the black van following. No. Just the open road behind, and the open road ahead. Lush green meadows stretched for as far as the eye could see, with clusters of trees sprouting up like soldiers guarding the land. She tightened her grip on the steering wheel and clenched her jaw. There is a butcher's knife on the seat next to her. His tool to taunt had become her weapon.

Two bags of clothing, a beat-up old car, a key and a butcher's knife.

She rubbed her temples with her right hand, keeping her left hand on the steering wheel. She knew this feeling. A migraine was coming on, probably from clenching her jaw so tight. She reached into the glove department for pain killers. She'd left them in the bathroom. Damn! She'll have to sleep this one off in the dark, once she arrived.

Alice said to plan her escape. She said: find a secure place of succour to move to. Pack lightly, take only the essentials. Leave when *he* is not home, she said. Buy another cell phone and give the number to only five people you trust. Only five. Smash up your old phone. Leave with the intention of never returning. Ever! She gave Sian a card to a women's refuge in Lakesford. But Sian was lucky to have another option. A house, no it's more of a shack that belonged to her Great Aunt May. Sian inherited it when Aunt May died two and a half years ago. She had failed to attend the funeral which riled her mother. The excuse she gave was she was too busy at work, and there was no-one to cover if she took the day off to travel there. The real reason was, she wasn't allowed to go anywhere alone without *his* approval. She never told *him* about her Great Aunt May. She also kept from *him* that she'd inherited May's shack. Maybe deep down in her subconscious, she knew that one day she will need to go there to start again. The childhood memories of her summers spent in Woodville at Aunt May's were far too beautiful to be tainted by *him*. She had to keep some things sacred.

It will be a mess. She expected to see a crumbling shack, a spring wind away from falling down, with mice scurrying through the kitchen cupboards and cockroaches hiding in the plumbing. She expected to see windows smashed and the garden overgrown with wild grasses.

Two bags of clothing, a beat-up old car, a key, a butcher's knife and a run-down shack.

Sian brought a new cell and gave her new number to no-one. She had loved ones, friends and family. But her safety was dependant on *him* never knowing where she was. And if *he* tried to throw his weight around, like *he* was so good at doing, by threatening those Sian cared for, they might break. Therefore no one will know she was planning this, although most will be relieved for her.

No one knew except Alice, her councillor. But even Alice doesn't know about Mayfields.

ONE

Four Days Later

It was better than Sian imagined, only just. The windows were intact and the building itself was solid - the nearby forest a good wind breaker. But there were signs of mice, trails of little black poop in the cupboards and on the wooden floor and larger poop, possibly from a stoat or cat, piled up in corners. No signs of roaches, yet.

The room upstairs was Auntie May's bedroom and that was strangely perfect. Her bed was made, the duvet cover smoothed down without bumps, exactly how she liked it. The only things out of place were a few autumn leaves lying on the floorboards from an open window. The black and white photograph of Great Aunt May's parents, the Fields, still hung on her bedroom wall opposite the bed, and a painting of green and brown swirls on the wall opposite the window. 'Aunt May's attempt at abstract painting,' Sian remembered her mother saying.

This was where she died. Overnight and in her sleep. This was the house she was raised in, an only child who grew to be a spinster, rarely leaving Mayfields to stay elsewhere. In fact, Sian was certain that the only travel May did was into town for groceries. Her parents the Fields, named their only daughter after the land they lived on and she remained there until her death - Mayfields. May Fields. You got to love their humour.

Sian was pretty sure she was happy that way, too. Not everyone hungered for relationships and adventures in big cities. Sian smiled as she brushed the dust off the photograph. May was a happy woman. She was robust and independent and perfectly contented just staying where she was, reading her books and weeding the vegetable garden. Sian reminisced about the small selection of particularly interesting children's books that May read to Sian when she came to stay. Sian remembers the voices she'd use for the different characters; the characters were animals, animals that May said all live in the forest.

A cool breeze whistled through the open window and Sian shivered. She stood up to close the window, gazing down at the expanse of green forest. A memory of a boy named...she scratched her head, trying to remember. He was a kid from the neighbourhood, from a large family. Their house was on the west side of the river, opposite the forest. *What was his name?*

Turning her back on the forest she looked again at May's comfortable bed, and wondered if she was game enough to sleep there tonight. Up until now she had been sleeping on the couch downstairs, just because it unsettled her to sleep in a bed someone died in, especially someone she knew and loved. There's a small bedroom downstairs, where Sian slept as a child. But it's now jam packed with boxes and books - Aunt May always had a ton of books, but no bed in there.

The couch was pretty rough. It sagged in the middle and the fabric was worn at the corners. It also smelt of cat piss. Aunt May had a cat called Benny, no, Benny was the name of the boy in the forest. The cat was called Charlie and he was black and white, and doted on. His grave was by the forest. May painted a mouse's face on a small grey rock to use as his headstone. This was a perfect example of May's sense of humour. Even when her best friend Charlie died she still had something comical to say. 'Here lies the mighty assassin of mice, and conqueror of trees.'

At night the house seemed to speak. This chilled Sian's already tightly wound nerves. She slept lightly with the butcher's knife on the floor next to her. With every creak and every whistle, she'd sit bolt upright ready to attack.

The first night here at Mayfields, although exhausted from driving all morning, she still failed to sleep much more than an hour at a time. Her head pounded and her eyes were heavy, still she could not sleep.

In fact when she had first walked through the door, she felt like she was trespassing, as if someone else had moved in while the place stood empty. But there had been no obvious sign of anyone taking up residence here. It was nothing but a strange feeling that came over her and still comes over her now. She did have a dream that first night, of people standing over her watching her sleep. When she woke there was no-one there, only a lingering scent of damp earth and decaying wood, and scratching sounds on the roof. Probably a possum, or a morepork. Hopefully not a rat. She'll head down into town one day and get a cat to hunt the rodents, and to keep her company.

The thought of getting a cat warmed her heart. She avoided having pets and children while she was with *him* for fear of what *he'd* do to them. *He* wanted children, and she quietly took the contraceptive pill. When he found her packet of pills hidden in her handbag, he punched her throat and she dropped to her knees, gasping for breath. She still remembered the look of pleasure on his face as she gasped for air.

She immediately brushed the thought of *him* from her mind. '*He* does not exist,' she whispered. '*He* does not exist.'

***

The days were spent cleaning and mending, bringing Great Aunt May's house back to the cosy place it once was. The nights were spent in fear of moving shadows and impending doom. She had to keep reminding herself that no-one knew where she was. That was part of the plan. She was to start again. Perhaps create a new name and invent a past much more colourful than her real past, the past that has now been eliminated from her mind.

She always liked the name Ingrid, one of those old-fashioned names that have made a comeback, like Nancy and Betty. Okay, maybe not Betty. Yes, Ingrid will work. And surname? Ingrid Bergman. No, can't use that. She gazed over the author names of the many books Aunt May kept in her bookshelves. The shelves lined the walls in the living room. There are more shelves than wall and more books than shelves. The leftover books are stacked on any available surface, the floor, tables and in cupboards.

'Bone,' she whispered, picking up a fairytale book, of a boy stuck inside a wood unable to escape until the magic word is spoken. She couldn't remember this book from her childhood. When she turned to look at when it was published, she was surprised to see that it was only four years ago. *Maybe she brought it for a friend's child,* Sian thought. The author name was Marion Bone. 'Ingrid Bone. That will do.'

Down the dark, musty hallway was a mirror covered in dust. For the first four days Sian avoided looking at herself, dropping her eyes as she walked past to the bathroom. This was the only mirror in the entire house, not even the bathroom had one, and Sian thought that this only added to May's eccentricities. The mirror was oval in shape, its frame gold and twisted like treacle. Her aunt said she stole it from the evil witch when Snow White was saved by the handsome prince. The witch became so ugly and contorted from bitterness, she couldn't stomach to look at herself. So Aunt May said she did her a favour by taking it away from her.

Sian chuckled. The memories of the summers staying with Aunt May returned thick and fast. Some were hilarious, some a little scary, most were comforting like fat, warm arms wrapping around her thin body. All of these memories were welcomed.

On this particular day, Sian decided to look at herself as others see her. She pulled her long, dark hair away from her face, and inspected the creature in the mirror that looked back at her, horrified that she could be so brazen. *He* liked her hair long. She liked to wear it long to hide the shame tattooed on her face. Today, she will cut it off. She found a pair of dress-making scissors in Aunt May's kitchen drawer and began to cut. She fancied a pixie cut, but with absolutely no experience of cutting hair, she decided to cut it to a short bob at chin level. Of course it turned out to be a crooked disaster, and she ran up to Aunt May's room to find a scarf in one of her drawers.

It wasn't in Aunt May's nature to wear silk scarves or any type of pretty accessory. If it wasn't practical, she saw little point in it. While looking in the drawer, she found a red woollen winter scarf folded neater than anything else in there. When she unfolded the scarf, a reel of yellow ribbon was hidden within. Sian ran her fingers along the silky smooth ribbon wondering why May had put it in here. Ribbon didn't seem like May's style. She left the ribbon in the drawer without another thought, and wrapped the woollen scarf around her head, tying it up at the back. She'd only need to wear it when she went out, and the first place she must visit in town was the hair salon.

The window was open even though Sian swore she shut it. Pulling it shut again, she glanced down at the forest that stood hauntingly below. There was someone standing on the edge of the trees, looking up at the window. Sian pulled away from sight and tried to remember where she'd left the butcher's knife. The doors were locked and the windows bolted. She knew that much.

As she raced to the stairs something made her turn back to look at the black and white photograph of Aunt May's parents, the Fields. She swore last time she looked at it, the Fields were in front of a white wall, a typical studio shot of that era - May's mother sitting in a chair, her husband standing next to her, his hand on her shoulder. This time the background was dark. When Sian peered more closely she could vaguely see the outlines of what looked like the trunks of trees. She crept back to the window and peeked out. The person on the edge of the forest had gone.

TWO

S ian spent some time screwing knobs onto the kitchen cupboards and drawers. She couldn't cut hair, but she could blot pinholes in the walls with putty, build kitset furniture, and use a screwdriver - the basic handy-person stuff. In her earlier life she was a qualified horticulturist, but worked in an utterly mind-numbing, boring job as a receptionist in a large dairy firm called Hillocks. Sian only took on the job to cover her rent when she was made redundant at the garden centre she worked at. This was where she met *him*, Brendon Durie - CEO of Hillocks and an utter bastard. Not that he showed signs of being an utter bastard to start off with. Or maybe he did, and Sian was too starstruck to notice.

She hated the job and wanted nothing more than to leave. But *he* wouldn't let her. *He* said he liked to keep her close. The real reason was because *he* had trust issues, always thought she was flirting with other men. She couldn't even talk to other men without *him* making a nasty comment later on. But that was another time, another life, and not worth cluttering up her mind with. *Focus on the kitchen knobs.*

For some strange reason, all of May's kitchen drawers and cupboards were without knobs. How she worked around this was to keep them open a fraction, so she could slide her fingers inside to pull the drawers or cupboards open. To have a couple of knobs missing was one thing, but to have the whole lot gone was another, and to add to the oddity of it, Sian found one of the drawers contained all of the missing knobs, every single one. She could only put this down to May's mental state as she aged. There were no visits from Sian in summertime anymore. They stopped when she preferred to spend her summers with friends from age fourteen. No... summertime visits really stopped when the boy from the forest told her to go away and never come back to Woodville. He didn't arrive at their meeting place by the stream. She was thirteen, he was the same age. When she finally found him, he was distressed and frightened, and told her that she mustn't return. But she did return. She returned the following summer, desperate to see him. She searched for days, calling his name, hot tears streaming down her cheeks, her young heart splintered.

Sian was too focussed on screwing in knobs while reminiscing of her past at Mayfields, to notice someone come up to her front door. Mayfields was the last house on Tucker's Road, a long, unsealed rural road that has only three houses on it, surrounded by expansive green paddocks. The road stops at McCrae's Forest, a native forest that stretches for miles. The chance of a stray visitor turning up was slim to none, which was why Sian liked being there.

The visitor knocked on the front door and Sian started. Her instant reaction was to hit the floor, and crawl to a place where she couldn't be seen from the living room window. She found the butcher's knife where she'd left it under the sagging couch cushion, and gripped the handle tightly. She waited a few moments for the visitor to leave, but then she heard a child's voice. A child? A child is safe. But is the child alone? She crept to the front door and peered behind one of the curtains that hung over the narrow window either side of the door. A woman of about thirty stood at the door holding a casserole dish. A blonde child clung to her side. Sian placed the knife on the kitchen bench and opened the door a crack.

13

'I'm so sorry to disturb you,' the woman said. 'My name is Rosie and this is my daughter Chloe. We live down the road and I thought I'd be a kindly neighbour and bring some nourishment as a welcome to Woodville.'

'Thank you,' Sian said, then introduced herself as Ingrid Bone and reluctantly invited them in.

'I'm so glad someone has bought this place. I didn't know it was up for sale,' Rosie said.

'I inherited it,' Sian said, instantly regretting it.

'Oh! I didn't think Ms May had any family.'

'We weren't close blood relatives. Actually, I'm not completely sure what the blood connection is, something on my mother's side. But I spent most of my summers here as a child swimming in the lake and running through the forest.' *I've said too much. She may be working for him.*

Rosie nodded. She seemed genuinely nice, but looked at Sian with a hint of suspicion. To be fair that may have had something to do with the fact that Sian couldn't take her eyes off her. Rosie was one of the most impressive looking women she'd ever seen. Her fringe was cut severely across her forehead, dyed a claret colour, and her eyes were made up beautifully with plenty of black eyeliner. She wore a 1950's style skirt covered in little diagrams of ice cream cones, and her black-buttoned shirt was rolled up to the elbows, showing some striking tattoos. Sian could only describe her as 'domestic burlesque dancer' and she definitely would not be an associate of Brendon bloody Durie.

Sian could also tell that Rosie was no idiot and could possibly see through her lies. Ingrid Bone? A headless chicken could see through that lie.

'Well, I made a mushroom cottage pie, I'm vegetarian,' she said, placing the pie on the kitchen table next to the butcher's knife. She glanced warily at the knife, then refocused her attention on Sian.

'I've cut back on meat to save the planet, and all,' Sian said, feeling completely inadequate in Rosie's presence.

Rosie smiled warmly. 'It all seems like doom and gloom at times.' She looked at the oven which was grimy and ancient. 'Does it work?'

'I haven't tried it yet. So far I've been living on cereal and bread. I'm a little scared in case it blows. Besides, there's probably a family of mice living in there,' she said, looking down at Chloe who was taking great interest in the oven. She had barely noticed the little cutie.

'I won't hold you up,' Rosie said. 'We're just down the road if that ol' oven does blow. You can heat the pie up in our oven. Or you can just stay for dinner, anyway.' She hesitated. 'It can get a little lonely around these parts. My husband is away a lot and...' shrugging, 'you know how it gets.'

'Yes,' Sian said.

Rosie walked to the door with child in tow, and hesitated again. 'If you need anything, I'm just down the road, like I said.' She glanced at the butcher's knife again, then slid her hand into her skirt pocket and brought out a folded piece of paper. 'That's got my number on it. Ring me day or night if...,' glancing again at the butcher's knife, 'if you ever find yourself in trouble.'

'I will,' Sian said, taking the paper. 'Actually, there is something you can help me with,' untying the scarf from around her head to reveal a mop of dishevelled hair underneath.

Rosie's mouth dropped open in shock. 'I'm sorry, but who did this to you?'

'No-one did this. I did it to myself. I got sick of long hair.'

'Let me sort that out,' Rosie said, reaching for a strand of Sian's hair that was quite a bit longer than the rest, a strand that had obviously escaped the wrath of the scissors. Sian pulled away. 'Come over to my place tomorrow. I'll sort that out, hon.'

'One more thing,' Sian said, 'I need a cat for the mice.'

Rosie chuckled. 'You can borrow one of ours, if you like. We've got three cats, a dog and a guinea pig.' She pointed to the sweet child who stood silently next to her. 'She loves animals,' she whispered. 'Every stray, every damaged soul ends up at our house for some reason.'

***

After Rosie left, Sian had a sudden urge to venture outside. Since she had arrived at Mayfields, she had kept herself closed up for fear of being seen. But the great outdoors beckoned, and it was such a lovely day that she put on her running shoes to take a look at what else she had inherited.

There was a fence behind the property that was now lost in tall wild flowers and grasses. Behind the property was farmland, grazing cows mooing softly in the distance. On the right side, beyond the fence was a meadow of lush grasses that stretched to the neighbouring house, Rosie's. But on the left side beyond the fence was the forest, and this was where Sian had spent her summers with the boy, Benny.

When she began to run, her legs felt like lead to start with. It's been a few weeks since Sian has been for a decent run, so she had low expectations of her physical fitness. First she ran inside the Mayfields boundary, clambering through the tall grass, stumbling over unseen rocks hidden by the weeds, and twisting her ankle when stepping in holes, also unseen. During her short adventure, she discovered a raised vegetable garden, now nothing but dandelions and nettles and a tin shed, the door rusted shut. Always in the background was the forest, dark and intimidating and encompassing, but the horticulturist in her was dying to take a look at what species of native plants grew in there.

She ran down alongside the fence parallel to the forest, then froze! A shadowy figure stood still, watching. Only, when she took a step to the left the shadowy figure became a tree. The problem was that trees became people and people became trees, it's the trickery of the anxious mind.

But the returned memories of the boy in the forest only spiked her curiosity. She raced back inside to grab the butcher's knife, coaxing herself along by listening to Alice's rational voice in her head. She climbed over the fence and stepped cautiously in the forest.

THREE

It was deadly quiet just a few feet in until a bird belted out an alarm call, disturbing all the other birds and small creatures. A plethora of fluttering and swooping followed, while birds chirped sharply in fear and aggravation. It seemed that danger had arrived in the form of Sian Tanner, no, Ingrid Bone.

Ignoring all the fuss in the branches above, Sian tried to remember the location of the meeting place. It was by a stream, she remembered that much. There was a large rock too. It was shaped like a bearded man's head only giant size, and the rock was white stone. It's all coming back to her.

Benny taught her how to make a fishing rod and a bow and arrows out of thin branches. He was clever and practised with those sorts of things, even as a child. When he caught a trout, he knew how to gut it and then cook it. On one occasion he killed a rabbit, which upset a young Sian terribly. Benny was so horrified that he had upset his friend, that he swore he'd never kill a rabbit in front of her again.

'But you're still going to kill them?' she asked, as a seven year old.

'I have to. That's what we eat. I will just do it when you're not around.'

'We?' Sian asked out loud, as she trod cautiously on soft, black earth, still with the butcher's knife in her hand, ready to use. 'Who were his parents?' She could still remember the look on his face when she began to cry. She tried really hard to hold the tears in, but the cute creature was grazing peacefully nearby, only for an arrow to plough into its side. The blood flowed and so did Sian's tears.

Benny looked as if he'd had the life kicked out of him when he saw those tears. He didn't quite know what to do about it. It was obviously something he had never experienced before, a girl crying. Had he never been around a girl before? Because all girls cry, whether out of anger, fear or sadness.

'You are never to do that again!' Sian demanded.

Benny obeyed. He never killed another rabbit in front of Sian. Although being the opportunist hunter that he was, there no doubt were many times when he really wanted to shoot his arrow.

Sian could hear a trickling stream nearby and headed towards the sound, only to stop dead when she heard her councillor's voice of rationality in her mind. 'The priority is to keep yourself safe.' Sian turned to see how far from the edge of the forest she was. It was far too easy to get lost in a place like this, and a crazy stranger could be lurking right now.

She was going deeper into the forest with every step. The deeper she went, the more dense the growth, blocking out the light of the sun. The forest floor was also disappearing beneath her feet, covered by a green sea of ferns, vines and other smaller plants that mask holes and rocks ready to break an ankle.

'This is becoming unsafe,' she whispered, and turned to leave.

***

It was a pasta dish that was served up at Rosie's with carrots, potatoes and beans. The pasta was gluten free with sauce, mushrooms and haloumi. Her house was a pretty white cottage, nestled in a pretty cottage garden of blooming flowers, with roses creeping up trellises. Her husband works on an oil rig off the coast of Sydney, and is frequently away. To help pass the time, Rosie cuts hair at the local salon, and creates fabulous art in the form of canvas and rock paintings, and craft jewellery.

'You know there's a job opening up at the local library,' she said, as she snipped away at the terrible mess of hair that sat on Sian's head.

'Is there?' Sian asked, genuinely interested.

'It's only a few hours per week, but it might be a way to meet some of the locals, if you're planning on staying a while, that is.'

'I'll go in and apply,' Sian said, imagining herself as a librarian, stacking the books neatly in alphabetical order.

'It's mainly run by volunteers, but volunteers can become unreliable, I guess. What's the point turning up for work when you don't get paid for it, especially if the boss is mean?'

'And is the boss mean?' Sian asked.

'I don't think so.' Chloe was playing quietly in the corner when a large, fluffy, black and white cat emerged from behind the sofa chair and pounced on her. She let out a high-pitched squeal in fright, only to crumble into a mass of giggles when she realised who the attacker was. 'That's the cat I thought I would lend you. Chloe calls him Popo.'

Sian laughed at the name, only for a sharp pang of pain to strike her jaw.

'Are you okay, Ingrid?' Rosie asked.

Sian rubbed her jaw. 'It's been a while since I laughed. My jaw was used to being locked in the non-laughing position.'

'Well I'm glad my daughter is breaking you out of the non-laughing phase,' Rosie said, then hesitated as if she wanted to say more, but stopped herself.

Sian knew she was a curiosity to Rosie and probably the village folk. This awkward girl in her late twenties turns up without warning in a beat-up old car, moves into the Mayfields house once owned by a spinster, cuts her hair short, has no visitors and keeps to herself. You'd expect that behaviour from an old, anti-social hermit, not a young, attractive person like Sian.

'You know the forest is haunted?' Rosie asked suddenly, after a brief silence.

'McCrae's Forest?'

'Yes. They say there are forest folk who live in there who can't leave,' she said, sarcastically.

'Why can't they leave?'

Rosie uses a dustbuster to vacuum up the fallen hair on the floor and over Sian's neck and shoulders. 'Apparently,' rolling her eyes, 'they turn into dust if they leave the boundaries of the forest.'

'Are they ghosts?' Sian asked, genuinely interested.

'Figments in old folks' imaginations, more like.'

'Have you seen anyone?' Sian asked.

'That forest is creepy,' she said. 'Sometimes it feels like you're being watched.'

'And you saw someone watching you?'

'Well no, not really. There was this one time when the dog, not the current dog but our last dog Baron, went missing. Nate and I went looking for him, at night. That dog was my husband's pride and joy. I think he loved him more than me. Anyway, we drove past that forest and saw several lights amongst the trees, like torches. So we got out of the car to take a look. The lights suddenly went out and Baron appeared from nowhere wagging his tail. From that day onwards, Baron would take himself for a walk, heading straight past your place into the forest. He'd stay in there for two to three hours, then head back home. My husband hated Baron going in there, I think he was jealous that the dog liked the forest and the forest people more than home. So he chained him up to his kennel. But Baron became depressed. The happy lifeblood just seemed to drain out of him. Until one day, he just died.'

'Do you think the forest people were feeding him?'

'Possibly feeding him something nicer than what we gave him. I wondered if it had something to do with your Aunt May. She liked to go into that forest, too.'

'You saw her go in?'

'I've seen her go in a few times. One time when I was walking the dog down to the end of the road, I saw your Aunt May acting peculiarly, with a crown of flowers in her hair and long strips of yellow ribbon in her hands, dancing and singing. I've also seen her having an animated conversation with an invisible person. She always stood in the canopy of the trees.'

The yellow ribbon.

'How did you know they were invisible if they were hidden in the trees?'

'Because I crept around the side to take a look at who she was talking to, and there was no-one there. I'm sorry. I hope I'm not offending you. I bet you were close to your Aunt.'

'I was back when I was a child. I loved her. I longed for the summer holidays, just so I could get away from my mother and come here to see her, and venture into the forest. But I hadn't seen her for years. My Aunt was always odd, eccentric shall we say, but never mad. What you saw sounds like madness, losing her marbles.'

'Maybe,' Rosie said, then paused a moment. 'You may call it madness but she was happy. I didn't know her long. She died not long after we moved here, so you could say I didn't really know her at all. But I remember her being happy. She'd go into the forest an old lady, and come out with a spring in her step and flowers in her hair.'

'Mad people are happy because they're living in the past,' Sian said, then thought about it a moment. Aunt May's life consisted of reading books, gardening, running the house and going into town. She was a spinster recluse. What was in her past that would make her so happy? Perhaps it was the summers spent with Sian. Or was there a side to May no one knew about? A mystery. A secret.

Sian was reluctant to talk about the forest boy she played with as a child. Benny the forest boy, who was her first kiss and her first love. The forest boy, who was becoming more vivid in her mind as the days passed by at Mayfields. Whatever happened to him? *It's a secret.*

FOUR

Sian woke to a gentle kiss on her cheek. Popo the black and white cat borrowed from Rosie and Chloe, was purring like a chainsaw, and the morning light was streaming through the crack in the curtains. This was the first night since she arrived at Mayfields that she had spent a night in a bed, May's bed, and it was also the first night in months that she had slept the entire night.

The man who kissed her cheek was only a dream, she was sure of that. Although that same damp-earth scent lingered as it had before. It felt like someone was in her room, and the window was open again, which made Sian a little panicked thinking *he* had found her. She rushed down the stairs and checked the doors. They were all locked. The windows were shut and nothing had been tampered with.

'We're okay,' she said to Popo. Popo didn't care; he was more interested in breakfast.

Rosie told her that Popo was a good guard cat. If someone was trying to break in he'd scratch the carpet, jump on you, meow and do whatever it took to wake you up. This made Sian wonder why she chose a cat for her that would do that, if Rosie didn't suspect Sian was running away from something, or someone. One day she'll confess everything to this new friend, even her real name. But for now she had to keep hidden and out of the way of harm, and trusting people would come gradually.

Sian caught her reflection in the witch's mirror. Her hair was the pixie style that she requested from Rosie, short and cute, too short to hide her shame, too short to hide a bruise. If *he* was to find her, she would be prepared to fight to the death. *His* death, not hers. Hence the butcher's knife, that had been her ally and refuge up until now.

It was raining lightly by the time Sian had showered and dressed. The sun still shone in the part of the sky not covered by menacing cloud, which made the soft rain sparkle like glitter. It was a beautiful sight and while looking out at the forest, she swore she could see someone standing there on the edge of the trees, looking her way.

Sian shook the image from her mind, jumping into her car to head into town to pick up an application form at the library, and pick up a few supplies from the hardware store. She needed sandpaper to scrub the old olive coloured paint off the kitchen cupboard doors and drawers, and to buy fresh paint. She fancied a light aqua colour for the cupboards and a butter yellow for the walls. Immediately, a small voice in her head ridiculed her colour choices, only for Sian to say out loud, 'It's my house, I can paint it whatever I like. Besides, you don't exist anymore.'

The trip into town was met with many friendly greetings, especially from retired old men, and some suspicious looks and whispers, mostly from retired old women. She picked up the supplies she needed and asked for an application form at the library. An old woman with the name 'Mavis' on her name badge glanced at her over her spectacles, and asked if she was the lass who had moved into the Mayfields house.

'Yes, I am. I inherited the house.'

'And your name is?' cocking her head at Sian. Her hair was long and silver and pulled up tightly into a bun. When she shook her head, her silver bun wobbled, which Sian found quite amusing to watch.

'Ingrid Bone,' Sian answered.

'That's a strange name.'

'Yes, my mother is a strange person.'

'Only child are you?'

'No. I have an older brother who never spent any time with Aunt May, so he inherited diddly squat.'

The old woman glared at Sian for a moment as if reading her thoughts, and then her stony face cracked into a smile. 'I think I like you,' she said. 'Have you had any experience in a library?'

'No.'

'Do you read books?'

'Yes.'

'Have you ever been inside a library before?'

'Yes, many times.'

'Then you have had experience. Do you know your alphabet?'

'Yes.'

'Good. You've got the job.'

'But I...'

'You'll start on Monday. We need you here two hours every day, Monday to Friday. You can choose which hours of the day you want to work, it doesn't really matter.'

'Okay, great. Thank you.' Sian paused, before she turned to leave.

'Yes?' the librarian peered at her over her spectacles.

'Did you know my Aunt?'

'Yes, everybody knew your Aunt.'

'I mean did you know her properly, as a friend.'

'Yes, I did. In fact we had been very good friends for years.' She dropped her eyes to scan the form Sian had filled in. 'I remember going for tea a few times while a child relative was staying there. I don't remember May ever calling her Ingrid.'

'Might have been a different child relative,' Sian said, feeling the rise in temperature in her lying cheeks.

Mavis glanced back up at Sian over her spectacles, and then cocked her head ever so slightly when she noticed the change in colour in Sian's cheeks.

'But I guess my memory is not what it used to be,' Mavis finally said.

***

'Hello?'

'Alice it's me, Sian.'

'Ah! Sian! I've been thinking about you. You got away okay?'

'Yes. I'm safe and sound. Found a place to hide out in, until I sort my life out.'

'Good.'

'I've cut my hair short.'

'Have you really?'

'I'm thinking about dying it, too. Maybe a bright red,' she said, thinking about her new neighbour's bright, red hair. She wouldn't have the guts to dye it that bright, maybe a muted burgundy.

'Good. Listen I can't talk long as my next client has just walked in. But I am pleased that you're doing well. Remember if you're feeling scared, find someone safe to stay near. Your safety is paramount. Please always remember that.'

'Has *he* been to look for me?'

'I'm sorry, I have to go.'

Click.

The conversation fell flat. Sian sat at the kitchen table for several minutes staring at her cell phone, reflecting on the short conversation with her therapist. Sian understood that Alice was a busy woman, her days packed with clients with all sorts of problems, many worse than Sian's. But there was something cold and strange about Alice's tone. Had *he* threatened Alice? Sian kept her visits to the therapist a secret from everyone. Only Alice knew.

The neighbours called the police the last time he beat her severely. They heard the usual screaming and yelling, terrible swearing that upset their children. A female officer, Sergeant Louise Ratahi, took

Sian to the hospital while *he* was arrested. She had two broken ribs, a sprained wrist and a ton of bruising. Her left eye grew the size of a baseball. That was when she met Alice. She remembered sitting in the waiting room of her clinic, a Woman's Refuge brochure on the coffee table which said that *33% to 39% of women in New Zealand experience either physical or sexual abuse.*

A Government campaign poster on the wall opposite read *1 in 3 women experience abuse. That's not OK.* The faces used for the campaign were all men, mostly well-known sportsmen and local celebrities. But one man they used was an ex-abuser. Sian remembered this raising quite a bit of controversy at the beginning of the campaign. The Woman's Refuge felt he was a poor example, yet others said he was an excellent example of how someone can change. He admitted quite frankly how abusive he was, and how sorry he is now, and wishing he had got help sooner. Either way, men fighting for their women, is what this campaign is supposed to convey.

Sian looked at them with a sense of indifference, as if they had nothing to do with her. Why don't they just leave?' she thought.

'He just gets angry sometimes,' Sian said to Alice on her first visit. 'You can hardly call it abuse.'

Alice raised her eyebrows.

'Sian, what you experienced and continue to experience is abuse.'

Sian felt a sudden rage burn up inside her. 'I'm not part of the statistics! You're just trying to turn this into a big deal, when it's not.'

'He could've killed you.'

Sian rolled her eyes. 'But he didn't. Besides, I was punching him as much as he was punching me.'

Alice paused. 'Sian, being a victim doesn't make you weak.'

A stray tear fell from Sian's eye.

She hadn't cried since that day, when the floodgates opened, reality hitting hard. The following visit to see Alice was when they decided to plot her escape.

That was why Sian felt uneasy by the short, flat phone conversation she had just had with Alice. Perhaps she had come to rely far too heavily on Alice's good, rational advice and emotional support. She was not a friend, she was a therapist. And counselling was what she did, and now that Sian had gone from her sight, perhaps Alice had simply lost interest as newer clients came in. That's all Sian could put it down to. She was only one woman, one therapist; she can't be everywhere all the time.

To put the conversation behind her, Sian began sanding the old faded olive coloured paint from the kitchen cupboard doors and drawers. There was nothing like good physical work to take your mind off things. Underneath the olive paint was a creamy coloured paint and underneath that was the wood. So, she was sanding two coats, of probably lead paint, and she paused to debate in her mind whether she should be wearing a mask to avoid inhalation. She'd have to go back into town to get it, but couldn't be bothered wasting more petrol. Instead she wrapped Great Aunt May's red wool scarf around her nose and mouth and continued sanding. Before long one cupboard door was bare with another seven to go, plus four drawers. This was going to take a while.

The pohutukawa tree that stood gnarled and twisted on the edge of the forest had broken into flower, a scarlet bottlebrush colour that attracted every nectar-sucking bird and every bee in the entire area to a party in its branches. That sight and the sounds the birds were making was breathtaking. Sian rushed up to Aunt May's bedroom to get a bird's eye view of the forest, to find that other flowering trees such as the rata and yellow flowered kowhai had also broken into flower. The green broccoli-coloured tops of trees had exploded overnight into a feast of colour, that changed the feel of the forest from shadowy and intimidating into a joyous extravaganza.

This was most unusual, though. The pohutakawa was known as the Christmas tree, simply because it broke into flower around late December, summer in New Zealand. The only possible reason for this early bloom was that the forest had its own unique eco-climate, which was not unheard of.

While in Aunt May's bedroom, she couldn't possibly avoid the elephant in the room - the photograph of Aunt May's parents. Sian had covered the photograph with a white lace handkerchief she found in Aunt May's drawer. This was to stop herself being freaked out every time she looked at it. Also the frame was fastened so tightly to the wall, she couldn't prise it off.

The problem with spending too much time alone at home with an over-active imagination, was that it could often play tricks on an already vulnerable mind. Far too often though, curiosity prevails and she just had to look. Like on this day. If she had been able to take it off the wall and toss it under the bed to forget it, it wouldn't be there to taunt her.

In all fairness, Sian doesn't have anything against the photograph; in fact she really liked it. But if she was going to make Mayfields her home, she wanted her things on the wall, not her dead Great Aunt's. That also goes for that strange swirling mess on the canvas, also tightly attached to the wall opposite the window that never liked to be closed.

On this day, Sian took a quick peek under the handkerchief. Mr and Mrs Fields were still in their same posing positions. Mrs Fields was sitting on a chair, Mr Fields standing next to her with his hand placed on her right shoulder and they were wearing the same clothes of that era. But the trees behind them were now more obvious and...

Sian started, dropped the handkerchief back over the photo and began pacing back and forth to calm her anxiety. 'This can't be happening. This can't be happening. I'm losing my frick'n mind.'

She went to open the window to breathe in some fresh air, but it was already open of course, so she stuck her head out to suck in the cool, fresh air to calm her racing thoughts. Sian knew that she was not imagining this now. The background trees were like those that grew in the forest. They were ancient and native, not the trees folk planted here in the early days like gum and redwood pine. They were natives, unique to New Zealand. The Fields were standing in the forest. And the forest floor was a sea of red, the fallen pohutukawa and rata flowers.

After calming her nerves a little, Sian had to take another look at the photograph. It was a black and white photograph, yet the forest floor was red. No. She had to have gotten it wrong. Perhaps it was the reflection from the red scarf she wore. Yes, that's it. She drew Aunt May's scarf off her neck, took another deep breath and peeked under the handkerchief.

The forest floor was red. The fallen bottlebrush flowers from pohutukawa and rata trees had covered the floor a blood red. Yet, Mr and Mrs Fields and the trees that stood tall behind them were still black and white.

FIVE

The Therapist

Alice Granger sat wearily at her desk in front of a stack of envelopes. Most of them looked like bills; electricity, rates, internet usage, telephone etc...same ol', same ol'. The five year lease was coming up on her office space and she was considering not renewing it. Her husband had been badgering her for years about taking a year off work to travel the world. They had plenty of money to act on this dream through his high income as a large business accountant, and his talent for investing in profitable ventures. Her income was tiny next to his, but her devotion to her clients and to the cause, was what got her up in the mornings. Not the money. Never the money.

Lately though, she had been feeling drained. It seemed like a never-ending battle against a system that wasn't in favour of the victim. There were support places; Women's Refuge and others set up by religious groups such as the Salvation Army and the Anglican Church, but a victim was never truly safe, and these organisations relied heavily on public donations to keep running. The abuser could still contact his victim while in prison, terrorising her, or send a 'friend' around to sort her out. The sentence served was never long enough, before long the abuser is out walking the streets, searching for his next victim on Tinder or some other dating site.

Sometimes at night she imagined shooting the abusers in the head. It's an easy fix and solved the problem for everyone involved. Even the children of an abuser are better off not knowing what kind of animal he was. Even better, the victim won't go back to an abuser if he's dead.

This, of course, was the crux of the problem for people like Alice who worked with the victims of violence. Sometimes, no often, they go back. This can be heart-breaking for families and friends and especially the children of the victim. There are many reasons why victims go back to their abusers. It's not because they are weak. It's because they or their family have been threatened, or they were raised in an unhealthy, violent environment, and violence was what they were used to. The abuser might convince the victim that he has changed and is sorry, and she believes him. He may have changed and worked hard to control violent outbursts, only to return to his fist punching self later down the track.

Alice reflected on the client she'd had in earlier. Her name was Cheryl Chandler. She'd been coming in to see Alice off and on for years. She had lived with a charming, good-looking man who had violent tendencies, for years. They had three children together, three girls, two of the three girls attracted boys just like their father, rough and disrespectful. The third girl disowned her family and ventured in a completely different direction. She was the first person in the family to achieve a university degree to become a school teacher. It worked for her to divorce her family, as it was far too painful to be involved with their life choices.

Even though this daughter rarely contacted her mother and never contacted her sisters, Cheryl Chandler spoke about her as if she lived just around the corner, her face lighting up with pride. What Cheryl didn't know was that her favourite daughter, Marie, was also one of Alice's clients. Alice knew the truth about Marie, while her mother made up stories to cover up the pain of losing her child.

33

On Cheryl's fortyfifth birthday, she left her abusive husband for good. She had tried many times before, but he only threatened her by taking off with one of the daughters. What triggered this escape was when she found he had been sleeping with a work colleague, and had another daughter with her. This had been going for three years before she found out about it. The child was two years old and was kept a secret. At this point her teenage daughters had all left home to go flatting, and her best friend Sue had moved away, so she was free to take the leap.

Like with other women who long to leave their abusive husbands but refuse to head to a women's shelter, together Alice and Cheryl plotted her escape. She had to set up a bank account and tell no-one, putting small amounts of money away every week. Cheryl's best friend, Sue, was her support person and the person she would be staying with. Alice also gave her the contact details of the Women's Refuge in that area, and a therapist who specialises in abuse victims like herself. It was a five hour drive to where Sue lived and they doubted her husband would bother to hunt her down. Only her daughters knew where Sue lived, but the chance of one of them opening their big, stupid mouths was high, so they had to be vigilant.

While Cheryl spoke in her white trash, dreary way, Alice thought again about the imaginary hand gun, pointing it to the head of Cheryl's husband and pulling the trigger. If only she could get away with it. Then he could never seek her out, ever.

Cheryl seemed positive about her move down south to Sue's place. She spoke about Sue getting her a job in the supermarket she worked at as a check-out operator, maybe climbing up the ladder to check-out supervisor. Sue worked in the office as an accounts clerk and would put in a good word.

Alice could see the glimmer of hope in her eye. But she had doubts about it all. Cheryl had been with her husband since she was nineteen; she was used to him being around. It annoyed Alice slightly that it was only when she found out he was cheating, did she find the strength to leave him. She and her daughters had put up with years of manipulative behaviour, slaps around the face, ferocious, unpredictable outbursts where he'd throw chairs across the room, punch holes in walls or kill the family pet. It seems odd to someone standing on the outside of an abusive relationship, but Cheryl will miss her husband. She might natter on about how much he betrayed her, and spit venom when his name is mentioned, but at the end of the day she will consider many times about going back to him. Women often do. They have high hopes for their men, only to be disappointed over and over again.

Cheryl Chandler gave Alice a hug when she left and thanked her for the many years listening to her go on about her brainless husband. Alice said that was part of her job. This was meant to be their last session together as Cheryl was moving on. Alice advised her to avoid returning to the city, as the chance of bumping into her husband again is high, considering that they have three children together, and the social circles they dwell in - low class, low income, down and out - overlap.

Alice brushed thoughts of Cheryl Chandler aside and began to tear open an envelope that contained a card. She often received *Thank You* cards from her clients, past and present, clients that have moved on to a better life. Some just needed a gentle push in the right direction. Others, like Cheryl Chandler, required years of therapy before they finally left.

The card inside was of a golden Labrador puppy wearing a Santa Claus hat, the card read *Have yourself a Merry Little Christmas*. It was early October, mid Spring, a little too early for Christmas gaff, but she smiled at the picture anyway. When she opened the card it took a while for her eyes to adjust to the large words spread out across the pages. She reached for her reading glasses and took another look. They were words typed on a computer, printed, then cut out and glued onto the card. The words read: *I know where you live.*

Alice reached for the envelope. The address was also typed, no handwriting to identify anyone by. If it was a past or present client who wrote this, she could compare the handwriting to the Initial Consultation form that is filled out by hand. More than likely it was an abuser who sent it. His life ripped to shreds after Alice filled their wife's, girlfriend's, boyfriend's, son's, daughter's head with lies about him. Now everyone is against him and he's blaming Alice for it. This was nothing new to her. In the past, she has had restraining orders against abusers fresh out of prison, and had to call the police more than once on the partner of a client, who let himself into her clinic to let her know what he thought of her.

Most of the time, they're dim-witted with large fists. She thought again of the hand gun. How easy it would be wipe out an entire generation of violent offenders. Their fathers were like that and so are they. This was the likely cause of why she was feeling drained. There had been some nasty cases this year. A baby brutally killed by a jealous partner, the mother of the baby was seeing Alice at the time and continues to do so, although she's now drugged up on anti-depressants and street drugs to numb the pain. An elderly woman abused by her son. Each time he visited, he'd beat her black and blue, stealing her ATM card to withdraw money from her account.

And then there was Sian Tanner, her partner was a Durie. Brendon Durie. Clean exterior, charming, very good-looking. Born into money so had status, with good rugby-playing genes. He played top-class rugby, three years at the Super Rugby level, one degree below becoming an All Black and playing for New Zealand, before he retired after a chronic groin injury. He then went on to become CEO of a major dairy corporation, Hillocks, a rarity for one only in his early thirties to achieve at that level. But then, he was a Durie after all.

Behind the scenes Brendon Durie had a cunning and cruel streak to him. His abuse was often planned, and drawn out. It took Sian months to gather the courage to leave him. Alice shuddered at the thought of the hell Sian went through, only for him to serve no prison time due to his lawyer uncle getting him off on a technicality. Alice had to admit that most violent offenders were thick as pig dung, but when you come across someone like Brendon Durie, you have to treat the situation a little differently. He was smart with a high IQ, and had money and power. To escape someone like him, you'd have to go to the next level, change identity and flee overseas, or even fake your own death. Believe it! Some women have faked their own deaths to escape the fist of their husband, who in the end probably would've killed them. Some women have committed suicide to escape the fist of their husband, who probably would've killed them.

So this pissy, little card from some jumped-up crack pot was nothing new, nothing to lose sleep over, definitely nothing to be frightened over. But for evidence's sake, she thought it wise to hold on to it and slipped it into her drawer.

SIX

Sian was laughing hysterically when Benny planted a kiss upon her lips. A fat wood pigeon had gorged itself on red berries and hastily pooped them out, the majority of the red slush landing on Ben's head. It was a bit gross being kissed by a boy covered in red pigeon poop, but she didn't pull away. She couldn't pull away. He was too quick, anyway. One moment he was cursing like a sailor, wiping that red stuff from his eyes, the next he was there, his lips on hers. Lovely. *It's a secret.*

Sian smiled as she lay on the sagging old sofa, the children's book by Marion Bone opened on her lap. They were about eleven or twelve at the time. 'I wonder what he looks like, now.' The mystery of why he didn't want to see her any more was a curiosity she'd like to delve into. But where does one start? All she knew about him was his name was Benny. He had told her his surname once, but she can't quite remember it, although she felt it started with the letter S. He came from a large family. Sian remembered meeting the odd brother or sister but Benny didn't want them hanging around. She did remember Benny showing her his house across the river one day. It was too far away to see what sort of state it was in, but when she said she wanted to cross the river to meet his parents, he refused to take her. *It's a secret.*

***

It was Monday and Sian was heading into Woodville town to start her new job at the library. If she had the opportunity, she would ask Mavis about the boy in the forest. Sian vaguely remembered a woman visiting for tea a couple of times. This woman, she thought, was a school teacher. She definitely had that headmistress vibe of old, when they were severely strict and dealt out the strap frequently. Back in the days when scaring the students into submission was how to discipline, and memorising the times tables was achieved.

Sian wore the only nice clothes she had packed. In fact they were the only nice clothes she owned. It was a pair of blue dress jeans and a short sleeved white blouse. She brushed her short pixie hair with her fingers and stepped into the small library, where she was immediately greeted by a plump woman with three wobbling chins and an enormous bosom. She was from farming stock, Sian assumed, as her fingernails had dirt lodged under them and her hair was lank and greasy. But Sian took to her instantly when a rich Irish accent emerged, from a seemingly New Zealand exterior .There was also a strong motherly vibe to her, a magpie mother who'd fiercely protect her young and her territory, no matter what it took. Until she needed to protect them, she'd watch them closely, letting them stray only so far.

'So you're the one Mavis hired without consulting any of us?' she said with hint of wit, as if she expected nothing less from Mavis and only pretended to be offended.

'Yes.'

'My name is Genevieve. The kids just call me Genny, because it's easier to say. I'm the manager here. Everyone else who works here is a volunteer, so you'll see many faces come and go. I'll show you to the return shelf,' which was only a couple of feet away in this small building. 'All this position requires is someone to put these books back where they came from in alphabetical order. It's a piece of cake really. Probably more suited to an afterschool job for a student, but Mavis has spoken and she chose you. I have to admit she's always been a good pick of character. After all, she hired me all those years ago.'

'Is Mavis here today?' Sian asked.

'No. She's feeling poorly. But she sends her regards.'

'I hope nothing serious?'

'I hope not, too.'

'Was this a house once?' Sian asked, to break an uncomfortable pause in their conversation, only feeling stupid after she spoke. It's obvious that it used to be a house, as it looks like a character home on the outside but painted several bright colours, and has a sign out the front that reads Woodville Library.

'Yes,' she said. 'It was a homestead surrounded with paddocks for as far as the eye could see. Now our little town of Woodville is growing at an exceedingly fast rate. You know, local land owners have had a permit approved to build two hundred houses down Winchester Ave, while a hundred houses have just been finished down North Street. The pony paddocks are all gone and so has the piggery. People are moving here from the city for peace and quiet and cheaper real estate, since it's only a twenty five minute drive to the city. Except that the land has increased in price, due to the demand.' Shaking her head, 'It's a strange world, I'll tell you that. But if this little town gets any bigger I may have to leave. As you can probably guess, I'm not fond of the city and the way this town is growing, they'll meet in the middle in no time.' She took a breath to change tack. 'Mavis tells me you used to stay with dear May Fields back in the day.'

'Yeah. I started staying with Great Aunt May over the summer when I was about five or six. I loved it. I had so much fun.'

'Well...your Aunt May was quite a local celebrity at one time. I don't know if you knew that. She even got into the papers in the city.'

'No.' *What was it? Knitting jerseys for chickens? Growing the town's largest pumpkin? Or, rescuing and hand raising native birds?* Sian remembered Great Aunt May doing all of these things and much more. The chickens she brought cheap from a poultry farm. They were a sorry sight to behold, looking more like buzzards, mostly featherless. So she started knitting jerseys to keep them warm until their feathers grew back. The pumpkin was pure magic and a ton of fertilizer, a special recipe, and the rescuing of native birds was often out of the jaws of Charlie, the oversized cat.

'She wrote a book. Did you not know that?'

'No.'

Genevieve chuckled. 'She wrote it under a pen name, actually. But word got out and it became a best seller in New Zealand. Then someone let the cat out of the bag. Journalists came to interview her, and as you'd probably know, she didn't like that at all. She'd rather spend her days under the branches of a plum tree, she would, than have her face all over the papers.'

'What was the book called?' Sian asked, finding this terribly exciting.

'Ah! I have it over here in the kids' section. It's still a big hit with the youn'ins.'

'The Boy in the Woods,' Sian said, when Genevieve held up the book Great Aunt May wrote and published. 'By Marion Bone. There's a copy of that book at home.' Then she felt her face burn red at the sudden thought that she had taken her surname, Bone. Damn it!

'I see on your application form that your surname is Bone, too,' Genny said. 'That must be where she got the idea for the name, from your family.'

'Yeah.' *Sure, let's stay with that story.* The Boy in the Woods was an intriguing title, even more so now that she knew Great Aunt May wrote it. *Did she know about the boy? Did she see us play together?*

The story was of a boy who was stuck in the woods and couldn't leave unless someone said the magic words. A simple, yet typical fairy tale type story that is dark as much as light. The consequence of staying in the forest is that he never aged. He became friends with children, in particular a little boy called James who grew up before his eyes, eventually growing out of playing with the little boy. Then one day he met another little child, a girl called Daisy, who somehow figured the magic words, so he could leave the forest. He grew up like everyone else, which he didn't mind. He got a job, married and had a family. It was when he became old and crippled with arthritis that he returned to the forest to become young again, only for the forest to turn him away. He died that day and was buried under fallen leaves and twigs.

Was this boy Benny? Did Great Aunt May write about Benny? Nonsense! This is nothing but a fairy tale.

Sian put The Boy in the Woods book back down, and began to sort the many books read and returned by the local small-town residents of Woodville. It was after 3pm before she knew it, and a hoard of primary school children filed into the library in their little blue uniforms, with matching hats to protect them from the sun. Unexpectedly, Sian felt a rise of anxiety. The library was now packed with people; children and parents and other folk. It became unsafe. Libraries are open to the public, which means anyone can walk in and anyone included a violent woman-beater that she was trying to hide from.

'*He* doesn't know I'm here,' she tried to console herself. 'No one knows I'm here.'

Because she was new, and it was a small town where everyone knew everyone, she quickly became the focal point of interest for the children and their parents. Many came up to her to ask questions and strike up conversations. Others just stared at her from across the room. None of this helped ease her anxiety.

Before long it was time to leave and this was a great relief, but she will have to return tomorrow, perhaps in the morning when the children are at school and their parents at work.

***

Popo was sitting at the front door when Sian drove up the drive. This cat was supremely confident and if a cat was capable of arrogance, he was it. She unlocked the front door and stood at the doorway. This was a little habit she had got herself into, for fear that someone has broken in and was somewhere in the house waiting for her. She would quietly tiptoe around the house armed with her butcher's knife that was kept under the sofa cushion. She was also fearful of entering or leaving the house through the back door, as a large, woody hydrangea that grew next to the house was great cover for a stranger waiting to pounce on her.

Popo though, indicated there was no-one home, and walked straight in with his tail in the air, demanding food. She knew if a madman was lurking in the house, Popo would let her know in his way. Right now he was relaxed until...

Popo sat on the kitchen floor and stared past Sian in the direction of Aunt May's bedroom. He flicked his tail and Sian gripped the butcher's knife tightly. She could hear nothing, but Popo had forgotten his stomach and was instead engrossed in something she could not see. She then followed the cat down the hall to the stairs that led up to Aunt May's bedroom. The cat sat at the bottom of the stairs, green eyes transfixed.

A banging sound came from Aunt May's bedroom. Popo flew up the stairs to the closed door, then began meowing to get inside.

'On the count of three,' Sian whispered, still clenching the butcher's knife. 'One, two, three!' She flung the door open and in a flash the cat raced in after a fluttering, terrified bird that in seconds was in the jaws of the brute. The bird had gotten in through the open window. The window she always closes before she goes out, only to find it open again later. Sian threw the knife onto Aunt May's bed and went after Popo and the poor bird. She managed to grab the cat while he was under the bed, pulling him out hissing and howling. Carefully she took the bird, a spotty song thrush from Popo's nasty grasp and freed it out the window. Luckily it could still fly, although it probably had had the fright of its life.

She closed the window, glancing briefly at the forest. Many trees were still in bloom, with birds flying excitedly from tree to tree drinking the nectar. Again on the edge of the forest someone seemed to be standing in the shadows, but Sian convinced herself it was a smaller tree, or a play on shapes. 'Minds play tricks. Tricks pray on minds.'

Popo went back downstairs in a huff after losing his bird, but then began calling for his tea. He was forever hungry this cat, and his round stomach was showing signs of greed. Sian wondered if she should change his diet. Rosie gave her a bag of dried cat biscuits, but Sian had read on the internet that some cats respond well to a raw diet. Perhaps she could pick up some raw chicken necks and beef mince next time she was at the supermarket. She had a savings account that was slowly shrinking, mostly going on house maintenance. It was part of the escape plan put into place by Alice the therapist, to save up as much money as possible, an emergency fund. The small income from the library job helped, but very soon she'd have to do something more.

This debate going on in her mind was only a distraction from the fact that something was bothering her. The photograph. The bottom right corner of the handkerchief had gotten caught up on the top right corner of the photo frame, revealing some of the Fields family photo. Sian assumed this happened when the window was open and a gust of wind blew the handkerchief.

With a shaking hand Sian lifted up the handkerchief, so she could see the entire photograph. She gasped, dropped the handkerchief, took a step backwards and sat heavily on Aunt May's bed.

There was a third figure in the photograph.

SEVEN

He stood behind the Fields, partially nestled in the forest. Sian lifted the handkerchief again to take a better look. The young man's eyes were a striking blue, staring directly at the camera lens which made it look like his eyes were following you. His hair was slightly messy, dishevelled, as if he didn't care about such things. He was an outdoors lad for sure, but what the hell was he doing in this photograph?

The forest floor was still blood red from the fallen pohutukawa flowers, and his eyes were a vivid blue, but everything else was in black and white as it should be.

Popo was calling dramatically from downstairs and Sian left to feed the animal, but the man's face and his shining eyes lingered in her mind. As soon as she had fed the bottomless pit, Sian raced back upstairs to take another look at the man with the beautiful blue eyes. This time she noticed he was holding a broomstick, no, she leaned in closer. There was a glimmer of something shiny, a curved blade. He held what looked like a scythe. The grim reaper? Or maybe a farmer ready to cut hay by hand, even though there are plenty of machines these days that you can hire.

'This is too weird,' she said, releasing the handkerchief to watch it fall gracefully back over the man and the Fields who...

She lifted the handkerchief again. 'Was this a depiction of their deaths? Was this man about to kill them? I know the Fields are already long dead, maybe I'm being shown their murderer. Wait!

Were the Fields murdered? I don't think so. I don't remember Great Aunt May mentioning that.'

Something brushed against Sian's leg and she leapt in fright. It was just Popo, who had inhaled his food without chewing, and was back for more. The silent assassin. *The mighty assassin of mice and conqueror of trees.*

Sian couldn't help herself. She had to take another look at the young man who stood behind the Fields. This time she noticed Mrs Fields who was seated, had her head slightly turned, as if she had just heard something and was momentarily distracted. It may be Sian's imagination but Mr Fields' right hand that hung by his side was now clenched into a fist. The other hand placed on his wife's shoulder hadn't changed.

She was pulled back to the blue-eyed face of the young man again, and to the scythe he held upright in his left hand. He definitely wasn't on the attack, or showing signs of a desire to kill the good people in front of him. He just simply stood there relaxed, partially nestled in the trees, staring at the camera.

***

The sun was falling, creating an orange glow across the western skies and tingeing the dirty white panels of the Mayfields house. Sian went out for a run, once again reluctant to leave the boundaries of Mayfields, running instead along the fence line. The endorphins kicking in made her feel invincible, leaping over clumps of prickly thistles and weaving through the umbrella head yarrow. This feeling only lasted a moment before she came to the fence that separated Mayfields from the forest.

She climbed over the fence but froze when she heard a rustling sound coming from behind her. Her anxiety was instantly relieved when a fluffy black and white tail emerged from the undergrowth. Popo, Sian's feline protector, had decided to join her, which was good because he needed the exercise anyway.

Popo trotted under the wooden fence rail, while Sian jumped over the top and together they ran to the edge of the forest. Popo, now full of beans and sprinting about the place like a kitten, raced into the forest while Sian stopped at the outside.

'It's getting dark,' she said to Popo.

Popo flicked his tail at her and waddled confidently further in.

'Okay, I'll go just a little way in.' She followed the cat, who stopped to sharpen his claws on a rotting log. 'I probably should have my knife with me.'

The cat said nothing.

In the canopy of branches above was a chorus of hundreds of birds with several different bird calls, getting ready for bed. On the floor below was a mix of brown bark and black soil, with a sprinkling of blood red bottle brush flowers fallen from the pohutukawa and rata. Further along were yellow flowers from the kowhai tree, and nestled under the kowhai was a manuka shrub covered in tiny soft pink flowers.

The further in they went the darker it got, and the forest floor became a hazard of fallen logs, and knobbly roots and vines that easily caught the foot of someone unfamiliar with this type of terrain. When the floor suddenly dipped downwards, Sian thought it was time to head back home. It was a single light in the distance that changed her mind.

'What's that?' she asked Popo, who had vanished from sight. 'Popo!'

Popo reappeared at her feet, completely at ease with the failing light and dangerous footing. Carefully she stepped towards the light, closer and closer. Finally she could see it, a little lantern tied to a tree, moths and other night insects fluttering around it. Further on was another light and beyond that, another.

'Are we being guided?' Sian asked.

This time Popo meowed.

'You speak!' Sian laughed, as she slapped a biting insect from her arm.

Slowly she ventured towards the next lantern, and then on to the third to hear a trickling sound nearby. The stream. A forth lantern lit up next to a large rock. As she drew nearer, she could see that it was a rock shaped like a bearded giant's head. This was the meeting place. This was where Benny would wait for her, and she would wait for Benny, before they'd disappear into the depths of the forest frolicking and giggling, creating adventure with their imaginations.

Sian picked up the lantern from its spot next to the giant's head, and searched for the tree with a face carved into its trunk. Benny did this one day while waiting for her. She was running late, as Great Aunt May had a visitor and she had to stay a while to be polite. If she remembered rightly the visitor was Mavis the librarian, and for some reason Aunt May didn't want Sian going into the forest. Why? She didn't mind every other day.

While Benny waited, he sculpted the face of a girl he said was her into the trunk of a tree. But this tree was a mighty kauri, which seeped gum that made the girl look like she was weeping tears. By the time Sian arrived, he was fed up and just about to leave. She saw the carving, and ran her fingers over the dried gum and cuts in the wood. She was so taken aback by the beauty of it that she kissed him on the lips. This kiss latest longer than the others; their embrace lingered. They were thriving adolescents, and without them realising, it would be the last summer they would spend together.

Sian found the carving in the dark and held the lantern close. As she had done many times before, she ran her fingers over the cuts in the wood. It had been over fourteen years since he carved it into the trunk, and the tree had healed over some of it. Her eyes were still clear, but her lips and nose had faded.

A morepork hooted in the tree above. Popo rubbed against her legs, and she took this to mean that it was time to go. Getting out of the forest, although dark and daunting, took much less time than going in. Popo dashed about full of spirit, while Sian jogged using the light of the lantern to show her the way. Careful not to step in a ditch or trip over a tree root, they were soon out in the clearing under the orange glow of the falling sun. Sian jogged to the fence that separated Mayfields from the forest, and left the lantern on a fence post. This was a deliberate ploy to see if anyone emerged from the canopy of the trees to retrieve it. Hopefully when they do so, she'll be watching from either the kitchen or Aunt May's bedroom window.

Rosie and Chloe were waiting for them at the front door when they arrived back. Popo sprinted up to Chloe who giggled excitedly.

'Bloody hell! I've been knocking for ages,' Rosie said. 'I was starting to get worried.'

'Come in. Have a cuppa,' Sian said, apologetically. 'The cat and I went on an adventure in the forest.'

'Find anything interesting?'

'No,' she lied, then feeling guilty, 'an old lantern. We didn't go too far in as it was getting dark.'

'Was the lantern lit when you found it?' looking over Sian's shoulder to the glowing light perched on the fence post.

'Yes. Strange, aye? There were several of them.'

'Yes, very strange. So you don't believe that forest is haunted?' Rosie asked.

Sian paused a moment, as she unlocked the front door and let Rosie and Chloe in. 'Sometimes I think I see people.'

Rosie smiled. 'I sometimes think I see cake.'

Sian laughed. 'Where do you see cake?'

'Everywhere. Chocolate cake. Chocolate caramel slice. Chocolate forest cake. Chocolate mint slice. You name it, I see it. I'm type two diabetic, insulin resistant, and must steer clear of sugar. I contracted it while pregnant with Chloe. I grew the size of a house while pregnant with her. The problem is, all I think about is sugary foods. Because I'm not allowed it, I want it more. It's like a rebellion against myself.'

'You're not the size of a house, now,' Sian said, filling up the jug from the water faucet.

Rosie scoffed. 'Have you seen the size of my arse, lately?'

'I'm not in the habit of looking at people's arses. Coffee or tea? I have a chamomile peppermint blend that I bought to soothe upset stomachs.'

'Why not? It can tell you a lot about the person. Like, how much cake they eat. I'll give chamomile and peppermint a try, thanks.'

'What would happen if you did eat cake? Even a small slice?'

'I get this carbohydrate addiction kick to eat and eat until I almost burst, and even then I'm rarely satisfied. I also get dizzy spells, migraines, sudden drops in energy, rashes, and I gain weight easily.'

'Sounds similar to a night out drinking,' Sian said.

Rosie laughed. 'Similar. Anyway, the reason I'm here is the Spring Market next month. I have booked a stall to sell my art and jewellery and pottery. I'm asking...well actually, begging you to help me out.'

'Yes, of course!'

'I haven't told you what's involved yet. Nate usually helps, but he won't be here for this one. Oh! I forgot to ask, how was your first day on the job in the library?'

'Great. It's not much of a job. I have to put the returned books back into the shelves. No brainer. Even Chloe could do it.'

'Each book would be covered in saliva if Chloe had that job. She loves to put anything and everything in her mouth. I caught her putting the blade end of one of my shavers in that gob the other day. Luckily, it still had the protective cap on it. I don't how she got it. I usually leave things like that out of arm's reach.'

Sian then remembered the Marion Bone book, The Boy in the Woods, and got up to grab it off the couch.

'Have you read this to Chloe?'

'Yes, we have our own copy. It's a nice story, a little sad and dark, but life is sad and dark sometimes. We shouldn't raise our children in a fantasy world of candy floss and purple unicorns, where everyone is good and kind and nothing bad happens.'

'I agree. Did you know who really wrote this book?'

'Oh yes! The book sellers told me when I bought it. Your Aunt May. Marion Bone was her pen name. How fantastic, to have a famous author in your family.'

'I didn't know she wrote a book. I feel guilty, because I drifted out of contact with her when I hit my teenage years. I wanted to hang out with my friends and boys, rather than come to small-town Woodville to hang out with my eccentric Great Aunt May. Now, I feel really bad about it. She was living here alone, slowly going mad.'

'Like I said before, if she was going mad she was pretty happy being that way.' Rosie screwed her eyes up, trying to catch a memory, shaking her head. 'It doesn't make sense. She was so sharp at times. But you shouldn't feel guilty for being a teenager. The teen years are meant to be selfish and indulgent. It's the last period in our lives we can be that way, until we meet the man of our dreams, get married and have children. Then everyone else becomes more important than you.'

'Rubbish!' Sian scoffed.

'I'm not seeking sympathy. My life is good now.' She played with her dangling earring, and her mind seemed to be a million miles away. 'Did I tell you, it was us who found your Aunt? Well...it was my husband.'

'No,' Sian felt another pang of guilt. Instead of wasting her life away with *him* in the city, she should've been here looking after Aunt M. 'I'm sorry.' The jug boiled and Sian poured the hot water into the teapot that contained dried, loose chamomile flowers and peppermint leaves. She hadn't read the packet on how many scoops of herbs per cup, and had assumed that a teaspoon per cup was similar to what's found in a teabag.

'Why? We hadn't seen her for a while so I went to check on her. To not seem like a busybody, I took the dog for a walk past her house near the forest. I never go in that forest, it gives me the creeps. I couldn't see her and knocked on her door. Her old banger truck was still up the drive. Are you going to do anything with that truck? You might be able to sell it to classic car collectors.'

Sian wondered if that old truck still worked. The engine probably hadn't turned over since the day Aunt May died. Starlings have taken up residence in there now. She'd seen them come and go, their chicks making a heck of a noise as the parents come in with food. Sian brought Aunt May's teapot over to the table with two mugs, and poured the tea.

'Aren't you supposed to let it steep a bit?' Rosie asked.

'Oh?'

Sian sipped her tea. It had a hint of mint flavour to it, but mostly it was tasteless and may as well have been a mug of hot water.

Rosie continued. 'Anyway, I went back home and when my husband came home he went to check on her again. Eventually he knocked the back door down. He found her upstairs lying in bed, perfectly at peace.' She sighed. 'I think my husband is having an affair.'

Sian almost choked on her insipid tea.

EIGHT

'You know, I always found it strange that this house has only one bedroom. There were three people living here at one time, maybe more. So where did May and her siblings, if she had any, sleep?'

'Wait a frick'n minute!' Sian said, slapping her hand down on the table. 'What did you just say?'

'Where did May sleep?'

'No, before that,' then leaned in to whisper, so Chloe couldn't hear. 'You said you think your husband is having an affair.'

'Oh right. Did that slip out of my mouth?'

'Impossible,' Sian said, and meant it. Rosie was a striking woman, tough and clever. A painted woman, with bright red lipstick, dyed red hair and tattoos all along her arms. Her frocks were classic fabrics, and colourful. She reminded Sian of a burlesque dancer. Would her husband be stupid enough to cheat on her? You'd never find another like Rosie, ever. But under those painted lips and blackened eyes, was someone just as vulnerable as any other woman.

'Why is that impossible?' she asked.

'Because, look at you.'

Rosie laughed, and gazed out the kitchen window. 'Hey!' she stood up and pointed out the window. 'Someone just grabbed the lantern thing off your fence and ran back into the forest.'

Sian raced to the window. 'Who was it?'

'A man.'

'We haven't finished this conversation,' Sian said.

'Yes, we have. I'm just being silly.'

'Stay here,' Sian said, 'I'll be right back.' She ran outside and paused on the back door step. The night was looming. The sun was still falling, creating an orange glow over the sky. In a few minutes it will be completely dark. She could see flickers of the light from the lantern moving through the trees, then vanishing. She stepped out onto the overgrown grass, suddenly aware that she was wearing only socks, the wet dew making them quickly sodden. She turned back, deciding that she'll look in the morning. The dark worried her, made her anxious. To be watched by someone you can't see was a great concern. "Keep yourself safe," Alice always said. "Find a support person." She decided Rosie was the support person here in Woodville, even though she doesn't know it yet. '*He* doesn't know I'm here,' she reminded herself. 'No one knows I'm here. I can't let *him* govern my life.'

Sian, feeling like a wimp, turned to go back inside, but then spotted Aunt May's Redline gumboots sitting perfectly by the doorstep. She felt so close at times, Aunt May. She slipped her feet inside the gumboots, which fit perfectly. Ignoring the lump inside the left boot, which may or may not have been a cockroach, Sian ran to the fence, climbed over and stood on the edge of the forest.

'Hello!' she called. 'Is someone there? I had your lantern, I'm sorry about that. I was borrowing it.'

Popo rubbed against her leg, giving her a fright. 'Where did you come from?'

Sian turned to look back at the house. The backdoor light was on and she had left the door open. At the kitchen window Rosie stood watching, her arms wrapped around a wriggling Chloe. The inside light was on and the blind hadn't been closed. Since Sian had arrived at Mayfields, as soon as it became dark enough to need a light on, she'd close the curtains and pull the blinds. It's far too easy for someone to stand outside under the cover of darkness, and watch their victim through a lit-up window.

Again Sian brushed that thought aside. '*He* doesn't know I'm here. Stop thinking about *him*.' Refocusing on the task at hand, Sian stepped further into the forest. The usual chatter of birds preparing for bed had died down with the failing light, and been replaced by the chorus of cicada and crickets, and hooting morepork.

A flicker of light in the distance was a pull on her heart strings. It appeared, vanishing as the carrier of the lantern walked behind trees, only to reappear again several feet away from where she last saw it.

Sian took a couple of steps inside the cool forest. The smell of damp bark and sweet flowers that lay on the forest floor rose up into the air with every step she took. Spotting the flicker of light again, she called out. There was no reply. The light was moving further away now. She watched it, mesmerised by the cicada chorus until it was gone. She stood transfixed for a moment, then turned to leave, only to walk into someone.

She screamed and stepped back. A man had been standing right behind her. She didn't hear him. How did she not hear him? How did she not sense him?

'Stay away from me!' she threatened him. 'I have a knife,' she lied. She had left it inside under the sofa cushion. She couldn't make out his face properly in the dark. But he seemed unfazed by her threats and just stood there, arms relaxed by his sides, tall and straight like the tree that stood next to him.

A whistle cut through the air, and he vanished into the night, leaving the scent of sweat and leather behind him.

'Did you see anything?' Rosie asked, when Sian clambered back inside, wrestling the gumboots off her feet. The lump in the left boot was flicked out the door without Sian looking at it. She'd rather not know, besides her heart was thudding against her chest.

'We need to talk,' Sian said, as she took her place back at the table. 'There's something I need to tell you.'

'Let me guess,' Rosie said, placing Chloe back on the floor. Popo suddenly appeared from nowhere to play with the fraying sofa fabric. That cat never failed to amaze Sian. For an animal so round and heavy, it could run like the wind. 'You saw a ghost. Just what I need - more scary thoughts to keep me up at night.'

'No. I mean yes, I think I did see a ghost. Actually, I'm not sure what he was. A man in the forest,' she began doubting what she saw, 'or it could have been a tree, there's plenty of them in there. Although, I haven't seen many trees run before.'

Rosie wore a bemused expression on her face. 'You saw a man in the forest, but it could have been a running tree or a ghost?'

'Yes. But that's not what I want to talk to you about.'

Rosie sat opposite Sian at the table, only for Sian to get back up and close the blind at the kitchen window, then all the curtains in the living room and dining room. She'll worry about the bedroom window later when she got up there.

'I'm on the run,' Sian said, when she sat back down.

Rosie said nothing. Her perfectly painted eyes assessed Sian for a moment. Then she glanced down at her mug, filled to the brim with insipid tea that she had barely touched. Sian was convinced those eyes could see through the thickest of bull-crap.

Sian continued, 'I need a support person. I mean, my therapist said that people like me need a support person.'

'You're on the run from an abusive relationship?' Rosie asked, completely nailing it.

'Yes. My ex. He has problems with violence.'

Rosie's nostrils flared in anger. 'You mean he's a narcissist arsehole?'

'I guess you could call him that. He doesn't know I'm here. I had to escape without telling anyone.'

'Not even your family knows you're here?'

'No,' she said, as a heavy pang of guilt struck her. 'It sounds awful, but he might-'

'-Threaten them into telling him where you are,' Rosie interrupted. 'If only I had pursued my alternative career.'

'What was that?'

'Killer of arseholes.'

Sian fell silent. She could sense the suppressed fury within Rosie. Women hate seeing other women being abused. It's a thing. We become equally enraged and protective at the same time. In matriarch-led societies, such as hyena, elephant and dolphins families, male against female abuse or infant abuse doesn't exist. Why? The females protect other females and their infants by creating a tight community around them. If an adult male were to intrude aggressively he'd get a swift boot, and be immediately excluded from the herd. Or in the hyena's case, be ripped apart, since males are smaller. It's an instinctive female reaction. It's a form of protection.

'I'm joking,' Rosie said finally. 'Actually, I'm not joking. It had crossed my mind to fill the gap the police and the law can't fill, by taking down some of these sub-humans.'

'Like a vigilante?'

'Yeah, but to answer your question, yes, of course I'll be your support person. I knew something was making you nervous, and I did have a hunch you were hiding from something, or someone. But Ingrid, - is that really your name?'

'No. I'm just scared all the time. I probably shouldn't be living alone, 'cos every little sound makes me jump.'

'That explains the butcher's knife under the sofa cushion.'

'Oh! You've come across it?'

'No, Chloe did.'

Sian gasped in horror.

Rosie waved her ringed hand as if it was no big deal. 'She's fine. What you keep under your sofa cushion is your business. I have cake crumbs under mine.'

Sian laughed. A warm feeling of happiness came over her. She felt lighter and freer for telling Rosie, and she couldn't pick a better hyena to be her support person. 'Sian is my name.'

'Sian? Great name!'

'It's Irish, spelt S.I.A.N. But it's pronounced Sharne.'

'Cool! I love it.' She suddenly turned solemn. 'I guess after being in an abusive relationship you became distrustful of men.'

'My life is dictated by my past. Threats he made... I guess it will fade away over time.'

'Time heals all wounds, so the saying goes. It's a brave act living alone out in the middle of nowhere.'

'I'm constantly scared of my own shadow. I tell myself a thousand times a day that *he* doesn't know I'm here. But still, I get jumpy and check the doors are locked several times per day.'

'What would he do if he did find out you're here?' Rosie asked, clenching her fists.

'Kill me. I'm pretty sure of that. It was my therapist who told me I had to have an escape plan, or end up as another statistic.'

'Why is he not in prison?'

'He was in custody for a short time, then he was released and he hunted me down. There were complications with the case and he got off. Witnesses recoiled due to threats etcetera, and something else to do with contaminated evidence. He comes from the Durie family. I don't know if you've heard of them. There are five brothers who have done well in their chosen careers. One is a lawyer, another is a sports physician, a school principle, a financial speculator and a sports broadcaster. My ex, sorry but I shall never utter his name, is the son of the sport's physician. But they're all the same, apparently. Clean and shiny on the outside, but peel back a layer to find rust and scum on the inside. And when one Durie falls the others gather to pick him up. The lawyer came to the rescue and unfortunately for me, he was a very good lawyer.'

Rosie shook her head, horrified by what she was hearing. 'I guess I'm lucky to have my husband. He may be a cheat, but he'd never lay a hand on me.'

'Are you sure he's a cheat?' Sian asked, still finding it hard to believe the man could be so stupid.

'No. I have no proof. He works very hard and I punish him by accusing him of having another woman.'

'Have you accused him to his face?'

'No. I would never let my vulnerabilities show. First, I would have to gather evidence, to make the accusation. Anyway, enough of talking about me...you said you saw a man in the forest?'

'Yes. But you see that's my problem, he could've been a perfectly nice man, but I yell and scream at him saying I've got a knife.'

'Because you're assuming he'll be like your ex, Durie?'

'Yes.'

'He could've been the man of your dreams,' she said, nodding in the direction of the forest. 'or, one of the Sorensons.'

'Who?'

'The Sorensons. They're hunter and gatherer types. They often go into McCrae's Forest to hunt possum or goat.'

'Sorenson,' Sian said slowly, the name rolling off her tongue. *Benny Sorenson,* she said in her mind.

'Did he say anything to you?' Rosie asked.

'No. He stood right behind me, and I turned around and walked into him. The light wasn't good.'

'And he said nothing? That's pretty rude, and a little creepy. That could only mean that he was a Sorenson.'

'Sorensons are creepy people?'

'Uncouth, uncultured, unclean, uncivilised. I could keep going if you like.'

'What would he be doing in there at night, anyway?' Sian asked.

'What were *you* doing in there?'

'I was trying to catch the person that those lanterns belong to.'

'Why?' Rosie asked, curiously.

Sian shrugged. 'Because it's all so mysterious. And I wonder if my Great Aunt knew something about that forest that we don't.'

'Like, it's a magic forest?'

'It may be.'

'It's a creepy forest. But your aunt seemed to love it.'

Sian pondered for a moment, her imagination going wild. 'I wonder if it's not just birds and lizards that live in there.'

'You think a village of people live there?'

'Maybe.'

'Wouldn't we see them, if that was the case? Wouldn't they venture out of the forest, and head down to the shops or to the takeaway bar?'

'They could be self-sufficient,' Sian suggested.

'No-one is that self-sufficient,' Rosie argued.

'If I head further in I might find houses and a vegetable garden.'

Rosie smiled. She enjoyed the company of someone idealistic. Sian probably had that same romantic idealism towards her Durie ex-partner. *He's an artist. He's complicated. He has difficulty expressing his emotions. He gets angry sometimes, we all get angry.*

'You might come across leprechauns and Taniwha, as well.'

NINE

'Not to your taste?' Mavis asked, as Sian cringed at a couple of romance books, the classic covers with a woman falling into the arms of a big handsome man.

'No. Do people really read this pseudo rubbish?' Sian asked.

'Oh yes. Romance is a very popular genre, mostly for women of course, who long to escape the humdrum of everyday life.'

'But life is never like this.'

'Of course it's not, that's why people read them.'

Sian slid the books into their correct place on the shelf in the *Romance* section. 'Tell me about my Aunt.'

'Well, she was a little crazy.'

This comment made Sian chuckle. 'The common theme of my Great Aunt,' she said.

'She had a big heart. She knew quite a bit about wildlife, the native plants and birds as well as the introduced species.' She paused to collect a memory. 'She had many little sayings and old wives' tales. I remember one thing she used to say when the shining cuckoo began to call, "Sian's birthday". She'd stop mid-sentence at the sound of the bird's song and say, "Sian's birthday".'

Sian's cheeks burned red.

'Sian's birthday?'

'Yes. I always thought her great niece was Sian. But you're her great-niece and you're Ingrid. Sian was probably an old cat or dog.

The shining cuckoos begin to call at the beginning of October. Have you heard them?'

'No.' Sian's birthday was on the 3rd of October, the day she left the city and *him,* for good.

'I'm sure you have, but you may not identify their call as anything special. You'll also hear the grey warbler singing their song. It's a great song for such a tiny bird. Now you're living next to the forest you should try to identify your neighbours. You'll be spending quite a bit of time together. How long do you think you will be staying here in Woodville?'

Sian immediately thought of the man in the dark, rather than birds. 'Ah, I'm not sure.'

'You're not going to sell May's place, are you?'

'No. I haven't thought about it. I just wanted a fresh start. I recently broke up with my boyfriend and thought, why not come down to Woodville and check out my inheritance.'

'The first time you've been here since she died?'

'Yes,' she said, feeling guilty. But Brendon Durie wouldn't have let her come, even if she did tell him about it. Her mother came, yet she, the one who May left her house and land to, couldn't manage to get here. Her mother, Bev, was bitter about the inheritance and couldn't at all understand why it was given to Sian alone.

Mavis turned and pointed to the non-fiction section. 'There's a book on New Zealand native birds. You should take it home and study it. The young ones in the Woodville Kiwi Club tell me there's an app you can download with all the bird calls on it. Anyway, it's quite an impressive story about the shining cuckoos. They fly all the way from the Solomon Islands to lay their eggs in the nests of the tiny grey warbler. When the cuckoo chicks hatch, they instinctively know to throw the warbler chicks and eggs out of the nest, so the poor warbler parent has only big cuckoo chicks to feed. They're quite exhausted when the season is over.'

'That's awful!'

'It depends how you look at it. It could be deemed awfully cunning, or cleverly wise.

'So parents take no responsibility for their chicks?'

'Nope,' she chuckled. 'Lay them and leave them.'

'So are the grey warbler numbers good?'

'Remarkably good, considering what they have to deal with. I guess there are some nests that cuckoos miss. Cats and stoats are a bigger problem than irresponsible cuckoos. Anyway, there's an old Maori belief that if the tail end of the cuckoo's call drops down, then expect rain. If it goes up and is higher pitched, expect it to be fine and sunny.'

'I'll listen out for it,' Sian said.

'Then tell me if the Maori legend is true. Considering their relationship with the land, it's likely to be fairly accurate. Probably a better weather prediction tool than what that lot use on the TV.'

'Do you know if anyone lives in the forest?'

Mavis frowned. 'That's a peculiar question!'

Sian shrugged.

'Perhaps the question you should ask is why anyone would want to live in the forest. It's damp, cold, and you can't grow anything in there unless you create a clearing. I haven't seen any evidence of people coming and going, but I rarely visit the forest these days. I take it you've seen people in there, or else you wouldn't have asked.'

'It was just a discussion I was having with my neighbour.'

'Your Aunt used to mutter strange things like that. You've obviously inherited her imagination. There are plenty of local rural kids that go into the forest and hunt wild turkeys, and fish from the river and streams. You know when a fool lets their domesticated animals go free, they don't die like they hope, but live on. They learn to survive and now we have a turkey problem, apparently. They tell me there are pheasants and chickens in that forest, as well. You'll see plenty of people going hunting closer to Christmas for their dinner.'

'That explains a lot.' Ben, the boy from her childhood, often had a bow slung across his shoulder with a pouch full of handmade arrows, and a pocket knife to kill the prey if the arrow was ineffective. It wasn't to Sian's liking, all this hunting and killing. Whenever she was with him, he was always on the alert for rabbits, possums, trout in the stream and small lake, anything edible. She remembered his eyes flicking back and forth, his pale head cocked to the side, as if he could hear and see something she couldn't. Of course, this was likely the case. He only ever killed a furry creature once in front of Sian, but never again, due to her distraught reaction. He must've really loved her in his own child-like way, to cease hunting in front of her.

***

When Sian arrived home from working in the library, she checked the photograph of the Fields, hidden behind the handkerchief. The photograph had not changed, just like this morning, when she woke from a good sleep and checked. The rugged-looking man still stood behind the Fields holding his scythe, and the Fields, the focus of the photograph, remained in front - Mrs Fields sitting in a chair, Mr Fields standing with one hand on her shoulder. Her head that had turned slightly a couple of days ago, was still in that position, while Mr Field's hand is still clenched into a fist.

Considering how eerie this changing photograph is, most nights Sian sleeps well here at Mayfields. The fear of being pursued was slowly crumbling away. She had made a good friend in Rosie her support person, got a pretty good job working with people who were likely to help her if needed. She was doing well. She was okay.

As she sat on the edge of Great Aunt May's bed, watching the handkerchief billow up and down in the gentle breeze that flowed through the window that never wants to shut, she thought about what Rosie said about the Sorensons. She wanted to ask more questions about this infamous family, but Rosie seemed uncharitable towards them, and possibly for good reason.

It was a conflicting situation for Sian. She was eager to find out what happened to Benny the forest boy, and was convinced that his surname was indeed Sorenson. And yet there was something holding her back. He could have grown to be someone uncouth, uncivilised and unclean - just like Rosie said, and her romantic thoughts of him as a kid, would merely crumble into dust. Or worse, the beautiful boy grew into a beautiful man and meeting him may be absolutely terrifying.

She brushed those thoughts of fear from her mind, and recalled something else Rosie said. Why does Aunt May's house only have one bedroom? Sian forgot to mention that there was a second bedroom but it's tiny, and on the ground floor.

The Fields' house was unusual architecturally, not your normal New Zealand rural house. For one, a house this small would be built on one floor. There'd be little point in a having a single bedroom upstairs, going to all that effort to build a staircase, and strengthening the foundations to accommodate the bedroom. It's not in a farmer's nature to bother with all that effort, when it would be so much easier, and more importantly, more practical, to have the bedroom on the ground floor. Secondly, why have only one and a half bedrooms, when most New Zealand homes have three to four bedrooms.

As she pondered on this abnormality, she recalled as a child of about seven or eight coming up to Aunt May's bedroom at sunrise, and knocking on her door. She wanted to ask for permission to fetch eggs from the chicken coop, as that was something Sian loved to do. When there was no reply to her knocking and calling through the door, she turned the handle and let herself in. Aunt May's bed was empty and neatly made. She was always an early riser as she loved to rise with the sun and the birds. In fact it was the birds' constant chatter and singing she said, that woke her most mornings. But being alone in the house worried a young Sian, and she fled back downstairs to look for her. She ran about the place calling out her name. She wasn't in the bathroom or the toilet. She wasn't in the chicken coop, or out harvesting vegetables and fruit in the backyard.

When Sian ran back inside, hot tears streaming down her face, she was about to dial 111 for the police on May's old telephone, when May came briskly down the stairs from her bedroom.

'Why the tears?' May asked. She was wearing her dirty, blue gardening trousers and checked buttoned shirt.

'I couldn't find you,' Sian said, wiping the tears from her wet cheeks.

'I was in my bedroom,' May said.

'But I checked, and you weren't there.'

'Oh!' wrapping her arms around the small child, 'you mustn't have looked hard enough.'

The wind whistled through the guttering, making Sian shiver. She didn't look in the wardrobe for her. But you wouldn't expect a grown woman to be in there. Even at age seven, she was no fool. Even now, she wondered where Aunt May had been, perhaps there was a hidden room.

'A hidden room?'

Sian got up off the bed and opened the wardrobe doors. It was a double wardrobe for two people, May's parents perhaps. Inside May's clothes were hanging, which were mostly trousers made out of corduroy and tweed, along with some nice, flowing skirts. Sian thought Rosie might like these skirts. She could hand-paint patterns and flowers on them, or just leave them as they are. Rosie could pull anything off, except beige. Rosie was definitely not a beige person.

Feeling a tad ridiculous, Sian reached to the back of the wardrobe and knocked on the back panel. It sounded like a normal wall, no little doors, no little door handles as far as she could tell. There was nothing suspicious, just an ordinary wardrobe with hanging clothes and piles of shoes, most of which were very dusty. There were a couple of pairs of men's dress shoes, black leather, in good condition. They were a small size and extremely well made, and Sian assumed they were May's dad's shoes.

Something furry in the corner moved giving Sian a hell of fright, but it was just Popo in his typically nosy fashion, coming to investigate what Sian was doing.

On the shelf above the clothing was a shoebox of a brand of shoes that had long since folded. She reached up and pulled the box down expecting to find another pair of ancient shoes in great condition. Instead, when she flipped the lid it contained old photographs, mostly sepia black and white. The next hour vanished as she inspected each and every photograph, recognising only one individual, Aunt May. The rest of the people in these photographs were strangers, possibly relatives. Some of the pictures were staged studio shots, which probably would have been expensive at the time. Most of them were people captured while doing everyday things, such as standing in a field, sitting at the beach, at a wedding and other celebratory moments.

One photograph was of a couple standing in front of a house, arms by their sides. Sian leaned in closer. She recognised the house, and the couple were younger versions of the couple who are in the photo hidden behind the handkerchief. They were standing in front of Mayfields back before the gardens were dug up and flowers, shrubs and fruit trees were planted. It was just a house sitting on bare land. She had her dark hair done up into a loose bun, while his short dark hair was parted and slicked over. She wore a long, dark skirt down to her ankles and a white, long sleeved blouse, while he wore a white buttoned shirt and dark trousers. They looked to be in their early twenties, and going by the fashion, the photograph was probably taken in the early 1900's.

'This photograph could be a hundred years old,' Sian muttered to Popo, who couldn't care less. Written on the back were the words, *Mum and Dad,* probably written by May, as she seemed to be an only child. Something Sian must ask Mavis about.

Nervously, Sian lifted the handkerchief to compare the couple in the photograph in her hand, to the couple in the framed photograph on the wall. Definitely the same people, just forty years difference in age.

TEN

After having a quick lunch of a crunchy peanut butter sandwich - the peanut butter she brought from Chad's Bulk Bin in Woodville, which has a machine that grinds salted peanuts into butter - she decided since the weather was bright and clear and no rain was forecast, that she'd go down into the forest and spend a few hours in there. This time she thought it would be wise to take a back pack with provisions such as a bottle of water, her cell phone, the butcher's knife and snack food if she lost her way and got a little peckish. It had crossed her mind to tie a long piece of rope around her waist, the other end tied to a tree on the edge of the forest, so she could find her way out again. But finding a piece of rope long enough was a bit farfetched.

She hoped that Popo would come along with her for company and security. It was a strange thing to think that an oversized cat could protect a human. Of course he wouldn't be interested in actively protecting her, but he was alert and noticed things that she was oblivious to. Rosie did lend Popo to her for protection, and in his aloof, disinterested way he was protecting her when he protected himself.

She had her on good running shoes that were light-weight with good tread, but they were not suitable for very rugged terrain like hiking boots would be. But she didn't have hiking boots, she had running shoes and if hard pressed, she could run pretty fast if she needed to.

Sian stepped into the forest, the canopy of trees blocking out the warm rays of the sun, making it cool and foreboding. Like she hoped, Popo who was tremendously confident and ludicrously nosy, followed behind full of beans, scampering about like a kitten. Soon she got to the place where the forest floor sloped downwards to the trickling stream and the kauri tree that Benny had sculpted her face into, stood tall and mighty.

Being a horticulturist, Sian knew that New Zealand doesn't have many deciduous native trees. Many more introduced species which were brought over by early settlers, and later avid gardeners who wanted a slice of the motherland in their new home - shed their leaves. So when you walk through an ancient forest in New Zealand, you walk on black volcanic soil covered in native ground covers, small bushes and fallen flowers and berries, all sheltered by the larger trees. The leaves that have fallen would do so through force, strong winds and heavy rains, and of course, disease.

She found her face in the weeping trunk of the kauri that Benny carved so long ago, and the small stream that overflowed after rains. Up until now she hadn't ever gone further than this point. With one eye on Popo to see if his behaviour changed from playfulness to fear, she stepped over the trickling stream and into thick bush.

Overhead, tui and wood pigeon flew from tree to tree, their wings making a remarkable whooshing sound. A curious fantail came down low over Popo, peeping and squawking, flittering quickly from one branch to the next, diving and dashing about playfully. Popo's large green eyes were transfixed onto the bird. *An easy catch*, Sian thought, watching the bird swoop low over the cat, teasing and taunting, its feathered tail spread like a fan.

The further into the heart of the forest, the more difficult the terrain to walk on. Her feet were quickly sodden in her running shoes which were not waterproof, and she wondered if it would've been wiser to wear Aunt May's Redline gumboots. Regardless, she clambered on until she came to two totara trees, both with pale bark, almost identical. Sian stood back gazing up into the branches. Both trees had catkins, a slim cylindrical flower cluster, which meant they were both male. Twins. Brothers.

She walked round the circumference of The Brothers to find strange symbols like arrows, carved into the wood on the other side. These symbols weren't familiar to her and didn't trigger a memory. She ran her hand over the symbols and wondered what they meant. Perhaps they communicate direction, or a meeting place. While she was transfixed by the symbols, a strange whistling sound followed by something crashing into a nearby bush, startled her. She searched for Popo who was nearby staring at the bush, so she assumed it was a bird.

Carefully she stepped over to the kawakawa bush of large green, heart-shaped leaves and parted the foliage to find an arrow wedged inside. Immediately, she dropped to her knees on the ground to avoid being shot at again, and dragged her butcher's knife from her back pack. She could hear tramping feet stepping through low lying bush coming nearer, stopping right by her head on the other side of the kawakawa bush.

'If I wanted you dead, I would've aimed for your head,' a man's voice said.

Sian stayed low and hidden in the foliage.

'Get up!' he demanded. 'Get up! I'm not going to hurt you.'

Sian slowly got to her feet, still holding the butcher's knife tightly in her hand. She had imagined one day using it to defend herself in case *he* were to appear, but the thought of actually stabbing someone in real life was frightening, and just not in her nature.

'What do we have here?' he asked, bemused. 'A boy, and he's carrying a dagger.'

This comment had Sian staring square on at the man to see if he was talking about her.

'That's no boy,' another man's voice called. 'And that is no dagger.'

The man closest to her looked at her again, sizing her up. 'What knife is that?' he asked.

'It's a butcher's knife for gutting cows and sheep. It's very sharp,' she answered.

'There are no cows and sheep here,' he answered.

The second man cackled at this remark as he stepped forward out of the shadows of the thick foliage. He was thick necked, unshaven and with a large protruding belly. They were both dressed in green and brown camouflage clothing, not army skivvies, but clothes hunters would wear. The larger man with the thick neck struggled to fit comfortably inside his.

'Why did you try to kill me?' she asked.

'Like I said before, if I was meaning to kill you I would've aimed for your head. Instead, I chose to let you live,' he stared at her with his green eyes, frowning as a thought occurred to him. 'Why are you here?'

'This forest is state owned. Anyone can come in,' she said.

He frowned at her again.

'Are you boy or girl?'

'I'm a girl, a woman. I'm twenty nine.'

'Yet your hair is cut short like a man,' he said, mockingly. 'Are you hiding from someone?'

'No,' she said, even though it was a partial lie. She *was* hiding from someone and cutting her hair short was part disguise, part therapy.

'Pretending to be a man so you don't get found,' he added.

'No. Women can wear their hair any way they want these days.'

'Why do you carry a knife?' he asked, swiftly taking the knife from her hand before she realised what had happened. He ran his finger along the blade and felt the weight of it in his hand. He then tossed it to his hefty friend who caught the handle easily, then threw it swiftly at a nearby tree to see how sharp it was.

'Impressive,' the hefty man said.

'I ask you again, why do you carry a knife?'

'For p-protection,' she stuttered.

'What from?'

'Anything.'

'Anything? Like us?'

She shrugged.

He looked at her face as if seeing her for the first time, his expression softening slightly, but then tensing up again when the sound of a car horn bled out, vibrating through the foliage and startling the birds. He turned to his friend who had become agitated, and signalled. Turning back to Sian with his mind now elsewhere, his expression hardened again.

'Bugger off!' he said to Sian cruelly, and took off in the direction of the horn sound. His friend pulled Sian's knife out of the tree, tilted his head in a slight bow to Sian and then vanished into the thick greenery, taking her knife with him.

ELEVEN

The Therapist

'I think you're right,' Alice Granger said to her husband at breakfast. He was an overweight man of good humour considering the load of his work responsibilities who, in all the years she had known him, ate the exact same thing for breakfast every day. A bowl of cornflakes, no milk, covered in two teaspoons of sugar, swimming in juicy canned peaches. He had a dairy allergy. He'd then finish it off with a mug of black coffee. He didn't like to eat much for breakfast, as the evening meal that he went to bed on was rather large.

He looked up from reading the newspaper, a spoon of cornflakes hovering near his mouth, a boyish look of wonder on his face. 'I'm right?' he asked, grinning. That's good to hear, doesn't happen very often. What exactly am I right about?'

'That we should take a year off work and see the world.'

'Are you serious?' he asked, gleefully.

'Yes. What about next year, 2020?'

'So soon?' he paused, scrutinising Alice's movements. But she was difficult to read. That came from having to be a straight therapist, never revealing your true thoughts, never letting your emotions show. 'What is this really about?'

'I'm getting tired. It's been a tough year.'

He nodded in agreement.

'And?'

She sighed. He had noticed her exhaustion lately and wondered if she was feeling poorly, or worse, having menopausal problems, a subject he avoided discussing.

'I've been doing this a long time,' she said finally, looking up from her herbal tea.

'That's true,' he agreed. 'And you feel like a change?'

'A break. I feel like a break.'

There was something she wasn't saying; he could see it on her face. He'd been married to her for almost forty years; he could spot an internal conflict a mile away. He stayed silent.

'It seems like a never-ending battle at times. For every woman I help, there's another five waiting to be helped. The prison sentences aren't long enough; the cycle of violence is rarely broken.'

There was a momentary silence between them, as he clapped his chubby hands together, making Alice jump. 'Right, let's do it! Let's plan our escape for 2020. It may have to be mid-year, after the end of the financial year.'

'Not sooner?'

'What's your hurry? There's a lot to organise. The flights, accommodation, and we'd have to get a house-sitter to feed the cat for a year. Do you think Sarah would do it?'

'I was thinking about going after Christmas Day, say Boxing Day. The kids are coming home just for Christmas Day then heading off to Mount Maunganui for New Year's Eve. Sarah has to move out of her flat anyway in January, so she may as well move in here, and live rent-free for a year.'

'I don't know about rent-free,' said the accountant. He glanced at his watch. 'I have to go. We'll discuss this at length when I get home.'

After he left, Alice began clearing away the dishes as she had done for the last 28 years. It was no big deal these days, just rinse the dishes and place them in the dishwasher. A notification came through on her cell phone, and she trembled. Anxiously she picked it up, it was from Dave. *I hope you're OK*. A sweet, thoughtful gesture. From a man who knew her so well.

She was struggling to tell him about the threats that had been occurring lately. A week ago she had received another Christmas card addressed to her clinic. This time it was a kitten in a green elf's hat on the front, only the face of the kitten was covered over by a picture of Alice's face. What disturbed her was that the photograph used was a private one of her and Dave sitting on the beach in Bali, drinking cocktails. This could only mean that the person sending these threats had been inside her house. It gets more disturbing as inside the card the typed name, *Damon Ridge* was glued.

It was a name she had pushed to the back of her mind. A name she hadn't thought about for nearly four years. She assumed that no-one knew of her connection to him. She thought she had covered her tracks and left no paper trail, no phone messages, nothing. No-one saw them together, she was sure of that. She then began to doubt herself, reliving that evening over and over again in her mind. No one was there, except her and Damon Ridge...and Birdie. *How could I forget Birdie? There's no way in hell he'd ever tell anyone.*

The day after receiving the kitten Christmas card, a text came through on her private phone. *How is Damon Ridge?*

She entered the number the text was sent from onto the internet to see if there was a match. Nothing. Where were these threats coming from and what do they want? Whoever was doing this knew they had her cornered. She couldn't go to the police and she couldn't tell her husband. She's going to have to face this individual head-on, and alone.

Who is this? She sent back a text, after several moments tossing around in her mind the best way to deal with this.

Five long minutes later, a text came through. It was a photograph of her and Damon Ridge, standing under a street light. She knew the location. It was the car park outside Stanley Sports Stadium at about ten minutes after midnight, 8th February 2016. There were no cars parked there apart from hers and Damon's, and no people lurking in nearby bushes. She knows this, she checked. She was smart about it. She deliberately chose this meeting place because it was out of the way on the outskirts of the city, no homes nearby, only bush-covered hills in the front and the beach behind. She had it all planned out to the letter. She'd be there early, check if there were any parked cars or night bathers, or kids trying to break into the sport's stadium. Due to it being a weekday night, the place was deserted, exactly how she wanted it. She had contacted Damon on a cheap cell she picked up for $20. Apart from secret meetings, their only communication was on this phone. What happened? What did she miss?

Taking a deep breath, she replied to the pic with, *Shows us talking. So what?'*

Moments later another text came though, this time a pic of something more incriminating. Alice panicked, holding back the tears. Her work cell rang, startling her. The number was a client, Cheryl Chandler. She'd have to make this quick, her next client was due and these recent threats were putting her on edge. Not the ideal temperament a woman escaping an abusive relationship needs in a therapist.

She took the phone call, trying to sound supportive without coming across rushed, and ended it when she heard her next client come in to the waiting room. Cheryl Chandler was having a weak moment, and was close to contacting her ex-husband. Alice reminded her that she was to contact her local therapist now, and then calmly went through the routine; distract yourself by keeping busy, read out the affirmation card - *I am worthy* etc, phone the help line.

What do you want? She sent back a text to the stranger as she spoke to Cheryl on the phone.

A trade for information.

What information?

An address.

Whose?

I destroy these pics of you and Damon Ridge for the address of Sian Tanner.

Alice swallowed a lump in her throat. Brendon arsehole Durie.

I don't know where Sian Tanner is.

This was the truth. Sian wanted no-one to know of her whereabouts for fear that a friend or family member would pass the location on to Brendon Durie. She had even kept this information from her best friend Nigel, who owned the Brownhouse Bay Cafe. It broke Sian's heart, but she felt she had no other choice.

Brendon: *Liar!*

Alice: *I'm telling the truth. No one knows where she went. She dropped all contact with everyone.*

Brendon: *Find her!*

Alice: *I can't. It breaks code of conduct client/counsellor privilege.*

Brendon: *I want her address by 6pm tomorrow or these pics go live!!!*

TWELVE

'How did you meet him?' Rosie asked, as she stitched a square of blue floral fabric onto a brown corduroy skirt to somehow make it look rather funky. To take an ordinary, dull, unloved piece of clothing and revitalise it through patchwork, was a skill in itself.

Sian was miles away, gazing at a beautiful scene painted on a rock of a field of yellow and red wild flowers, and two lovers holding hands in the distance. Rosie had painted several river rocks, most of them could fit into the palm of a person's hand. Yet the paintings were intricately detailed, obviously done by a steady hand with a tiny paint brush.

'Hello!' Rosie called, 'Is there anybody out there?' knocking on the table to break Sian out of her little spell.

'These are fantastic,' Sian said, pointing to the painted rocks. There was another rock with a frog painted on it, its reptilian skin was painted in such a way you'd swear it was the real thing. Another had a grass snake wrapped around the rock as if it was attempting to suffocate it. Once again, it was cleverly done. Another was of a cute little mouse, yet another a scene of frothing waves coming in to shore, blue skies, and a rocky cliff to the left of the painting with a lone pohutukawa tree on top. 'How much do you sell them for?'

Rosie shrugged. 'Twenty bucks.'

'How long did it take you to paint them?'

'Not long. The rocks that I don't sell, I leave about the place for kids to find.'

Rosie had invited Sian over for lunch to go through the inventory for the goods they would be selling at the Spring fair. She had up-cycled clothing, the rocks as well as canvas paintings, mostly abstract, and funky jewellery. She'd hand-made the jewellery using a clay-like substance that sets in the oven to shape into weta, mantises, beetles, moths and a variety of other ugly insects. Once again they were thoughtfully crafted with great detail, even though her choice of subject may not be to everyone's taste.

'I'm not a blue butterfly and pink fairy sort of person,' Rosie said. 'I love the ugly, weird and wonderful.'

'These insects are ugly for practical reasons,' Sian said, loving this eccentricity about Rosie. Sian had come from a world where she was severely controlled. She was told how to have her hair, what to wear and who she could speak to. Everyone thought they were a perfect, happy couple socialising with high profile elitists. But she wasn't even allowed to speak to his work colleagues and their wives and girlfriends without asking. *He* wanted Sian to look perfect and beautiful - whatever he believed beauty to be, which would change from week to week.

'I hope you don't mind me asking,' Rosie said, 'I understand if you don't want to talk about it.'

'About *him*?'

'Yeah. How did you meet him?'

'We worked together. I got a job as a receptionist at the main reception area at Hillocks and he asked me out not long after. I was flattered at first, and it was a distraction from my incredibly boring life. I have a degree, believe it or not in Horticulture.'

'Oh wow, very cool. What were you doing at Hillocks then?'

'I was made redundant from my job at the garden centre I worked at. I loved that job. So I took on the Hillocks job thinking I would just stay until I found something better.' Sian paused to reflect on when she started at Hillocks, and a memory rose of a couple of female workers cornering her one day in the smoko room. 'I was also warned against him, you know.'

Rosie raised her perfectly plucked eyebrows.

Sian added, 'They said he was an egotistical prick.'

Rosie broke into a sharp laugh. 'And they were right,' she said.

'They were. But at the time I thought they were jealous, or something,' she said, rolling her eyes at her own ignorance. 'He's a very handsome man, wore the most beautiful suits, his shoes were so shiny and he drove an expensive sports car. Up until that point, the only men who showed interest in me, had dirt under their fingernails and grubby tee shirts.'

'There's nothing wrong with blue collar blokes.'

'I know that now. I guess I took it as a complement when he, from a well-known family, showed some interest in me.'

'So I guess you don't see your friends, anymore?' Rosie asked, sympathetically.

'No. On the sly I visited all my loved ones and told them I was leaving. My mother couldn't understand it as she thought *he* was the bees' knees - rich, handsome, powerful. Kynn and Nigel knew what was going on. They didn't like *him* from the start, especially Nigel. He's highly suspicious of all handsome, clean cut men in suits.' Sian chuckled, thinking about her gay friends arguing in the back kitchen while the diners listened in. Their volatile relationship was a draw-card for many patrons who loved to listen to them squabble. And they, Nigel and Kynn, loved to be on stage... well...Kynn loved to be on stage, Nigel just went along with it. 'There was also an ex-girlfriend of *his*, who warned me against *him* as well. She was a beautiful, blonde, curvaceous legal secretary, who I thought was trying to steer me clear of *him*, so she could have *him* back. How stupid of me. I remember that meeting like it was yesterday. She made quite an effort to hunt me down just so she could tell me that *he* was a "controlling narcissist."' Sian paused when she thought of this woman, what was her name, Lori, looking Sian up and down, slightly confused by *his* recent choice. The word 'narcissist' has been bantered about so often these days, mostly towards men, it seems to have lost its meaning. 'Lori even gave me her contact details, and said if I ever needed help to call her. I tossed them away as soon as she turned her back. "Once you're caught in *his* net, it's hard to get out." is what Lori said, and she was right. I now wish I had kept her details.'

'Did he go to your friends' bar?' Rosie asked.

'Yes, just, now and then. It wasn't his regular, and I know after meeting up with me he preferred we go to the bar all of his work colleagues and friends go to, a snotty upper class bar called Metro owned by his Uncle Mack.'

'Ah yes, I know that bar,' Rosie said, her painted face creasing into a dark scowl. 'I wouldn't step inside that place if you paid me. I keep meaning to tell you that I have a wee connection to the Duries.'

'Tell me more?' Sian asked, eager for gossip.

Rosie continued, 'Mack Durie was the one that pushed his wife down the stairs. She broke two ribs and her left ankle,' shaking her head in disgust. 'He got away with attempted murder practically, returning to his job after a stand-down period of only two months. The stand-down period was only enforced due to public disgust. Otherwise he would have gone back to his sports commentating job pretty much after the weekend he pushed her.'

Sian knew all about this. It was all over the news for days. Women took to the streets in protest at Mack Durie getting off without even a slap on the hand. His wife was paid to shut up, and the charges were dropped. *He* had a different take on it and said it was all lies. 'Women always lie to get money,' Sian remembered Brendon bloody Durie saying to her: 'It's part of their nature. The truth is that she deliberately slipped down the stairs and blamed Uncle Mack so she could sue him for a pay-out, and ruin his career.'

'That's a lot of effort to ruin someone's career,' Sian had said timidly. 'She could've killed herself.'

'Pity she didn't,' *he* said, leaning over her shoulder to inspect the news article on Mack Durie that Sian had up on her laptop. An ex-girlfriend and a brothel worker were interviewed. The ex-girlfriend had plenty to say about Mack, none of which was pleasant, whereas the brothel worker had a fairly benign opinion of him. The fact he visited a brothel was juicy enough for the newspapers. 'And that's all lies too!' he yelled, fury rising in his tone. 'Uncle Mack should sue for defamation.' He snatched Sian's laptop out of her hands to take a closer look. He stood for a moment staring at the screen. It was one of those silent pauses that shook Sian to her core, as she couldn't predict what he was going to do next. What he did do next was hurl her laptop against the wall in anger, and forbid her to ever read or discuss his uncle with anyone. Just before left the room, he ordered Sian to clean up the broken computer. After all, it was her fault. She'd forced him to smash it because she was reading that trash of lies.

Rosie continued. 'Apart from being a wife beater, he had also been pulled up by the SPCA on more than one occasion for animal neglect. He had a Shetland pony that was brought for his granddaughter. When she grew too big to ride it he forgot about the poor thing, and it was just left in a paddock of gorse and with no water, to fend for itself. Anyway, the pony was found by SPCA staff undernourished, and her hooves were so long she could barely walk. Sadly, she had to be put down. When he was asked by a TV journalist why he neglected the pony, he simply said, "Out of sight, out of mind." I'll never forget that. I'll never forget the way he shrugged, like it was no big deal. The amount of suffering and pain that pony would've been in, and he just shrugged, indifferently.' She growled furiously. 'He got a fine for that. Should've been thrown to the hyenas, instead he just got a bloody fine. He had also been pulled up for neglecting sheep a few months before. They were malnourished and full of maggots and he was just as apathetic about that, too. So my vegan friends and I spray-painted his Metro bar with slanderous words such as "wife beater"... "animal abuser"...etcetera. I spent the night in prison for that, and I don't regret it one bit.'

Sian clapped her hands together after Rosie had finished her story. 'You're the best!'

'Not really. I just like justice to be served, and I don't think animals should be treated as lesser beings, when they're not. I mean, look at Popo,' nodding towards the large black and white cat stretched out in a sliver of sunlight, 'he definitely does not believe you and I are better than him.'

'He certainly does not,' Sian laughed.

'But it's a small world,' Rosie said. 'Your ex is the nephew of my enemy. I used to live in Lakesford. My parents have lived there most of their married lives. I wonder if we'd met in Lakesford, would we be friends?'

'Any potential friends had to be approved,' Sian said.

'Approved?'

'By *him*.'

'Geez! What a jackass. What about old friends?'

'They were treated with suspicion. I had to ask permission to see my friends and family,' Sian said shamefully. 'Looking back now, I don't know how I managed to survive.'

'If you were my friend, I would've created an intervention.'

'Nigel tried. He was really worried when I didn't answer his messages. We were really close. *He* smashed my phone and forbade me having another one. I did get another one and when he found it he smashed it across my head.'

Rosie gasped, then uttered several swear words in anger.

'So I went without a phone for a while and lost touch with a few people I cared about. I did finally get another phone, not long before I left.'

'I can see now why you had to plan your escape,' Rosie said, snapping a piece of orange thread between her teeth. 'And do it carefully. *He's* an utter control freak and should be hung up by his balls. It must've felt like you were in prison.'

'For a crime I didn't commit,' Sian added.

THIRTEEN

All day and all of the last two nights, Sian couldn't get her mind off the wild men in the forest. After work at the library yesterday, she spent the rest of the day over at Rosie's helping organise her crafts for the Woodville Spring Fair. His green eyes and wheat coloured hair were on her mind for much of the time, until Rosie brought up the subject of Brendon bloody Durie. *He,* whose name she refused to utter. Mentioning *him* was like smearing faeces on a De Vinci painting. A beautiful thing ruined by a terrible desecration.

But Rosie wasn't to know that, although she wasn't born yesterday, and had noticed that Sian was away with the fairies quite a bit.

What threw Sian into this stunned, preoccupied state was that she felt she had seen the man in the forest before. Not the hefty man who stole her knife...*God! I've got to get a weapon!* But the other man, the one who did most of the talking, the man who shot an arrow at her - let's not forget that! *What a loser!* She wondered if he was Benny. But so many years have passed, it's hard to tell. Every man of a similar age was becoming Benny.

Benny, her childhood friend, the boy from the forest. But the man in the forest looked at her as if she was a stranger. Had he forgotten her? It has been fourteen years since they last met. Fourteen years. Had she changed so much that he couldn't see that fun-loving girl of the summer, behind the pixie haircut and shy temperament? She wasn't shy when they were together, and her hair was long and untamed.

If that was Benny, the boy she loved as a child, she wanted to know why he cruelly told her that he couldn't play with her any more, back when she was thirteen and longed to see him. When she returned the next summer, aged fourteen, he told her he never wanted to see her again. He was different that summer. Then he vanished from her life. She hunted high and low for him, calling out his name as hot tears streamed down her cheeks. The only replies she received were calls from the tui and bellbirds, leaping like monkeys from flower to flower licking up the sweet nectar. She even tried to find his house on the other side of the river, but couldn't navigate her way through the forest, and then became afraid that she might get lost.

He was gone forever, so she thought.

The longing that she had to see that forest man again made a deeper hole in the already empty feeling she had in her belly. She always felt empty and numb inside, an emptiness. She wished she was a little more like Rosie, colourful and fiery, fighting for a cause. Instead she was in between beige and colourful, a quiet wallflower.

She had been told many times that she was a natural beauty, but had little interest in her looks until Brendon Durie claimed her. Called her *his* project, dressed her in clothes he liked to see her in, classy and neat with a hint of cleavage.

You can't blame her numbness on him. She was already like that. Raised by her solo mother who'd frequently suffer with migraines, she had to be quiet; she had to be a good girl. She'd come home from school, and the house would be in darkness and no sound could be made. Her mother would lie in bed for days, just sipping on iced water. Sian would fix her own meals and school lunches, while attending to her mother's needs. Her older brother, Shane, fled overseas as soon as he was old enough, and rarely makes contact.

'He was his father's child,' Sian's mother would say.

What Sian wanted more than anything as she sat on the edge of Aunt May's bed, was to hear a friendly voice. Since she spoke about Nigel to Rosie, she had thought quite a bit about him and Kynn and their fabulous Brownhouse Bay Cafe. She wanted to tell him about Benny, and ask if she was losing her mind. To which he's likely to reply, 'Yes you are, my dear. And a mind without a head will get you nowhere fast.'

Sian held her phone in her hand and began to dial Nigel's number. She had entered four numbers into her new cell phone; Nigel's, Alice her therapist's, Bev her mother's, and now Rosie's. She pondered for moment, wondering if it was worth the risk. Alice and her mother both have landline numbers, so her cell number won't be detected. Nigel has only a cell phone. If she calls him, she may be putting both her life and his life at risk, so she'd have to destroy the phone she's about to use, and replace it with another.

She shook her head, thinking how ridiculous this all is. *He's probably found another victim to control by now.*

Sian took a deep breath and began entering Nigel's cell number into the keypad. She paused a moment, then pressed the big green button. It rang five times, then went straight to answer phone. She smiled when she heard Nigel's comical voice, 'Hey, it's Big Nig! Leave a message. I will get back to you when Kynn quits nagging. Tra-la-la.'

Sian paused, and finding it difficult to know what to say, cut the call.

'Big Nig,' she laughed. Nigel was below average height, balding and slim, but quick-witted and clever with food. Calling himself Big Nig was him being funny.

Just as she dropped the phone down onto Aunt May's bed, it rang. It was Nigel.

She answered the call with a cautious 'Hello?'

'You rang my cell?' Nigel asked, briskly. It was obvious in his tone that he hadn't caught on that it was Sian on the other end. Nigel always got twitchy when an unrecognisable number flashed up on his screen, especially when they don't leave a message. He can't help himself; he has to ring to find out who it is. Mostly it turned out to be a wrong number, or a charity organisation asking for donations. Kynn was always having him on about it. 'If it was important enough they'd leave a message,' Kynn would say.

Sian could hear plates clinkering, and people talking and laughing in the background. He's at the cafe. She looked at the clock on the wall. It was 1.30pm, lunch is still on.

'It's me, Sian.'

'Oh shit! Hold on.'

The background noise became muffled. A few seconds later a door slammed and the background noise vanished.

'Sian?'

'Yes, it's me.'

'I'm in the office. The door is locked so no-one can hear us.'

'Okay.'

'Are you okay, darling?' his voice high-pitched and urgent.

'Yes, I'm doing well.'

'I hadn't heard from you in a while and I got concerned, so I rang the police. I'm sorry if that was the wrong thing to do, but with your therapist ringing me looking for you, and then that piece of shit ex of yours making a little visit, I was starting to get worried.'

'*He* came in?'

'Oh God, he's so full of crap, darling. I'm so glad you got rid of him.'

'What did he do?'

'Oh! He was as sweet as apple pie, calling in like we're the best of friends. Kynn was in the kitchen making hissing noises at him. Not that he'd notice, far too confident to ever think anyone could possible hate him.'

'Did he say anything to you?' As Sian asked, she could feel her heart thud against her ribs.

'He just made conversation and asked how the business was going. Then he threw in a casual comment at the end, asking about you. I just said I hadn't heard from you, and I didn't know your number. Which is not a word of a lie, is it? '

'No. You're safer not knowing where I am at this point. No-one knows where I am, until I'm ready.'

'I think, darling, it's true to say that he's moved on. A girl came in to meet him. She looked about twelve but you know, each to their own. Anyway, they sat at one of the front tables by the window whispering and giggling, like newly courting people do.'

Sian was startled by a feeling of despondency over him moving on so quickly. Had she not meant that much to him? But then, he was a Durie; handsome, spoilt, successful - he probably had a hundred girls on speed dial, waiting for him to ask them out for a drink. *This is exactly what you want, Sian,* she reminded herself. She only hoped this new girl could see the signs of a sociopath, before it's too late.

'I hope she's going to be okay,' Sian said, meaning it. Sian was warned against Brendon Durie by an ex-girlfriend, and she felt it was her duty to perhaps warn any others. But she can't right now, she's on the run.

Nigel continued. 'Of all the bars and cafes he could've chosen darling, he chose our place. My only guess is he did that to send you a message through me, even though at the time I hadn't heard from you.'

'Did you say that my therapist was looking for me?' Sian needed to change the subject, as Brendon's moving-on brought up feelings she wished weren't there.

'She wanted to know if you had been in contact. I said that you hadn't, which was the truth, but she didn't believe me and went on about needing to get a hold of you.'

'Do you know why?'

'Well that's the thing. I asked the same question, and she said she just wanted to check up on you. Then she asked where you were living? I thought this was a peculiar question. Anyway, I said if you contact me, I could pass a message on to her. But she declined. I just feel something was a little off. I might be wrong, of course. It's just the timing of the *piece of shit* coming in with his new girlfriend, and your therapist ringing all in the same day, it was a bit eerie for my liking, darling.'

Anxiety rose in her stomach. She'd suffered with anxiety since a child, her stomach would be tied in knots, constantly apprehensive that something bad was about to happen. It was always there, the anxiety, like an annoying little sister. Brendon Durie only made it worse. Sometimes she'd vomit, or have panic attacks until she felt nothing. Nothingness followed a height of anxiety. Being numb was the best way to cope with his manipulations and sudden bouts of violence. It was like a game to him. His torturing her, and making her petrified about what he was going to do next, was his entertainment.

Sian said, 'I rang her on her work landline a couple of weeks ago. She seemed too busy to talk. Do you think I should ring her again?'

'It might be a good idea,' Big Nig said. 'At least you know she's on your side.'

'Yeah,' she said, though the timing also bothered her, and she wondered if Brendon had been in contact with Alice, and Alice was ringing to warn her.

'Darling, are you okay? I hope I haven't frightened you.'

Sian hesitated.

'Sian, are you still there?' Nigel asked, the tone of his voice rising higher, the more concerned he got.

'I hope he really has moved on,' Sian said, breaking the silence.

'We all do, darling. We all do. Tell me, are you eating well?'

'You sound like my mother.' When Sian is under stress she forgets to eat and can become dangerously thin. Actually, she says she forgets to eat, but the truth is, the constant nervousness makes her nauseous and food will just make her sick, causing a barrage of comments about food from both Nigel and her mother, when she was living with the Durie.

'Oh God, shoot me now!' Nigel gasped in horror.

'Yes, I'm very happy and I'm eating well,' Sian said, speaking truthfully. 'One day, sometime down the track, I want you and Kynn to come down.'

'Oh! That would be marvellous.'

They chatted a little longer, a quick catch up, when a knock at Nigel's office door cut the conversation short.

When Sian got off the phone with Nigel, she immediately rang Alice on her work landline. It went to the answer phone. The receptionist must've been busy. Alice was probably with a client anyway, but she thought she'd give her work cell a ring.

Alice picked up straight away.

'It's Sian Tanner.'

'Oh my, it's lovely to hear from you. Where are you? How are you keeping?'

The sickly sweetness in her voice made Sian nervous. This was not the response she got last time she rang Alice. In fact, this didn't sound like her therapist's calm, steady voice at all. Maybe Nigel was right, something was a little off.

'Have you found yourself a nice place to live?' Alice asked.

'Yes,' she answered, revealing little.

'Look! If you tell me where you are I can hook you up with a good, local counsellor.'

'I have the helpline number, and you gave me the website address of the list of therapists who specialise in women who've been in abusive relationships. I'll just contact one of them when the time is right.'

The line went dead.

'Hello? Alice, are you still there?'

'Yes, I'm here,' her voice had cooled somewhat. 'My next client has just arrived.'

'Okay, I'll go now,' Sian said swiftly.

'I'm genuinely pleased you're doing well, Sian,' Alice said, this time sounding like the therapist Sian was familiar with.

'Thank you for spending all that time helping me. My life is so much better because of you.'

FOURTEEN

The Therapist

Alice cut the call. She looked at the cell number on her screen, Sian's number.

If she was smart, she'll smash that phone now and buy another with a different number, she thought.

She leaned back in her chair and gazed up at the ceiling, while torturing thoughts circled in her mind. If Brendon Durie went to the press with those photos, her career and marriage are doomed. She glanced at her watch. It was 1.40pm. She had until 6pm to find out where Sian lived. Going by the conversation she's just had, Sian's not going to give up that information easily. She hadn't even told her best friend where she's living, so he said. But this was what they had planned for months, her escape. She had to sacrifice her friends, family, and career to start a new life out of reach of harm. They went through this over and over again. Every counselling session in the last twelve months before Sian left, was the planning of the escape. A new life with a new name; *never give your personal details out to anyone, have a support person you trust*, etc. Alice had taught her this and now the student had outsmarted the teacher.

Alice had two options; let Brendon Durie go to the press with the pics, or contact her friend Sergeant Louise Ratahi in the local police force to trace Sian's whereabouts. Knowing Sian's history, Louise will ask questions and want to know if she's in trouble. She's a good police officer, sensitive to Alice's work, and she's no fool.

However, there was a third option. She picked up her cell and rolled it around in her fingers, pondering the consequences of the third option.

Finally, she came to a decision.

She texted Brendon Durie, *I need more time*

Several minutes later, *Why?*

Alice: *I have a lead, but it will take time*

Brendon: *How much time?*

Alice: *3 days*

Brendon: *Three days is too long! I'll give you 24 hours.*

Alice fumed, slapping her hand on the desk. 'Little punk!' She took several deep breaths to calm her anger before replying. *Fine*

Brendon: *You've got until 6pm tomorrow*

Alice: *Fine*

She held the cell tightly in her hand, tempted to throw it at the wall in fury. Instead she released it from her grip to grab her handbag from under the desk. Inside the black handbag was a zipped up pocket that contained her make-up. She opened the pocket, and hunted around for the foundation concealer in a round, flat plastic container. Once she had it in her grasp, she flipped up the lid and dug her fingernail into the edge to lift out the false bottom. Underneath was a small piece of folded paper. She took it out and unfolded it. It read, *Birdie* with a cell number underneath.

Alice hesitated. Once she's dialled this number there's no going back. She re-read Brendon Durie's messages and clenched her jaw. A gentle tap at her door interrupted her thought process. It was Mandy the receptionist.

'Your client hasn't shown up, but there's someone else here to see you.'

'Who is it?'

Mandy mouthed, 'The Police.'

'Let them in,' Alice said, curious.

In a strange coincidence it was Sergeant Louise Ratahi, looking fabulous in that awful uniform. How can they bear to wear those awful, shapeless slacks? One design fits all it seemed, whether you're male or female. It's a miracle, but Louise managed to look good in them.

She comes in smiling, long black hair pulled back into a pony tail, dark eyes creasing as she smiles.

'How have you been, Alice?' Louise asked, pulling up a chair.

'A little tired, but...I was just about to call you.'

'What about?'

'Sian Tanner.'

'Actually, that's why I'm here. We received a call of concern from a Mr Nigel Blackley, one of Sian's friends, apparently.'

'Yes?' She had met Nigel a couple of times, when he came for counselling sessions after his father died. He wasn't close to his father since he'd come out of the closet, and his death had only raised unresolved relationship issues, rather than closure.

'He's concerned for Sian as he doesn't know where she is, and hasn't heard from her. He said that you had contacted him asking where Sian was. What concerned him was that on that same day, Sian's ex-partner Brendon Durie came into their bar, Brownhouse Bay Cafe, and was asking after her as well. So I guess Mr Blackley was getting worried for Sian Tanner's welfare.'

Alice swallowed a lump in her throat. 'I don't know why Brendon Durie went into Nigel's bar, and I haven't been in contact with him. I only know that he needs to be kept as far away as possible from Sian Tanner. He should be in prison, or on an isolated island a million miles away from women.'

'According to Mr Blackley, Brendon Durie has a new partner. So we'll watch that one closely,' Louise said, sternly.

'Will you? Like you watched Sian Tanner closely?' Alice said sharply.

Louise cocked her head. 'Come on Alice, you know we can only do what's within the law.'

It was a sore point for both women. Brendon Durie was an abuser through and through. If Louise and Alice had it their way, he'd be strung up by the balls. Instead he was arrested for assault and battery against Sian, but got off on an oversight. Brendon's uncle the lawyer, came in, picked up on the error of contaminated evidence, and saved the day, and saved the Durie name in the process.

'So have you contacted Nigel Blackley?' Louise asked.

'Yes. Sian rang a couple of weeks ago, on my landline. Unfortunately, I couldn't talk to her for long. I wanted to get back in contact, just to make sure she had followed the procedure. So logically, I thought her best friend would know where she is.'

'Does she sound like she's doing okay?' Louise asked.

'Yes. But it wouldn't hurt if you located her to check up on her. I have her cell phone number; she rang just this morning on my work cell. I'll write it down for you.'

Louise took the number. 'Did Sian tell you where she was staying?'

'No.'

'Did you ask?'

'Yes.'

'So it looks like she doesn't want to be found yet.'

Alice fell quiet.

Louise continued, 'I know quite a bit of effort and preparation had gone into Sian's escape, so I'm sure just as much thought has gone into her hideout as well.'

'She should've had police protection,' Alice said bluntly, frustration rising, as her thoughts returned to those days when Brendon was arrested, and then let off. They had planned her escape, knowing that his prison term would be short, a few months at the most. Sian had to have disappeared leaving no trace, by the time he was let out of prison. What they didn't expect was for Brendon Durie to serve no time at all. Sian had to leave immediately.

Louise ignored her tone. 'I'll look into this,' holding up Sian's number.

FIFTEEN

'There were a few times when she almost killed herself,' Mavis said, as she sipped milky tea from a cracked teacup. They were having morning tea in the library's small staffroom, and Sian had asked to hear more about her Great Aunt May. These stories calmed her as much as entertained her, but she couldn't get away from the mysteries that shrouded her Aunt; the book about the boy in the woods; the photograph of May's parents on the wall with the young man standing behind, scythe in hand; and her apparent deteriorating sanity, spending more and more time in the forest.

'Tell me,' Sian insisted. She wanted to block out the recent phone calls with her therapist and her best friend - both of which had unsettled her. Perhaps it's better if she doesn't contact them again. Not for some time, anyway. Like Alice had advised her, she smashed her cell and then buried it in the backyard. She was going to buy a new cell online, but talked herself out of it. That meant that the company she was going to buy the cell from would have her personal information, and she just wasn't ready to give that up yet. Not yet. Even though Brendon Durie seemed to have moved on and found himself a new victim, she still felt it was all for show, an attempt to make Sian jealous, perhaps. So it must have annoyed him when Nigel said that he didn't know where Sian was, and hadn't heard from her.

Mavis continued, 'The winds were awful. I've never known anything like it. I remember that day like it was yesterday, but it was really about eight or nine years ago. I took Trixie, my little foxy terrier, who sadly passed away three years ago, in the car down to May's place to check up on her. I don't drive anymore, my eyesight is too poor. On my GP's orders I had to give up. Do you have a doctor, Ingrid? I know Dr Hanson is still taking new patients.' She took another sip of tea. Outside the window a cherry tree was in blossom, and little silvereye birds were flittering from one crimson flower to the next licking up the nectar, while bees hummed and hovered about. Sian noticed a rata bush was growing nearby too, but that still had not bloomed. Yet the rata and pohutukawa trees had exploded into bloom in McCrae's Forest. Fascinating. One day she'd like to explore the ecology of that forest more closely.

'Yet, you can still read books?' Sian asked.

'I have to use a magnifying glass. Some titles I can read without it, but mostly I need the words to be rather large. Your Aunt had almost perfect 20/20 eyesight up until the day she died. Although other faculties were diminishing,' she stated, tapping the side of her head.

'My neighbour Rosie, thought Aunt May was pretty alert and sane.'

'She'd have nothing to compare May's behaviour to. She wouldn't know what May used to be like, when she was younger. Besides, isn't your neighbour that girl with the bright red hair and tattoos all over her arms?'

'Yes.'

Mavis grunted, her look of disapproval said it all.

Eager to return to the story about Great Aunt May, Sian asked, 'What happened on the day of the winds?'

Mavis continued, 'Oh yes! I thought the roof might fly off that old house you live in. Still do.' She shook her head, wearing an expression of perplexity. 'Such a peculiar shaped house, that is. I'm sure May's parents had something in mind when they built it. I just don't know what? So I drove in my old Volkswagen, the winds making my car sway back and forth. When I arrived, I knocked on her door. Gosh! I remember the winds were so strong I struggled to open the car door, the wind just kept blowing against it. Trixie didn't want to get out of the car and ruffle up her fur, so I left her in there. After knocking on the door a few times I started to worry, and wondered if she wandered off into that forest. She loved that forest. If she could've lived in there, I'm sure she would've. I heard what I thought at first was a cat meowing. When I looked up I saw your Aunt on the roof, holding on for dear life. The meowing sound was May, calling for help,' she chuckled.

'She screamed that the wind had blown the ladder over, so she couldn't get down. "What the hell are you doing up there on a day like today?" I yelled. But she didn't hear me. So I managed to walk against the wind to where the ladder had fallen, and tried to stand it back up. But I wasn't strong enough to lift it.' She paused to gaze out the window at the flittering silvereye birds. She seemed bewildered by something, and covered her gaping mouth with her hand. Sian looked out the window to see what amazed her so, and saw only bees, birds and a flowering cherry.

'It was rather odd,' Mavis said finally. Her eyes had glazed over. She was not looking at something outside the window, she was looking at something in her memory. 'I suddenly found the strength. It was as if someone had come up from behind to help me steady the swaying ladder,' she said, still gazing out the window, 'and prop it up against the house.' She pulled her eyes away from the flowering cherry, and chuckled. 'The old bird crawled along the roof to the ladder, then as she was about to climb down, the guttering damn-well snapped.' She gasped, breaking into laughter. 'But she managed to hold on, and down she came. When she got down onto the ground, she brushed the dirt from her hands and said, and I'll never forget this: "Now it's all fixed." She was up there in a hurricane fixing the roof!' she laughed hysterically, which made Sian laugh too, ignoring the pangs of guilt she felt for not coming to see her Great Aunt sooner.

Mavis suddenly stopped laughing when another thought came to her. 'I don't know where I found the strength, but if I hadn't come along when I did, I don't what would've happened to her. Call it divine intervention.'

'Do you know why she loved the forest so much?' Sian asked.

'I can only guess it's because of the wildlife. The trees are ancient species, there nothing like them anywhere in the world. But there may have been other reasons.'

'Rosie, my neighbour, said she saw Aunt May with a ring of flowers in her hair, dancing near the forest entrance. She said it looked like she was dancing with another person, or perhaps a ghost. Did Aunt May have a lover, do you know?'

'Are you saying your neighbour didn't actually see this person your aunt was dancing with?'

'No, she didn't.'

Mavis scoffed, swigging down the rest of her milky tea. 'And this was the girl who believed your Aunt was alert and sane?'

Sian shrugged. 'I was wondering, perhaps Aunt May was dancing with the memory of a past lover? Or...maybe someone Rosie didn't see?'

'Look, I've known your aunt since long before you were even born, much longer, fifty, sixty years. She never had a lover. My husband and I tried to set her up with men, farmers mostly, but she was never interested. She always seemed too preoccupied to be bothered. She always had some project on - writing a book, sowing seeds, growing seedlings in the glasshouse, or visiting that dreadful forest. If you look hard enough in all that wild grass in your backyard, you'll find the foundations to the glasshouse. She'd go around selling her vegetables from the back of her pick-up truck. They were great. Huge!'

Sian remembered this. As a child she'd sit in the front seat of that old V8 truck and they'd visit people with boxes of produce. She'd take a brown paper bag to put all the cash in. By the end of the day, that paper bag was stuffed with notes and coins, and they'd head on down to the dairy to get an ice cream. Sian would get mint with choc chips or boysenberry, and Aunt May would always get hokey pokey, every single time. Usually though, the hokey pokey got stuck in her teeth, and she had to use the prongs of a fork to get it back out again when they got home. Good times. They were the best of times.

This also reminded Sian of the time she took a jelly-tip ice cream to Benny in the forest. It was melting in her hand by the time he appeared, like he did, out of nowhere. He taught her how to whistle for him and still to this day, she remembered how to do it. Like the call of a Shining Cuckoo he said, and then performed his whistle, which was impressive. She then tried several times, only to make him laugh. They were 8 years old, innocent kids hanging out in nature.

But in the city where she lived with her weary mother, there were no cuckoos. You were lucky to see or hear tui. Only sparrows, blackbirds and starlings, the birds introduced by settlers from Britain, thrived in the city by living off breadcrumbs and mites. Over time she forgot what the cuckoo sounded like. When Benny told her he never wanted to see her again, she blocked his whistle from her mind.

Benny loved the jelly-tip ice cream. He couldn't disguise his delighted reaction when he opened the packet, and sucked up the soft sweet ice cream, and chocolate, and red jelly. Sian smiled thinking about that day, brown chocolate and white vanilla ice cream smeared all over his face, and dribbling down his chin. She found herself laughing out loud at it. Then a memory moved in like a wave from the ocean, carrying with it fear, fear that sat in the pit of Sian's stomach. That was the day he took her to that place, a secret place. Sian tried to recall where he took her. *It's a secret.* A hidden gravesite. Benny said someone was buried there. Sian's heart thudded against her chest. Then the wave retreated into the ocean, and the memory faded.

When Sian got home from work at the library, she thought she'd venture back into the forest in the hopes of bumping into the man who she suspected might be her Benny. She'd also make an attempt to whistle the cuckoo's whistle that he had taught her.

Once again Popo came along, his big fluffy tail waving in the air excitedly, and she found the kauri, her face carved into its bark. She whistled the cuckoo's call, and then waited. It was a warm day, but cool and eerie in the forest. Popo was acting peculiarly, not his usual confident, playful behaviour, racing under a fern and staying put. A cool breeze carrying whispers sailed through the branches, rustling the leaves. Sian shuddered. Popo seemed frightened, and this made her uneasy.

After waiting a little longer, she ran back out of the canopy of trees into the daylight. Maybe the whistle was wrong. Perhaps she was confused and had whistled another bird's song.

Back up in Great Aunt May's bedroom, which was really her bedroom legally, only it hadn't started to feel like hers yet, she had to check the photograph of May's parents. This was something she did every day, twice a day usually. She couldn't help herself. There it was hanging on the wall, the handkerchief billowing in the breeze that came through the window that never liked to close. It was like waving a red flag in front of a bull, a temptation one couldn't resist, even though it heightened her anxiety the moment she lifted the handkerchief.

They've changed.

She dropped the handkerchief back and took a couple of deep breaths to calm the nerves swishing in her belly. When she felt brave enough, she lifted the handkerchief again to take a closer look. The Fields, and the young man who stood behind with his scythe gripped in his hand, were all looking slightly to their right. The young man's eyebrows had also creased into a frown. Once again it was very slight, not a full frown, and Mrs Field's lips were parted as if she was about to speak.

Sian couldn't see what they were looking at, and once again she questioned her own sanity, anyway. Every time she noticed a change, she quickly told herself that she was imagining it and convincing herself that it was probably always like that. Deep down inside she knew the truth. The young man definitely was not there at the beginning. But he's there now, becoming clearer.

SIXTEEN

The Sergeant

Sergeant Louise Ratahi punched Sian Tanner's cell phone number into her work mobile. It made strange noises indicating that it was inactive. Sian must've cancelled her subscription with that cell phone company, and destroyed the phone - the actions of someone who doesn't want to be found. It's not as if Sian was doing anything illegal. The worse possible crime she may be committing is that she was possibly not paying her taxes, which is a problem for the Inland Revenue to pursue. Someone living their life under an alias and in hiding, may choose jobs where they're paid under the table, or may have to beg, borrow and steal to get by. It's not her fault. She's just doing what she can.

After speaking to Nigel Blackley about Brendon Durie, no alarm bells were raised in her mind. To her it seemed that Brendon wanted to get the message across that he had moved on. But it bothered her that he had all this freedom, while Sian had to give up her friends and family to hide from him.

Brendon Durie.

The Duries are all shitheads, the whole lot of them. They've run rings around the law and the police, and they'll do whatever it takes to get whatever they want. They're complete and utter shitheads.

Louise found the number of Sian's mother in the white pages, and gave her a ring.

'Sian's therapist has already rung me,' she said, her voice droning as if she's half asleep. Maybe she's taken some sort of sedative to knock her out. 'I'm feeling unwell, so make this quick.' Louise was aware that Bev Tanner suffered from migraines. She liked to let everyone know that, probably so they'd leave her alone.

'So your daughter hasn't contacted you?' Louise asked.

'Her therapist already asked me that. I just told you, no. Why would she bother contacting me anyway? She never cared. I'd be the last one on the list that she'd contact.'

'I know the reason she didn't tell you of her whereabouts was to protect you.'

'Protect me? Who from? From that nice, young man who made a home for her? Who looked after her with all of his wealth, and what did she do, bloody ran away from him. Accuse him of hitting her or something ludicrous. Good men are hard to find sergeant, and she lost a real bloody prize, that stupid girl!'

Louise bit her tongue. If only this woman knew what Sian had been through. Or maybe she did know, but thought the sacrifice was worth it. After all, money and a nice home was a good exchange for being locked up in a wardrobe for days because she smiled at Durie's friend, or going to bed to find hundreds of cockroaches crawling around in the sheets. He blamed her for that, like he blamed her for everything. He set her up and then used it as ammunition. Louise remembered reading Alice's notes and wanting to punch Brendon Durie in the face. Ugly him up little, he deserved it. He was too perfect, too arrogant. The notes read that he made Sian lie in the bed of cockroaches all night, while he sat in a chair next to the bed, to make sure she didn't move. His justification was if she was dirty enough to attract cockroaches, then she's dirty enough to lie in them. Then he made her clean the sheets and mattress in the morning.

'Do you have any idea where she is?' Louise asked.

'No. Why? What's happened?'

'Nothing's happened. It's just a routine check up.'

'So, like visiting the dentist?'

'Not really,' Louise didn't find her joke funny. There's was nothing funny about this situation at all. 'It's just to make sure she is safe and well, and has a good support person and plan in place.'

Bev grunted. 'I really have no idea where she'd be. Sounds like she's being a little drama queen, if you ask me.'

I didn't ask you, you heartless witch, she felt like saying. 'Is there anyone else who may know?'

'That gay friend of hers, who owns that fancy bar with all the shiny furniture, he may know.'

'Yes, Brownhouse Bay Cafe. We know that place.'

'Does Sian have any brothers or sisters?'

'A brother, but he wouldn't know. They haven't been in contact since they were teenagers.'

'Would you mind giving me his phone number?'

'Hang on.' A loud clunking sound came through the line, the phone being dropped abruptly. Louise could hear the sound of a drawer being opened, and papers rustling. After she waited several minutes, Bev returned. 'This number is old. He don't care about his mother, either. You give birth to these kids; go through all that pain and this is the thanks I get. Two spoiled brats.'

'The number please, Mrs Tanner.' Louise insisted.

Bev reluctantly read the number out and Louise quickly cut the call. She dialled Shane Tanner's cell number, and a woman answered.

'Is this Shane Tanner's phone?'

'Who's this?'

'Sergeant Louise Ratahi. I'd like to speak to Shane, please.'

'Is this a police matter?'

'Yes.'

'How do I know you're really the police?' Good point. But she wasn't about to fly all the way to wherever the hell they live in Australia, just to ask one question he won't be able to answer. Then she heard a man's voice in the background asking who she's talking to, and demanding to know why she's using his phone.

Then, 'Who's this?'

'My name is Sergeant Louise Ratahi. Is this Shane Tanner?'

'Yes. Why? What's happened?'

'I'm looking for your sister, Sian. Would you have any idea of her whereabouts?'

'No. I haven't spoken to her for a long time. Has she gone missing?'

'She's in hiding from an ex partner, and we just want to check up on her. We have reason to believe she may be in danger.'

'From her ex partner?'

'Yes.'

'Are we talking about that tosser in a suit that my mother always bleated on about?' he asked.

'Yes, I think we are,' Louise answered, finding his description of Brendon Durie spot on.

'White collar arsehole!' he grunted.

'You can't think of any place she may be hiding?' Louise asked.

'No. I left home at seventeen, and never looked back. I had to get away from... So I don't really know my own sister. Our mother probably scarred her for life. Have you spoken to Bev? A real doozy, that one.'

'Yes I have, and she can't think where Sian could be.'

'No, I suppose she couldn't. The last time I spoke to my sister was when she felt bad about the house...' his voice faded away.

'Hello? Mr Tanner?' Louise asked.

'I think I know where she may have gone. She inherited a house and land from our Great Aunt May. I don't know if we're actually related by blood, but Sian went there for the summers when we were kids. I went once and hated it, and never went back. Aunt May was a bit weird. Sian seemed to like all that make-believe, storytelling stuff. I just found it creepy.'

'Do you know where this house is?'

'I can't remember exactly. It was a real small town in the central North Island. Ask the old crank, Bev.'

'What was your Aunt May's surname?'

'Jeez! I don't even know that. I met her only a couple of times. Like I said, I don't think she was actually related to us by blood. I don't know the connection at all between her and Bev.'

'Thank you, Mister Tanner. That's been a great help.'

'I hope it all turns out well. I mean...we weren't close because our mother made life difficult, but I wouldn't want anything bad to happen to Sian.'

As soon as Louise got off the phone she rang Bev Tanner again, but there was no reply. She then rang Nigel Blackley, and asked if he knew about a house and land Sian had inherited.

'Oh yes! I remember now. I forgot all about that. It was years ago when she inherited that old dump. I thought she was going to sell it.'

'Do you know where it is?'

'I have no idea.'

SEVENTEEN

Sian sat on the end of Aunt May's bed transfixed by the handkerchief waving softly in the breeze. The air was starting to cool now, and she got up to leave the room. There was no point closing the window, as she'd find it open again when she came back up. Strange business.

When she left to run down the stairs, a whizzing sound made her stop and turn around. An arrow was sitting on the bed. It wasn't there before, she was certain of that. She picked it up and turned it over in her hands, then stepped over to the window. Someone was standing in the shadows of the trees. She leaned out and called, 'Do you want this back?' holding up the arrow.

There was a pause, then, 'Why are *you* there?' a man's voice called back.

'I live here,' she yelled back. 'Wait! I'll come down.'

The man kept standing in the shadows, and it wasn't until she had climbed over the fence and walked right up him, could she see who it was. The forest man, the man she suspected might be Benny, with a big gash to his thigh, blood seeping into his black trousers. She quickly assessed the scene, which wasn't a positive one. A hunting rifle was slung across his shoulder, and a string of dead possums lay on the ground. He was leaning up against a tree, his face pale.

'It's not as bad as it looks,' he said. Then a husky voice cut through the air like a knife, 'It's the girl disguised as a boy!' It was his companion, the one who took Sian's butcher's knife. He stepped out from behind a tree and moved in close to her, grinning. He was missing a front tooth, had shaggy dark hair and dark beard, and Sian didn't warm to him one bit.

As Sian stepped away from him, she noticed he had bits of food in his beard. He sniggered, then drew a knife from his scabbard and used it to pick food out from his teeth. Sian recognised the knife instantly. It was her butcher's knife, her protection, and here was this pig of a man teasing her with it.

She could feel the weight of the other man's stare. When she turned back to face him, his expression was a mix of suspicion and pleasure, his bright eyes the colour of a green sea on a clear day, his hair the colour of wheat. He was a rugged, good-looking man, with an underlying seriousness as if the weight of the world was upon him, much like Benny.

'Who are you and why are you in the old lady's house?' the wheat-haired man asked, abruptly.

'My name is Sian, Sian Tanner,' she replied, hoping to trigger his memory. He flinched slightly. 'She's my Aunt May. She died years ago and I inherited her house and land.'

'You're May's niece?' the toothless man asked in his husky voice, his eyes running over her.

'Sort of,' she stepped away from him a little more. He smelt like that blackbird Popo caught and left rotting in the backyard. No, he smelt worse than that. 'Are you Benny?' she asked the wheat-haired man.

He frowned, and the toothless man cocked his head in surprise. 'Benny?'

'I used to play here with a boy called Benny, who I thought lived in the forest.' She turned back to the wheat-haired man, and was greeted with a look of irritability.

'Benny's dead,' he said, abruptly.

Sian felt her throat dry up. 'Oh, how?'

'What's it to you?' the hefty, toothless man asked.

'I just remembered him and thought -'

'You thought Angus was Benny, obviously!' the hefty man said bemusedly, then broke into a crackling chortle that startled Sian.

'Benny died years ago,' Angus said, softly.

'When?' Sian asked, feeling her hands tremble.

Angus shrugged. 'About fourteen or fifteen years ago.' He grimaced when he moved his leg. 'The old lady let us stay here sometimes,' Angus said.

'And cooked us a hot meal,' the toothless man added. 'When the place was sitting empty, we kind of...how should I say...borrowed it now and again. Then we heard someone had actually moved in and so we backed off a bit, until now.'

'Where's your own home?' Sian asked, still in shock that Benny had died.

'On the other side of the river,' Angus answered. Sian remembered Benny showing her his house. Even from that distance she could see that it was battered and bruised, and probably freezing in winter.

'You're Benny's brother?' Sian asked Angus.

'We're both Benny's brothers,' the toothless man answered. 'There's heaps of us. The old man always had his leg over something. And our mother was blind, 'cos if she saw what our dad looked like she would've done a runner.'

'Really?' Sian asked.

'Ignore him,' Angus said, hobbling out towards the fence boundary between Aunt May's house and McCrae's Forest. 'Our mother wasn't blind, she was bullied.'

'Sorensons?' Sian asked.

'That's us!' the toothless man said, 'All the horrible things you've heard about the Sorensons are all true.'

'I haven't heard anything. All I'm interested in is finding out about Benny, and I guess I have now.'

Angus rubbed his chin. 'Benny is a long story,' he said, exhaustedly. It was clear that he didn't want to talk about it. 'When the old lady was living here, she would drive us home when we got stuck for transport.' Sian got the hint.

***

She awoke to something landing on her. She had fallen asleep on the couch, and Popo's furry face was only a couple of inches away from hers, his green eyes transfixed on her eyes. This could only mean that he was hungry, and he was always hungry. Right now he was a heavy weight upon her chest and she just wanted to get him off.

The sun was rising over the east, and she was suddenly struck with a feeling of terrible guilt. The Sorenson boys wanted to stay for a while. Sian shuddered at the thought of letting two men that she hardly knew, stinking of dead possums, into her house. This immediately put her in an unsafe position. And being safe was a priority. The only possible option was to drive them back to their house, which is what she did. But first she stopped off at the pharmacy to pick up bandages and manuka oil, to mend Angus's wound.

He fell and gashed his thigh on a hard piece of wood sticking out of the earth. He was chasing a goat when it happened, a red male, a prize. They both work for DOC, Department of Conservation, and are hired to kill pests - goat, possum, wild boar and deer. They get paid per head of animal, and then are welcome to do whatever they like with the meat and carcasses.

They said Sian's Great Aunt May was a big fan of their work and often had them over for tea, if they came by after time spent in the forest. Sian wasn't sure if they were speaking the truth or not, but it's her house now, and her rules. But she still couldn't help but feel guilty for being so unwelcoming towards them. They probably thought she was a prude.

In the car driving to their house, they mentioned coming over to 'the old lady's' when they were kids, and their old man was drunk. She took them in and fed them warm Milo and ANZAC biscuits, and said they can stay as long as they liked. Except they couldn't stay as long as they liked, because before long their old man would wake up with a slamming hangover and demand his sons work the farm, while he went to work as the local police officer.

'Your father was the police officer?' Sian asked, surprised.

'He was a drinker before Benny died and became a drunk afterwards,' Angus said. 'Then, he got the sack.'

'If it wasn't hell before, it was sure hell after,' his brother Sam said bitterly, then swore under his breath. It was clear he held quite a bit of resentment towards his father.

'How did Benny die?' Sian asked, as she drove across the bridge, the silver waters of the Manawatu River flowing rapidly beneath, carrying with it debris from a storm further north.

Sam growled in the back seat. 'We don't want to bring up the past,' he said irately, and crossed his arms as if to say, 'end of story.'

'One day, I'll tell you,' Angus said to Sian. Sian wasn't sure she wanted to see these two wild brothers again.

Sam grunted again. 'You don't even know!' he said to his brother. 'You weren't even there.'

'No one was!' Angus argued back.

The atmosphere turned icy and stayed like that for a few miles, until Sian turned onto their rural gravel road, Moffat's Road. The house was halfway down the road, an old homestead that had fallen to wrack and ruin. Sian kept her opinions to herself as she didn't want to appear rude, but how the heck did they manage to live in that place? It should be condemned and pulled down.

115

'Just stop here,' Sam ordered, when Sian turned into the drive. 'We'll walk the rest of the way up.'

'Are you sure? I don't mind driving all the way up.'

'Nah!' Sam said. 'The place is a tip. Needs a bit of dusting.' Sian could tell he was being derisive. Everything that fell out of Sam's hairy mouth was a mock or a tease, under a cloud of anger.

Sam climbed out first, and grabbed the rifles and dead possums out of the boot. Angus took a while to clamber out of the car due to his damaged leg, which was now tightly bandaged. Sian got out of the car to help him. She could see a woman coming down the drive with a baby on her hip, and Sian wondered if she lived in that decrepit, old house. With a baby! It'd be an utter health hazard.

Angus caught Sian watching the woman with the baby and said, 'Sam's missus.'

'Oh! I didn't want to know who she is, I just...'

'- His bark is worse than his bite, our Sam,' Angus said. Sian didn't care. She had no intention of seeing him again. Angus hobbled to the back of the car to grab his kill and his hunting rifle. As Sian climbed back into the front seat, he came around to her side and said, 'Benny's body was found in the river. When an autopsy was done they found he had a high blood alcohol count, and came to the conclusion he drowned drunk.'

Sian's mouth dropped open in shock.

'He doesn't believe it,' Angus said, nodding towards Sam, who was now walking with his girlfriend towards the house. 'He reckons it had something to do with the old man.' Angus shrugged. 'I guess we'll never know. He's down at the Woodville cemetery on Winchester Street, if you want to go and see him.'

It's a secret.

EIGHTEEN

The Therapist

I think I've found her. I just have no way to contact her, so I've contacted the local police. They said they know of someone who has moved into May Field's house, her description is similar to Sian's, only she doesn't have long, straight hair. Instead it's short but of similar colour. They're going to pay her a visit and then get back to me,' Sergeant Louise said to Alice Granger over the phone.

'That's fantastic news! You've got her address?'

'Yes. She inherited a house from her Great Aunt and we believe she may be residing there.'

'Where is it?' Alice asked, hoping that she didn't sound too desperate.

'In a little town called Woodville about a four hour drive from here.'

'Does it seem like she's living alone?' Alice asked, hoping that she was living with someone who could protect her. Like a sabre toothed tiger!

'I'm not sure yet. I'll get back to you on that one. We still need an accurate ID on her.

As soon as the conversation with Louise was over, Alice texted Brendon Durie, *I've been told you've moved on. So you won't need Sian's location*

Brendon: *You got what I want?*

Alice: *Almost. I'm waiting for an accurate ID. Meet me at Memorial Park midnight tonight, by the paddling pool*

Brendon: *The deadline was 6pm today. Give me the details of where she is now.*

Alice: *I want to see you destroy all evidence of those pics or the deal is off*

There was a long pause.

Brendon: *Are you trying to set me up?*

Alice: *No.*

Brendon: *I know you're in contact with that police woman*

How could he possibly know that? Is he watching her clinic as well as her house?

Alice: *I haven't mentioned you. How did you get those pics of me and Damon Ridge?*

Brendon: *I have my ways*

Alice: *Do we have a deal?*

Another long pause.

Brendon: *Fine. I'll meet you at Memorial Park tonight.*

She tried to squeeze information out of him about her meeting with Damon Ridge at the Stanley Stadium car park. How much did he really see? Perhaps he wasn't there at all, but someone else was who snapped shots of her and Damon Ridge talking under the street lamp. How did he get those pictures of them behind the stadium, though? They were alone, just them and the sea. That was an oversight and it can't happen again.

She unfolded the small piece of paper with Birdie's number on it, which was hidden in her pressed powder case. She took a cheap cell phone from her handbag that she had bought for this specific task.

Still on for tonight? She texted

Birdie*: Yes*
Alice*: Midnight at Memorial park by the paddling pool*
I'll send you a pic of him and his car
Birdie*: No need. I know what he looks like. I know what car he drives*

***

It was just after 5pm before Alice got home. She took the chicken and apricot quiche out of the fridge to heat up for tea. Dave texted to say that he'd be home at approx 5.45pm, so it was up to her to start tea. On the kitchen bench were travel brochures of Thailand, Canada, China, and canal tours through Britain and France. It all looked delectably inviting.

She glanced over them superficially, as her mind was on other things. Birdie had never let her down before, so why was she feeling so uneasy? She thought she had it planned out to the letter. She'd arrange for Durie to meet her at Memorial Park at midnight, only for Birdie to be there instead. Easy. Birdie was to make it look like either a suicide or a car-jacking gone wrong. The Durie family had plenty of friends in high places, but they also had plenty of enemies in low places. The police could pass his death off as an ambush by a vigilante group, or a revenge kill. Either way, the world was a better place with one less Durie in it.

Her personal cell beeped. It was Sarah, her youngest daughter, inviting herself over for dinner tomorrow night. Alice could only conclude that Sarah was broke and out of food.

6.09pm and Dave still hadn't arrived home. She texted him several times, but received no reply. The quiche was in the warming oven and would soon turn to rubber, so he better be home soon.

6.26pm and Dave still hadn't arrived. Alice was now getting concerned. He was such a busy man, and forgetting to check his

119

personal cell was normal, but to be running so late without calling was very unusual.

7.03pm Alice's personal cell rang. It was the hospital. Dave had been involved in a car accident. He's fine, just a bit shaken up and needs someone to pick him up and drive him home.

'What happened?' Alice asked when she found him sitting on a hospital bed, his right eye the size of a baseball, his arm in a sling.

'I fractured my elbow,' he said, pointing to his arm. 'It's nothing serious. Can't even remember it happening,' he said, in his usual flippant way. Nothing was ever a big deal to Dave. 'A guy went through a red light and ploughed right into me. He was apologetic and was insured, luckily. We exchanged details and went on our separate ways. Or should I say, I went to the hospital and he went home completely unscathed,' a hint of bitterness in his tone.

She took him home and fixed him a sandwich since the quiche was inedible by this time. It was after 9pm; only 3 hours until the deed was to be done. She watched the clocks pensively - the clock on her phone, the clock on the wall, and the clock on the microwave, all moving at the same ridiculously slow pace.

'Are you alright?' Dave asked, as they sat on the couch watching a wildlife documentary on Botswana.

'Yes. Why?'

'You seem very twitchy.'

'I was just upset by your accident. You hadn't answered my texts,'-

'And you thought something bad happened?' Dave asked.

'Well...yes.'

'I left work late and I can't find my cell. I must've left it at work. We should go there next year,' he added, nodding towards the television. 'Looks nice. I wonder if we could get up close to the elephants.' He glanced briefly at Alice, her eyes were glazed over. 'I met an elephant once. Said her name was Nancy. Nice girl, she was. But her nose kept getting in the way of everything.'

'What?' Alice said, picking up on the last part of his sentence.

'Big nose, Nancy had,' he said, then used his good arm to make a trunk.

Alice frowned.

'What are you not telling me?' Dave asked. 'You've barely heard anything I've said since we've come home.'

'I told you, there's nothing wrong,' she said, sighing. 'Sarah's coming over tomorrow night for tea.'

'She must have an empty fridge.'

That made Alice chuckle.

Dave wrapped his good arm around Alice and pulled her closer, then kissed her temple. Sarah came late in the equation. She was an unexpected surprise ten years after the last child, Jacob. While their first two children had moved on, married and had children of their own, young Sarah is still finding her feet, turning twenty one next year. A definite baby of the family - avoiding as much responsibility as possible, and relying on her charm and good looks to get places. And she had plenty of charm, just like her father.

Dave yawned, a foghorn sound exuded from his mouth as he did so, then another yawn, louder this time.

'I'm going to head to bed,' he said, after the third yawn.

'I'll stay up a bit,' she said.

It was 12.34am when Alice woke. She had fallen asleep on the couch, her eyes getting so heavy, she could no longer keep them open. Immediately, she checked her cell. The plan was that Birdie texted her once the deed was done. Her cell had no new notifications, so she texted him. There was a movie on the television, a horror, of a walking and talking doll that went around killing people. She watched it for a few moments, repulsed, yet captivated by the ugly little thing running about the place with a knife in its tiny hand. A hand grabbed her shoulder from behind and she jumped. It was Dave, wanting to know why she was still up.

'I'm not tired,' she said.

'Whose cell is that?' nodding towards the one in her hand, a cheap mobile.

'Oh! It's a client's,' she said, having to think fast. 'She left it in my office.'

He frowned. He didn't believe her and why should he? Since when does Alice bring home articles clients have left in her office? Besides, she was checking it as he was walking up to her, like she was waiting for a reply. Strange goings-on. He decided not to say any more and wandered back to bed.

Eventually, Alice followed the texts with a phone call to Birdie, since he hadn't replied to her text. The call went straight to answer phone. Perhaps he's out of range, or his batteries are flat. But then, the deal was $6000 to knock off Brendon Durie, $2000 as a down payment, $4000 when the job is done. She asked him to send pics of the dead body and then she'd transfer the $4000. This can only mean that he was unable to pull it off. *Damn it!*

NINETEEN

S ian woke in a pool of sweat. She'd had nightmares again about being locked in a small, dark space. It was so dark she couldn't see her hand in front of her face, only feeling along the four walls that confined her. She shuddered as she wiped the tears that fell down her cheeks, trying with all her might to brush the memories from her mind.

There was an empty wardrobe that Brendon Durie would lock her up in. The crimes were small; smiling at another man who merely said hello to her as she walked into a store, wearing something *he* didn't like, eating a high calorie food that may cause weight gain. The more she cried, the greater the pleasure he got from it.

On one occasion she stifled her tears, keeping completely silent throughout the entire ordeal. This only infuriated him. He threw the wardrobe door open, then sat on a chair that was strategically placed opposite her. Then he revealed a bag of pebbles that he slowly and deliberately tossed at her bare legs and arms, one at a time, until the silence was broken and she began to cry.

Other times he'd tie her up to a chair, bind her mouth, and then a lecture would follow on improper behaviour, or inappropriate attire, whatever she was being punished for. He was not a brutal thug. He didn't rage about the place smashing everything in his way, including his wife's face. No, Brendon Durie was cunningly manipulative, and organised. The punishments were planned out in his head before he actioned them.

Lesser punishments, although she pretended otherwise, were when he brought home a woman from work and had sex with her while Sian was locked and bound in the wardrobe. The whole time they were making their noises, she envisioned kicking down the door and shooting him in the head. The thought of his blood and brain splattered across the walls and across the woman, gave her a sense of calmness. Until she scolded herself. Violence was not in her nature and never would be, but spending far too much time with a masochist was changing her thought processes, something she hoped would dissipate over time.

However, Sian kept questioning whether it was wise to stay at Great Aunt May's, because eventually, someone will let slip that she inherited a house and land off her Aunt. Apart from the lawyers who executed the will, there are only four people in her other life that know about this inheritance; her mother, her brother, and Nigel and Kynn. She had kept it a secret from Durie for fear that he may convince her to sell it, or worse, develop it. He was such a know-it-all on investments. From the start, she kept that secret close to her chest. But it wouldn't take much for him to find out about it, if hunting her down was his intention. All *he* needed to do was threaten one of the four who knew, and one of them might tell. Even her closest friends, Nigel and Kynn, might mention the inheritance, if their livelihoods are under threat.

'*He's* moved on,' Sian reminded herself. She just struggled to believe it.

Ignoring the white cotton handkerchief that kept the photograph of the Fields covered, she rose out of bed. It was Saturday and she was to help Rosie set up her stall at the Woodville Spring market. Rosie said that the market had quite a name for itself, for the wonderful arts and crafts that attracted people from all over the area, even from the cities. Sian froze when Rosie said that, in case someone recognised her. But what are the chances of that happening? There had to be a point when she stopped being afraid, when the past, those two years of hell with *him,* are pushed to the back of her mind. For now, she's always on high alert, watching what she's doing and saying, all the while keeping an eye on everyone else. It's exhausting. At least now she had Rosie.

Sian gazed out the window that never liked to close. It was early, just after 6am. They'd have to start setting up in town about 8am as the market officially opens at 9am. It's a clear morning, no signs indicating rain. Her eyes drifted down to the forest, standing eerie and dark. Today there were no strange shadows, or ghosts waving, although she still questioned whether she actually saw anyone at all. She'd come to the conclusion that the last three years of high stress may have sent her a little demented.

She was feeding Popo in the kitchen, when she heard a car slow to a stop outside her house. A car coming this far down the country road was a rarity, as past her house there were only a few metres before the forest began. As soon as she saw it was a police car, she felt a prickle of apprehension. Why would they be visiting her? Several scenarios raced around in her mind. The most obvious one was that she was using a false identity, and suspicions may have arisen as to why an Ingrid Bone would be residing at May Fields' place, so long after she died.

By the time the officer had walked up her drive and knocked on the door, she was shaking like a field mouse. She turned to Popo, whom she had come to rely upon to indicate if danger was nearby. He barely glanced up from his bowl of food, when the officer knocked on the door. This can only be a good sign, and besides, the officer had already seen her through the narrow window by the door. So it would only raise suspicions if she fled out the back. He waved and smiled warmly through the window.

'A beautiful morning!' he said cheerily, as she opened the door a crack. 'I know it's early. I hope I didn't wake you. But I'm expected at the Spring Market by eight thirty just to oversee everything.'

Sian remained silent, waiting for him to say why he was there.

'Would you mind if I come in?' he asked.

'Actually, I'm quite busy,' she said, hiding her trembling hands behind her back. *Are you really a cop?* she thought. *Did he send you here to terrorise me?* That's happened before, the first time Sian escaped from Brendon and stayed with her mother, who protested against it. Bev always said that no relationship is perfect, and a boy like Brendon Durie doesn't come along every day, especially to someone like you, Sian. It was a nightmare staying there, as Bev was extremely sensitive to sound and light, forcing Sian to tiptoe about the place in the dark. The day Sian left her mother's house to move into a flat, she swore she'd never return to live, as her mother's moods were mostly gloomy, and her migraines were too frequent. Shane had the right idea, fleeing at age seventeen to Australia and never returning, leaving the burden of their difficult, ailing mother to Sian.

It was on day three that the police officer came to visit. He looked genuine enough, wore the correct uniform, used the excuse that he was a detective and that's why he drove an unmarked car. Sian knew that this was a fact; many police do drive unmarked cars, but it didn't stop her from feeling that something wasn't right. He said that she had to accompany him down to the police station for questioning.

'Questioning? What for?' Sian asked, horrified.

'For drink driving. We have a witness who took footage of you, obviously inebriated, climbing into this car,' pointing to Sian's old rust coloured station-wagon. He then checked her number plate to make sure it matched what he had written in his notebook.

'What?' she cried, 'I don't drink!' This was the truth. She hated the taste of alcohol. She thought it tasted like dog piss might taste. If you were brave enough to taste the piss of a dog. Besides, it only fed her anxiety, like pouring gasoline on a flame. It took only a couple of small sips for her heart to flutter madly, so she became breathless and dizzy.

Looking back, Sian suspected right then that he was faking, pretending to read something on a blank piece of paper. If she had trusted her instincts and run, things would've turned out a lot better. Against her better judgement, she went with the officer. His car stank of cigarettes as he cuffed her to the back of the driver's seat. Like she suspected, instead of taking her to the police station, he took her an abandoned warehouse, where Brendon Durie was waiting. The fake officer drove the car right inside the empty building, and then left her cuffed and vulnerable. In the corner of the warehouse was a large cage.

The officer from the Woodville Police Station drove a marked car. That's one indicator he was the real thing. The other indicator was, he was measured and calm, a composure that came with experience, even when under attack verbally or physically.

He raised his hand to show that he was there to cause no harm. 'It's okay if we talk out here,' he said, noticing her nervousness. 'We were told that someone had moved into May Fields' house.'

'I inherited it,' Sian said, still talking through an open crack in the doorway. The officer had a tanned face and silver hair, a bit overweight and was fairly laid back.

'It's been sitting here abandoned for years, we were wondering what was going to happen to it,' he said.

'Has someone been talking?' she asked.

'We were contacted by a Sergeant Louise Ratahi in Lakesford. Do you remember her?'

Sian immediately noticed the dilemma. He didn't ask 'have you heard of her?' He asked, assuming that she was Sian Tanner, 'do you remember her?' What to do? Lie or tell the truth?

Sian nodded.

'So you're Sian Tanner?'

'Yes.'

'My name is Sergeant Lee Cabot. Everyone around these parts just calls me Lee. I'm from the Woodville Police Department and we've been contacted by Sergeant Louise in Lakesford. She told us of your situation, that you're running away from a violent relationship,' he said softly. He was sensitive to this situation, probably visited more than enough homes where domestic violence has taken place. After all, one in three women have been physically abused in this country, according to the billboard posters.

'I'm trying to move on,' she said, hoping to come across tough, even though she couldn't trust the police officer enough to let him in to her house.

'Louise said you may be using an alias?' he asked.

'Yes. Ingrid Bone is a false name. I don't want him finding out where I am.'

'That's fair enough. Sergeant Louise wanted me to check that you're okay, that's all. She said you dropped contact with everyone including family and friends, to start a new life. That must've been difficult,' he asked.

Where is this going? 'Yes and no. I miss a couple of friends.'

He nodded. 'Now we know what your situation is, we can send an officer to stop by on the odd occasion, if that's alright with you.'

She hesitated as memories flooded back again of the fake officer in Lakesford. 'Yes,' she answered finally.

'But ah...' shaking his head disapprovingly, 'using a fake name isn't wise. It's a criminal offence to sign legal documents using...what was it, Ingrid?'

'I know, but I wasn't sure what to do, and my therapist said that I may have to use a pseudonym for a while, until I feel safer.'

He shook his head, 'You'll only dig yourself a deeper hole doing that. Either change your name legally through the courts, or go back to your original name. It's only going to cause you a headache in the long run, applying for jobs and loans...etcetera.'

Sian knew he was right. But to tell those people who have offered her nothing but kindness since she arrived in Woodville, that she'd been using an alias name may cause some upset, and probably raise suspicions.

'Do you live here alone?' Lee asked. Another question that frightened her.

'Um. Yes.'

'It might pay to get friendly with your neighbour, set up a neighbourhood watch group.'

'Oh! I have already become good friends with Rosie. She's my support person.'

Lee smiled like a proud father would smile at his daughter. 'Good,' he said. 'Perhaps getting a flatmate, someone you trust, or a dog. Dogs are great at barking when strangers come near, but it's got to be well-trained.'

'I have cat that does that.' Just as she said the word 'cat' Popo appeared, rubbing his large, round belly against the officer's legs.

'This cat, this cat barks like a dog?'

'No, I mean he indicates when strangers come near.'

'Have you had problems with unwelcome guests?' he turned stern and protective.

'No. Just met a couple of possum hunters in the forest, who work for DOC. Or so they said. They weren't a problem, just a bit uncouth.' She refrained from saying more. She didn't want to get offside with the locals by dobbing them in. Besides, now the possum hunters know that someone has moved into the 'abandoned cottage' they hopefully won't come back.

'Not the Sorenson boys, is it?' he asked.

No surprises that they're known to police, especially Sam Sorenson.

Sian nodded.

'They're alright, just a bit rough on the outside. They haven't had the easiest life. The possums are good at destroying forests, so the Sorenson boys are needed, and they're good at the job. Anyway, you're best to add our station number to your phone, so you can call us if anything untoward takes place,' Lee said, taking a business card with the local police station's number on it from his pocket, and handing it to her.

'Okay,' taking the card. *I've got to buy a new phone, or hook the landline up.*

'Well...I hope you settle in Woodville. There's a good mix of people who reside here, anything from artists to retired farmers. We even had a comedian living here for a couple of years. But on a serious note, if you need anything, like more security, a good therapist, self-defence classes, or even a good plumber, head down to the community centre and talk to Fred Anderson, he knows the best people to contact.'

'Okay, thanks,' she said. The community centre was next door to the library. It was open only three hours per day, run purely by volunteers, much like the library.

As he turned to walk back to his car, Sian had a sudden thought and called after him. He turned back, eager to be helpful.

'Do you know about Benny Sorenson?' she asked.

'Benny?' he paused, placing his hands on his hips.

'He drowned in the river about fourteen or fifteen years ago?'

'What about him?'

'Was it true? Was that how he died?'

'It looked like it,' he said. 'Did you know him?'

'Yes. I came here over the summer as a child, and we hung together a lot. And then his brother said that he died.'

Lee nodded, wondering where the conversation was going.

Sian continued, 'He had a high blood alcohol count. Were you here then?'

'I was hired soon after, when his father... It was an extremely sad situation.'

'But was Benny Sorenson a drunk?'

'I can't tell you that, because I didn't know him. All I can go on is his autopsy results.' He was holding back. He knew more than he was letting on. But he was a police officer after all, not the community gossip. 'Out of interest, did you sign an employment contract when you started that job at the library?'

'No,' she answered, honestly.

'That's good. You wouldn't want to betray Mavis by signing a false name to a legal document. She may be old and retired, but she's proud as punch and doesn't suffer fools kindly.'

TWENTY

Rosie had already jam-packed her sedan with canvases and shoe boxes of painted rocks, and handcrafted jewellery, by the time Sian arrived in her station wagon.

'I had the police around,' Sian said, apologising and opening the boot of her station wagon so they could stack more artwork inside.

'I saw him drive past and thought he was just doing a look-see round the area. I hope nothing untoward has happened?' she asked, placing a large canvas in the back, which only just fit.

'No. It's just that the Lakesford police were checking up on me.'

'Really?'

'Just to make sure I'm okay.'

'Oh wow! That's good service.'

'I guess so. But I'm worried about how easy it was to find me.'

'Do the Woodville police know about your past?'

'Yes.'

'Are they taking it seriously?'

'I think so. Sergeant Louise Ratahi from Lakesford updated them.' Sian sighed. 'Just when you think you're beginning to make progress, your past taps you on the shoulder, and all those horrible things I'd rather forget, resurface.' Sian caught sight of a silhouette of someone standing in Rosie's front window, waving.

'This Louise must be worried about you,' Rosie said, closing the boot to the station wagon.

'She knows what *he* is capable of,' she replied, waving back to the person waving at her.

'That's my mother,' Rosie said, smiling. 'She came down to look after Chloe. It's turned into a tradition for the Spring Markets, she adores Chloe and Chloe thinks my mother is absolutely marvellous. She might pop by the market later.'

'Where's Chloe now?'

'Asleep.'

They were one of the last to set up at the Spring Market, but Rosie had pre-ordered a white gazebo to shield the sunlight from her canvases, while many others had just settled for an open stall. Rain wasn't forecast, but in a country which could produce four seasons in one day, it was wise to be prepared.

There were three cafes and a bakery in Woodville that did a roaring trade whenever the markets were on. Coming from the city, Sian wasn't a fan of small town cafe food, which consisted mostly of pies, sausage rolls and white bread sandwiches. One cafe raved about its 'famous cheese rolls'; a slice of white bread with grated cheddar cheese, and a secret ingredient which many believe is mustard, then rolled up and placed under the grill until crispy. Sian found this low nutrient type of food nauseating. She'd rather munch on an apple or carrot and Rosie was a vegan, so neither of them had much luck looking for a bite to eat in a cafe in a farming town.

Before they had even finished setting up the stall, local customers had bought some products. The kids loved the rocks and they were normally the first to go. Canvases were big ticket items, likely to sell to city folk. Usually, people from Lakesford and Wellington drove all the way to Woodville for a day out, and so they placed a higher value on good artwork of any kind.

After two hours of busyness; some were buyers, but most of them were browsers, Sian took a break to calm her nerves. There was a tall man standing nearby with his back to her. He seemed to be doing nothing but hanging about, perhaps waiting for someone. From that *angle he was the spitting image of Brendon shithead Durie. When he* turned around, his face was marked with acne scars, and he was wearing glasses. It annoyed her that she saw him everywhere.

She had to get away for a bit, so weaved her way through the crowd to the large oak tree, which created a lovely canopy for the stalls underneath it. At the base of the oak was a small slab of concrete with a bronze plaque on top. Engraved into the bronze were the words*, In memory of a boy who was taken too soon. Ben Stokes. Disappeared in 1956, age 16*

Feeling no connection to the words she was reading, she was about to walk away when she sensed a shadow bear down on her, and she flinched. It was the possum hunter, Angus Sorenson, dressed in a tee shirt and jeans, and this time unarmed.

'When there's no body, it's the next best thing to a grave,' he said.

'Are you related to him?' she asked.

He chuckled at that. 'No. Not that I know of. I cut the grass every week and always wondered about him.'

'How's the leg?'

'Alright, thanks to you. It's Sian isn't it?'

'Yes.'

He chuckled. 'Scotland meets Ireland in New Zealand.'

Sian looked blank.

'Sian is an Irish name, isn't it?' he asked.

'Yes,' then the penny dropped. 'Oh right, Angus. Angus is Scottish.'

'I hope we didn't scare you the other day.'

'Well...you shot an arrow through my window, you were dressed in camouflage clothing and you accused me of trespassing in my own house.'

He smiled. He was a ruggedly good looking man and charming too, but Sian was not the slightest bit attracted to him. In fact, she avoided looking him in the eye to show her disinterest.

'Your aunt was good to us,' he said. 'She wanted to preserve the forest, and the only way to do that is by killing off invading pests. That made me and Sam her favourite people, along with the other guys. She was also active in setting up the Kiwi Club for kids to learn about the native forest, and took tours through there. I was one of the first members of the Kiwi Club when I was a kid. I was in the Scouts, too.'

'So do you think Sam is going to give me my knife back?'

Angus chuckled. He did have a lovely smile. 'He's a bit feral, our Sam, lives by his own law.'

'So he's probably known to the police then?'

Angus gave a sheepish grin.

Sian rolled her eyes. 'My knife, my only protection is in the hands of an outlaw.'

'He's not that bad. He won't hurt anyone, unless they hurt him first. What do you mean by "only protection"?'

'I live alone, don't I,' suddenly realising she just made a grave mistake. 'I mean, when my partner is away on boxing tournaments.'

'Partner? It looked to me like you live alone. Maybe you should buy a dog.'

'Maybe your brother should give me my knife back.'

It had quietened down when Sian returned to Rosie's stall. Rosie was doing a deal with a guy obviously from the city, dressed in branded jeans and buttoned shirt. He wanted two of her paintings at a cheaper rate, if they could agree on a price. Rosie may look like a burlesque dancer with her arms covered in tattoos, and scarlet fringe cut sharply across her forehead, but she's good at business. Sian could tell.

Noticing that the community centre was open, Sian went in and had a look around. There were half a dozen people asking questions about the best nature trails in the area, and the old man at the counter seemed more than happy to help. Together they hovered over the map, while Sian noticed an open door with a sign reading *Museum*.

Inside, the smell of old leather and rust struck her nostrils quickly. In a large, cool room was old farming machinery, vintage cars, and many photographs on the walls of families who established Woodville. The name Woodville comes from the wealthy English family that married well, becoming royals, in stark contrast to the town of Woodville where you'd be hard pressed to find a gold watch, let alone opulent jewels and sable fur.

In the corner of the room was a shrine to the Woodville men who went to war, both World War One and World War Two. At the time the population was very small, so only a handful of men actually went to war. One man died, the rest came home, got married and worked on farms in the area. There were sepia photographs of the men in their soldier uniforms, their complexions perfect, like plastic.

As she moved to the next display, she caught the face of Benny Sorenson. He was in a black and white photo, dressed in shorts and jersey, knee-length grey socks rolled down around his ankles, and black shoes with the laces untied. He was holding a baby rabbit in his small hands, his face cautious, as if he didn't want his photo taken. Behind him was nothing but fields, muted and grey in the photo. Underneath the photograph was a plaque that read, *The Boy in the Woods. Victim of nature, Ben Stokes vanished in McCrae's Forest, 1956. Even though there was a large scale search party, consisting of hundreds of volunteers from several towns, scaling miles of terrain over several weeks, his body still could not be found. He died aged 16. He was seven years old in the above photograph.*

It's a secret. Sian's heart pounded. This made no sense. Perhaps he *was* related to the Sorensons. They're so alike, they could be twins. Next to the framed photograph of Ben Stokes was a newspaper clipping, framed, and yellowing from the light. It was hard to read, but had a photograph of several people armed with shovels and torches, searching through McCrae's Forest. What she could pick up from the blurred words was that an article of clothing was found in the search, discovering later that it did not belong to Ben Stokes.

'It's not free entry!' a voice called out. It was Fred Anderson, the retired farmer who volunteered at the Woodville Information Centre. He walked with a stick, wincing with every step as if in pain. 'You're supposed to pay at the front counter before you go in.'

'I'm sorry,' Sian said, still breathless from seeing Ben gaze back at her through still, grey eyes. 'How much is it?'

'Five dollars, for an adult concession. Some of the income goes towards the RSA, the Royal New Zealand Returned and Services Association.'

Sian handed him some gold coin, money she was going to buy some lunch with.

'I see you're looking at the Boy in the Woods,' nodding towards Ben.

'He looks like a boy I used to spend my summers with,' she said, as a group of people walked straight into the museum assuming it was free entry, just as Sian had. Fred asked the people as politely as a grumpy old man possibly could, to wait by the counter. 'There's a book written about him,' he said, as he began to hobble away.'

'Yes, I know. The Boy in the Woods,' Sian called after him.

'She said she used to see him,' he said.

'Who? Aunt May?'

He froze, and turned around slowly to inspect Sian properly. 'May? You're the one who's moved into her house?'

'Yes. She left it to me in her will.'

'You've got your work cut out for you. That house sat abandoned for so long, rats and possums took up residence.'

'It's not too bad,' she called back. 'It does need a bit of work.'

He grunted, and was about to continue on his way, when something stopped him. 'May Fields had a niece who she said played with the ghost of Ben Stokes. Was that you?'

'I-I I don't know.'

He broke into a croaky laugh. 'It's a load of old codswallop! That woman was as mad as the hatter.'

TWENTY ONE

The Therapist

Alice barely slept Friday night, the last night of Brendon Durie's existence. Still, there no word from Birdie, which was highly unusual, and disconcerting. She had used Birdie's service twice before, and he hadn't let her down. Besides, she had too much on him. She had found out who he really was in his other life, due to an unfortunate event.

It was on the night Birdie knocked out, and then drowned a target in the sea. This was the first time Alice had hired him, the target's name, Paul Gleeson, another violent lowlife. As he pulled the body further out into the ocean's waves, he got caught up in the currents and swallowed some water. Struggling against the tide, he managed to pull himself free and dragged himself up onto the sandy shore where Alice was pacing back and forth in a panic. Under just a single dim light, she pulled off his balaclava to find an ordinary man underneath.

Two weeks later, she stumbled across him at a Christmas party in a bar that she and Dave attended, at first pretending not to notice him. But as the bar filled up with noisy, happily drunk patrons and the music grew louder, she struck up a conversation with him, while

Dave talked shop with a workmate. Birdie's natural reaction was to pretend that he didn't know her, but as he threw back another lager, the truth fell out of his mouth.

Birdie, real name Kenneth, or Ken Eagle, worked for an insurance company. Before then he was with the SAS, so he knew how to kill, and camouflage. He took up the part-time career of contract killing to "rid the world of scum." He'd grown up in a household where violence was an everyday occurrence. His parents fought like cats and dogs, his mother coming off second best over and over again. Eventually, his mother died at the fist of his drunken father. His father was sentenced to six years for manslaughter. Ken swore that when his father was released from prison, he'd hunt him down and kill him. Luckily for his father, he died in prison from a heart attack. In Ken's eyes, he'd gotten off scot free.

His first kill, outside of the army, was a Pakistani student doctor who'd killed his teenage flatmate. This flatmate, a girl of only seventeen named Penelope, was threatening to go to the police about his inappropriate behaviour towards young girls. She claimed to have evidence of him touching her cousin, a 5 year old, and she was also aware that there were other girls he'd abused. The student doctor already had a strike against him for inappropriate behaviour towards young female patients. If this information was to land in the wrong hands, not only would his career be in ruins, he'd also be deported back to Pakistan, shaming his entire family.

Ken Eagle's connection to the case started off fairly loosely. The step-father of the teenage victim worked in the same building as he did. They'd said no more than two words to each other previously, but when the girl was murdered and the killer caught, the truth came out through the courts showing what a real scumbag the student doctor was. Ken sat up and listened. In all fairness, if he was to stumble across the doctor in the street, he'd take great pleasure in beating the crap out of him.

'I want him dead,' the victim's step-father said one day to Kenneth at the cafe on the ground floor. Ken looked behind him to see who he was talking to. Ken was buying a ham sandwich, the victim's step-father was in the queue behind with an empty plate, probably lacking in appetite. He looked like he hadn't slept in weeks. 'Her mother has breast cancer. They reckon she's got only a couple of months. The stress of all this will shorten her life.'

'I'm really sorry about that.'

'Can we talk privately?' the man asked.

'Sure,' Ken said, curious to know what was going to follow. They moved to a corner table.

'Correct me if I'm wrong, but you were with the SAS?'

'Who told you that?'

He shrugged. 'Interesting career change, Secret Service to selling insurance.'

Ken couldn't help but laugh at the absurdity of it. Even his wife found it funny.

'You know how to kill people, leaving no trace.'

Ken wasn't sure if this was a question or a statement.

'Ten thousand dollars to kill the doctor,' the grieving man said.

'I don't do that sort of stuff.'

'But you could, if you wanted to.'

'Look! This doctor is going to get more than his fair share of torture while he's in prison, and then he'll be sent back to Pakistan.'

'Why should scum like that be allowed to breathe the same air that good people like us do? Good people like Penelope? If I could wave a wand...' his fists were tightly clenched, 'I'd wipe them all out. Every single rapist, child molester, woman beater...' he sighed, and slammed his fist down on the table. 'Think about it, and get back to me,' He stood up and left.

Ken went home and told his wife Marilyn, and was gobsmacked when she said, after little thought, 'I think you should do it. You're smart enough to never get caught.'

'Are you serious?'

She sat down next to him, took his hand in hers and said, 'We would all love for Spiderman, or Superman, or that big green man to really exist, but sadly they don't. The next best thing, are people like you. People who are compassionate, and know how to kill with one shot, then vanish. Simple.'

'You know this will make me a criminal?'

She laughed. 'Criminal. Shriminal. That is just a matter of opinion.'

'The opinion of the law.'

She released his hand and leaned back in the seat. 'Yes, but only if you get caught. Besides, the extra money would be rather nice, don't you think?'

'And, it's the Hulk.'

'Pardon?'

'The big, green man is the Hulk.'

'Oh.' She got up and patted him on the shoulder. 'Think about it. Just remember, I'll always be your support.'

And so it began...the alternative life of Ken Eagle.

His story was reluctantly told to Alice over several beers and she swore never to repeat it. After all he's a hitman. If she were to tell people about him, she'd be next on the list. He left out his wife's name in the story. Unbeknown to Alice, it was his wife who anonymously sent Alice the details of a hitman. Alice wasn't looking for one. In fact it hadn't even occurred to her to do that, until the text came. It was a simple solution to ridding the world of an on-going problem: Paul Gleeson. She still to this day did not know who the link was, but she suspected it may have been one of Paul Gleeson's clients. Apart from being a regular visitor to child brothels in Thailand, Paul was also a financial investor, and was a big fan of the pyramid scheme. Many clients lost money and Paul fled overseas. He thought he'd gotten away with it. He set up a new life in Bali, running a beachside resort that he bought using his client's money. But, one day, there a knock on his door. *Birdie.*

Birdie the hitman, who while killing, was always covered head to toe in black clothing including a balaclava, leaving only his hands and eyes uncovered. When he drowned Paul Gleeson though, he tripped up. Big mistake. He couldn't breathe, and Alice Granger, who happened to be holidaying in Bali - no coincidence at all - seemed to be someone he could trust. He had no choice but to remove his balaclava, so he could cough up the salt water that had filled his lungs. It was unfortunate, but he'd be dead right now if he hadn't.

They got away with the Bali hit. But unbeknown to them, someone was taking photographs of Alice meeting Damon Ridge under the street lamp in the Stanley Stadium car park. And, behind the building where Birdie was waiting in the shadows to knock the man out and pull him into the sea, the whole time Alice stood by and watched. This was unusual behaviour for a client. Normally, they play their role, which is minimal, mostly a draw-card to the target, and then quickly flee. But Alice Granger stayed the whole time, like she did in Bali. Perhaps she wanted to make sure the job was going to be done properly.

The best outcome is the disappearance of the target. No body, means no proof they're dead. Of course, there are unused bank accounts and cell phones, but the target could've fallen off a cliff, or taken their own life.

Pushing her concerns to the back of her mind, Alice set to work making lunch for Sarah and Dave. It's always special when an adult child comes home for a visit, especially if they bring the grandchildren. They've left the nest, moved out of Lakesford to build a new life, and are far too busy to visit often. Except Sarah, who still lives in Lakesford, finishing off her degree in psychology, taking after her mother, then she wants to do her big OE. The Grangers figured, since Sarah still has one more year left at uni, she can stick around and housesit while they spend the year travelling. Dave and Alice decided to reveal this to Sarah at lunch. Then if she was fine with it, they'd start booking their trip. The sooner they leave the better, Alice felt.

'Hellooo!' called Sarah, as she unlocked the front door. She walked in looking fabulous in skinny jeans and tee shirt, her complexion glowing. 'Hi guys!' she said, hugging and kissing her ma and pa. 'Sorry to land this on you...but...'-

'Oh no, what?' Dave cringed. 'Are you going to ask me for more money?'

'No actually, Dad. But if you have some spare cash lying around, I'd be grateful.'

Dave smiled, completely charmed by his youngest child, the apple of his eye.

'No, what I was going to say is I've brought a guest. I hope you've got enough food for one more?'

'Depends how big *his* appetite is,' Dave grunted, knowing full well that it's probably the latest boyfriend.

'We haven't been seeing each other for long, but he's...' lowering her voice to a whisper, 'quite a catch, if I say so myself,' sucking her cheeks in and swaying her hips. 'He's just parking the car.' There's a tap at the front door. 'That's him,' she says, suddenly becoming flustered, and darting to the door.

Alice chuckled, and set to work chopping cucumber and carrots for the leafy green salad, to go with the cold roast chicken.

'This is my new beau,' Alice heard her daughter say.

'It's great to meet you!' Dave said, stepping forward to shake his hand.

Alice looked up from the chopped vegetables to find a tall, striking young man wearing designer jeans and white buttoned shirt standing in her kitchen.

'This is my mother, Alice,' Sarah said, flushed.

Alice froze, tightening her grip on the knife.

'Hello Mrs Granger,' Brendon Durie said, as sweet as pie, holding out his hand for her to shake.

TWENTY TWO

The Therapist

That man is in my damn house!!! Alice texted Birdie, when she left the table to use the bathroom. *What happened last night?*

To avoid a scene, Alice played nice all afternoon, all the while wishing he was dead. She had to somehow pull Sarah away from Brendon, to tell her the truth. But they were glued together like newly courting couples, holding hands and whispering sweet nothings. This made Alice quiver in desperation.

He's supposed to be dead!!! She texted Birdie again. *And now he's dating my daughter.*

Alice stashed the cell back in her handbag and splashed cold water over her face. She had to get Brendon Durie away from her daughter. She had no choice but to tell her that he is an abuser, and a masochistic one at that. The glaringly obvious problem was that he had those pictures of her meeting with Damon Ridge at Stanley Stadium. Plus the shots of Birdie coming out of the shadows and whacking Damon over the back of the head, then dragging his body into the sea. All the while Alice stood by watching. In all of the pictures Brendon had sent her, Birdic was wearing his balaclava. He had taken a taxi to a nearby house, pretending to live there, then when the taxi disappeared out of sight, he'd run down the windy,

145

concrete steps to the Stadium car park. He changed into his hitman clothes behind the stadium, and waited for his target. He thought he had covered his tracks and it seemed he had succeeded.

Alice on the other hand, was easily identifiable in those photographs. All it would take would be for Brendon Durie to anonymously send these pics to the local police, and it's all over for her. Her marriage and her career, over.

Alice took some deep breaths to calm her nerves. Then she pulled herself together and stepped out of the bathroom. Waiting in the hallway was Brendon Durie. She froze as he moved close to her, his head bowing low, his lips almost touching hers. Then he pulled his head away and whispered in her ear, 'Your daughter is a good -!'

'-Get away from me!' Alice screamed.

Brendon laughed, and walked slowly back to the kitchen table. Alice could hear Dave asking if she was okay, as he appeared at the top of the hallway. Alice waved him over, dragging him into the bathroom.

'What's the matter?' he asked, as tears flowed down her cheeks.

'Do you remember me talking to you about a client called Sian Tanner?'

His face looked blank.

'She's the client that was hung up naked in an abandoned warehouse for several hours, while her attacker did the most insidious things to her. Even thinking about it makes me sick to my stomach.'

'Vaguely, wasn't there an arrest made?'

'Yes, but he was let off due to an oversight. The attacker's uncle...' rolling her eyes, 'is a high profile lawyer by the name of Mack Durie.'

The penny dropped. 'Shit! He's a Durie?' nodding in the direction of the kitchen table, where Sarah and Brendon were probably cuddling and whispering, 'He's related to the attacker?'

'No, my sweet man,' Alice said, taking Dave's face in her hands to look him directly in the eyes. 'He *is* the attacker.'

Dave pulled away. 'I'll kill him. I'll kill the bastard.'

'You can't. He's too dangerous. There has to be some way to make her understand what he's capable of.'

There was a gentle tap on the bathroom door. 'What are you guys doing in there?' Sarah asked. 'We're about to take off. Aren't you going to see us to the door?'

Dave swiftly opened the door and pulled his daughter inside the bathroom, locking the door behind her.

'You can't date him anymore. I forbid it,' Dave said sternly.

Sarah laughed. 'Why?'

'He's a psychotic masochist,' Alice said, seriously.

'Ooh! We are bringing out the big words today,' Sarah laughed.

'Listen to me!' Alice barked. 'You don't know what he's capable of.'

Sarah rolled her eyes. 'I know what you're referring to, mum. He's already told me all about that.'

'About what?' Alice asked, wondering if they were on the same page.

'He said a jealous ex-girlfriend accused him of doing all these horrible things, because he was going to leave her. He said she was a nut-job.'

'No! No! No! No! You've got it wrong, Sarah. She wasn't making it all up. She was my client, it went on for years. He's lying to you.'

Sarah cringed at her mother's ridiculous accusation, and pulled away from her to unlock the bathroom door. 'He said the judge didn't believe her either, and let him go.'

'That's not true,' Alice said, with conviction.

'Did he serve time in prison for abusing this girl?' Sarah asked, her arms crossed tightly over her chest in defiance.

'No, he didn't. There was an oversight, a lapse in legal procedure...'-

'So, he's not a convicted rapist then.' Sarah said, opening the door and leaving in a huff. 'Come on, let's get out of this house of demented people,' she said to Brendon, followed by the slamming of the front door.

'We're going to have to hire a hitman,' Dave said, pacing back and forth in a panic.

'I already had,' Alice mumbled.

'What?'

'Nothing.'

'Is there a possibility that he is telling the truth, and this girl, what's her name?'

'-Sian.'

'...Sian was jealous and decided to make up all this horrible stuff?'

Alice shook her head. 'She had been coming to me for over a year. I helped her put a plan into place for her escape from him. And she's succeeded. She's gone off and started a new life, happy and free from his... It was so awful what he did to her, I just can't bring myself to imagine it. And now the shithead is dating our daughter.'

'What are we going to do, then?' he asked, angrily. 'There must be something. I mean, Sarah is not an idiot, she'll come to her senses surely, and tell him to take a hike.'

Alice was barely listening.

'What are you not telling me?' Dave asked, reading his dear wife like a book.

She sighed, the emotional pain was unbearable. 'I might be wrong, but I think this is a set-up.'

'A set-up? What do you mean?'

'Brendon bloody Durie has contacted me on more than one occasion, asking for Sian's new location. He hasn't finished with her yet. I know he hasn't.'

'So why is he dating our daughter then, if he really wants his ex back?'

Alice rolled his eyes at Dave. 'To get to me!'

'Why?'

'Because he thinks I know Sian's location.'

'Do you?'

'No.'

'Can you get it?'

'That goes against everything I believe in,' she scolded him.

'I don't care! A violent psychopath is dating my daughter. Give him the damn address! Let him kill *her*, not my daughter.'

Alice fell silent, debating in her mind whether to tell Dave about the pictures Brendon Durie was bribing her with. For all his life experiences, Dave was a fairly naive man, much like Sarah. He was brought up in a happy, sheltered family, had a good education paid for by his parents, and went on to have a good career as a large business accountant. Everything he ever needed was there at his finger tips. He's never gone hungry, or struggled to find a job, never prematurely lost a family member, or had major health problems. How is this new piece of information likely to go down? How will he handle the fact that his lovely wife hired a hitman to wipe out serious abusers, and doesn't regret it one bit. How will Dave understand that now she is being bribed by someone, with photos of her watching on, as Birdie knocked out, then drowned their last target in the waves?

Before she had a chance to speak, her cell beeped. It was her personal cell, and she was hoping it was Sarah admitting that they were right and she was wrong, and that she was stupid not to listen to them. To her disappointment, it was from an unknown number.

'I think it's *him*,' she said, cautiously.

'How does he have your personal number?' Dave asked.

'Maybe Sarah gave to him.'

'Why would he want it?'

Alice opened his text. It was another photograph. Scarcely able to make it out, Alice enlarged the image only to discover it was something so vile, and so grotesque, she began to shake uncontrollably, her cell slipping out of her hand and landing on the carpet.

Seeing Alice's horrified reaction, Dave rushed to pick up the phone. He covered his mouth with his hand in shock, running to the kitchen sink to vomit. It was a photograph of a woman in a shallow grave, the lower half of her body covered in dirt, the top half bare and decomposing. But the most sickening thing of all, was a headshot of Sarah's beautiful smiling face stuck over the face of the dead woman.

'Now you know what he's capable of,' Alice said, as Dave came up for air after throwing up.

'We have to go to the police,' he said. 'What about your friend Louise? Call her! Call her now! Send her that photograph.' He began pacing back and forth again, stopping to cover his face with his hands and letting out a desperate groan. 'Send that picture to Sarah,' he blurted out. 'Then she'll know the truth.'

Dave handed the phone back to Alice, and with trembling fingers, she forwarded the image to Sarah. *Your lovely boyfriend sent this to me.*

An instant reply from Sarah read: *Unknown number. Not his. No proof. Stop playing stupid games. This is sick.*

I'm sure he has more than one phone, Alice replied.

Sarah: *STOP IT!*

Alice: *Please! Sarah, be careful.*

There was a pause then, *Why would anyone put my picture over a dead person's face?*

Alice: *Ask your boyfriend.*

Sarah: *NO! Talk to the jealous ex.*

Alice: *Why would my client send me pictures like this?*

Sarah: *Maybe she knows Brendon is dating your daughter*

Alice: *She wouldn't care. Please be careful, Sarah.*

The conversation went dead.

As soon as Alice put the phone down, there was another beep indicating a text, this time it was muffled and coming from her handbag. It was the cheap, throwaway cell, the cell she used only to communicate with Birdie. Knowing that Dave was watching she reached into the inside pocket of her handbag, and pulled out the old cell.

'Now you're answering your client's messages?' Dave asked, sarcastically.

'What?' she'd forgotten that he'd noticed this same cell in her hand last night. He hadn't seen it before, and she'd said it belonged to a client. She suspected that he didn't believe her.

Still with the weight of Dave's stare, Alice opened the message from Birdie. *We need to talk*

TWENTY THREE

The niece that played with the ghost of Ben Stokes, Sian repeated in her mind, as she weaved her way back through the crowd to Rosie's stall. She almost missed Rosie's gazebo altogether it was so crammed with buyers, the artwork and Rosie's claret hair were hidden from view.

It seemed Rosie was making a killing, so Sian thought she'd better help out. As hard as she tried, she couldn't stop thinking about Ben Stokes, and Fred's comment about her Great Aunt, "Mad as a hatter," he'd said.

Benny Sorenson was real, though. He was a solid boy with warm skin and soft lips. She knew this because they had held hands and kissed, and had teased each other, terribly. The blood from the rabbit he killed was real, as was the carving he made of her face in the trunk of the kauri tree. It's still there. She saw it, and ran her hands over the cuts in the wood. She remembered when the cuts were fresh, the gum of the kauri dribbling like it was crying. She'd touched the gum and it was sticky. No ghost can cut a solid thing, can it?

'How's it going here?' Sergeant Lee asked, holding out cash to purchase a painted stone. 'It's for my grandson. He's only two. He prefers trains and fire engines, but I guess a tuatara painted on a rock will do. This is pretty good work,' looking closely at the detail of the scales on the reptile. 'Did you do this?'

'No, this is all Rosie's work.'

'Ah yes, I know Rosie,' glancing in Rosie's direction. She was still trying to make a deal with the man from the city, who was now keen to have a third painting thrown in. 'Her husband is away a lot on an oil rig, so you two can keep each other company.'

'I had a look in the Woodville museum behind the Information Centre. There was information on a Ben Stokes, the missing boy who died in 1956. Do have any more information than that in your cold case files?' Sian asked Lee.

'Why, are you thinking about doing your own investigation?' he laughed, with a smirk.

'Just a curiosity,' she said with conviction. She had to get to the bottom of the mystery that is Ben Stokes. He looked so much like Benny Sorenson. And there was another thing gnawing away in her stomach...the photograph of the Fields. She'd have to take another look to clarify, but the young man standing behind the Fields with the scythe in his hand, could quite easily be an older Ben Stokes. If only she could find a photograph of Ben as a teenager. *It's a secret.*

'I'll take a look for you,' he said. 'There is very little on him. He walked into McCrae's forest, and vanished.'

'It's just that it doesn't make any sense to have that many volunteers searching for him, and find nothing, not even a shoe. It's not a big forest. You could walk from one end to the other in a day.'

He nodded in agreement. 'Apparently, the forest was bigger back then, some of it has since been burned down for farming. Besides, who said no-one found anything?' he asked.

'The newspaper clipping in the museum said an article of clothing was found, but it didn't belong to Ben.'

He gazed past her to a spot on a canvas, but he wasn't looking at the swirls of colour in the painting, he was trying to latch onto a memory of a past conversation, or something he'd read a while back. Rubbing his chin, he said, 'You need to check the archives of old newspapers in the library. It was pretty big news back then.'

'So you don't mind me investigating this mystery?' Sian asked.

'No, but don't be surprised if you come across nothing but dead ends. His disappearance was over sixty years ago, any evidence that wasn't discovered then, would be buried even deeper, now.'

'Sixty three,' she corrected him. 'It was sixty three years ago.'

'You're not going to find many people alive who were around then,' he said.

'Just Fred and Mavis,' Sian said.

Lee chuckled. 'Those two,' he said, shaking his head. 'Fred and Mavis should be called George and Mildred.'

Sian frowned.

He realised the joke was lost on her. 'Ah! George and Mildred. It was a television show a bit before your time. If you want to know something before it happens, ask those two. It's a pity they can't stand to be in the same room together like George and Mildred.'

'Why?'

Lee shrugged. 'I don't know. I have to say, it's pretty entertaining when they are forced to be in the same room. I've seen them in action a few times, with their constant snapping and little digs at each other. Fred calls Mavis a witch. Mavis calls Fred a cantankerous old fool. It's pure entertainment. And they never call each other by their proper names.'

'Fred didn't have anything nice to say about my Great Aunt May, either,' Sian added.

'Yeah, he was suspicious of Mavis and May. Thought they were up to no good. He called them the witches of Eastwick. As far as I know they were just good friends. But he did make a complaint about your Great Aunt not long before she died. Said she and Mavis were trying

to stir up the dead, accused them of grave robbery.' He laughed at
the absurdity of it.

'And were they?' Sian asked fascinated, but not at all surprised.
Great Aunt May was a wonderful oddity, who was capable of just
about anything out of the ordinary. Great Aunt May couldn't
possibly be ordinary if she tried.

'So, I went down to see if any of the graves at the cemetery had
been disturbed, and none were. I don't know what he was going on
about. He often makes mad claims about people. This was nothing
new. I suspect he doesn't like people much, and would rather live his
days alone with his dog. For some mysterious reason, he has an
unbending loyalty to the Information Centre and Museum.' He rolled
his eyes. 'It's not ideal having an impatient, bad-tempered old man
waving his stick at the tourists, but no-one can shift him from his
role. They've tried to gently ask him to work less days, but he won't.
"Only when I'm dead will you replace me." I remember him saying.
I guess he just likes to feel useful, just like the rest of us.'

'Which grave did he say my Aunt and Mavis were trying to rob?'
Sian asked.

Lee cocked his head at her, giving her a stern look. 'I don't see
what it's got to do with Ben Stokes.'

'It might have everything to do with it,' Sian said.

'Listen, I know you've made it your hobby to find out what
happened to that boy, but if you do stumble across something, you'll
come straight to me, won't you. You won't go sticking your nose in
where it doesn't belong, and end up upsetting people.'

'I won't deliberately upset people,' she promised. She had to keep a
low profile anyway, so creating a fuss and bringing attention to
herself was unwise. There was still that small voice that reminded
her constantly that Brendon Durie hadn't finished with her yet. Even
though some time has gone by, and he hasn't made any contact.
Even though, she's been told, he's moved on. Still, her voice of
reason was telling a different story.

'Know that there's a line you shouldn't cross,' Lee said sternly. 'then it becomes a matter for police to handle.'

'So you want me to do all the work, so you can get all the accolades?' she quipped.

'Accolades?' he was still serious. 'What planet are you on? That case is so old; you're not going to find much.'

'We just can't let his death go to waste,' Sian said. 'Besides, how do you know he went missing in McCrae's Forest?' Lee's attention was diverted by several noisy teenagers, a few metres away. They were encouraging a kid on a skateboard to jump the park bench.

Lee strode over to the group and had a quiet word with them. They dispersed, but not without an argument first. He came back to Sian and said, 'Drop by the station and I'll give you what we have on the boy.' His mood had shifted; he was back on the beat and the conversation was over.

'If I can get enough information, I'll write a book about it,' Sian said to Rosie, as they packed into their cars anything that hadn't sold on their stall.

'Great idea, people love historical mysteries,' Rosie said, running her hand over the paint on a canvas. 'It's been scratched. Look!' She held up the canvas. At first glance, it looked like red and yellow blotches and swirls, but the more Sian looked, the more she could see an image, a woman cradling a baby.

'Is that you and Chloe?'

'No. It's not based on anyone in particular, just a mother and baby. But can you see the big scratch?' Rosie asked, pointing to a mark about a foot long.

Sian ran her hand across it.

'Sabotage,' Rosie mouthed.

'Are you serious?'

'It has to be. It's a deliberate scratch with car keys, or something. If I looked hard enough, I'd be able to find the fallen paint on the ground, the cut is so deep.'

'Are there any more like that?'

'Yeah, one that rich city bloke wanted to buy, until he noticed the scratch. I sold it real cheap to someone else. They can paint over it for all I care.'

'Why would someone sabotage your work?' Sian asked, finding it all a bit hard to digest.

'Competition,' Rosie whispered, nodding towards a couple of middle-aged people loading canvases into their white van. In Sian's opinion, their paintings were amateurish compared to Rosie's. They were the type of paintings where the artist was trying really hard to make a sparrow look like a sparrow, rather than their interpretation of a sparrow, which is always far more interesting. 'Anyway, well done for helping me today. I'm sure you would have struggled with the crowds.'

'It wasn't too bad, surprisingly. I did need to get away for a breather, which was when I had a look at the Ben Stokes memorial. I have to admit *he*, who shall not be named, is always there at the back of my mind. Sometimes, every man is him. Sometimes he invades my dreams. But I'm feeling stronger, especially now I have something to occupy my mind, like this mystery.'

TWENTY FOUR

As soon as Sian got back home, she gathered a few essentials including water bottle and torch light, slid on Aunt May's gumboots, and disappeared over the boundary fence into the lush greenery of McCrae's Forest. For the first time in years, she had purpose in her step, and fire in her heart. Ben Stokes; an eerie similarity to the Sorenson boy also called Ben whom she had played with as a child. Both boys died in their teens. To be accurate, her Ben told her he didn't want to play with her anymore, and she wasn't welcomed back into his forest. He switched - went from hot to cold, just in one summer. But she had seen the changes in him coming for some time. He was always cautious, his eyes flicking this way and that searching for rabbits, or maybe enemies, but he grew distant and less interested in playing make-believe, and more interested in wrestling and war games. She remembered his fascination with World War Two. Many boys had a fascination with war, and ran about the place with wooden rifles, pretending to shoot the enemy. *It's a secret.*

When she found the massive trunk of the kauri tree with her face carved into it, she sat down with her back against the trunk amongst the small ferns. She shut her eyes in an attempt to quieten her mind. The chorus of bird song was all about her, like a halo of joy. The smell of damp bark and earth filled her lungs.

Then something brushed her leg and she jumped, opening her eyes. It was none other than the bottomless pit of a beast, Popo. *Of course it was the cat, what else would it be*? she thought, feeling ridiculous. Popo had caught something and was tossing it about like a toy. On closer inspection she discovered it was a horse-head weta, one of Aunt May's favourite insects. She found a large leaf and prised it away from the cat, who was most displeased. The weta had large pincers coming out of his long head, and could latch on to a finger with the intention of never letting go. It had a broken leg, probably from Popo's aggressive play, so she took it to a log, rotten from moisture, and placed it inside. Popo's green eyes watched her every move.

'You're lucky Aunt May's not here,' Sian scolded Popo, remembering her Aunt growling at her own cat for catching a fantail. Native species have little chance of surviving with all these introduced predators. But Popo was the king of the world, why would he care?

After the little drama of the broken weta, Sian closed her eyes again and thought about Benny Sorenson. There was one particular memory of buried bones, a shallow grave. The memory came in waves or spurts, eventually dissipating. She was sure she never actually saw the bones, but Benny said they were there. And then yellow ribbon. *Yellow ribbon? Aunt May has a reel of yellow ribbon in her drawer. What's yellow ribbon got to do with a shallow grave?*

Her busy, enquiring mind then reflected on the conversation she had with the old man, Fred Anderson. If what Fred said was true, and she was playing with the ghost of Ben Stokes, then perhaps she could conjure up his spirit. She began calling his name in her mind, her eyes snapping open when she heard distant gunshot. Hunters? Or it could be a local farmer killing something she'd rather not know about.

She closed her eyes again, and repeated Ben's name over and over in her mind, then whispered his name on the breeze. But it wasn't

Ben's face she kept seeing in her mind, it was Fred's creased face. Only two people were left in Woodville who were around when Ben Stokes disappeared. Fred and Mavis. George and Mildred, Sergeant Lee joked. One day she must Google George and Mildred.

It was getting dark. Tomorrow was Sunday, and she'll be spending the day helping Rosie sell the rest of her goods. If the museum is open, she'll pop in to see Fred and ask him a few questions about Ben Stokes, and what he meant about her playing with his ghost. She'll tell him that she's doing a research project, supported by the Woodville Police Department.

After checking that the windows were fastened and the doors were locked, she clambered up the stairs to Aunt May's bedroom, which was really her bedroom, it just felt as if Aunt May was still there. Strangely, Aunt May's presence seemed to strengthen, not dissipate, with every day. It's almost as if she was there in spirit to look after Sian. Well, that's what Sian liked to believe, the truth could be quite different. But, with the feeling of Aunt May's presence came the difficulty of clearing out her stuff, and she had a lot of stuff. The drawers and cupboards were still full of her personal belongings, the stacks of books in the living room, the cutlery and china in the kitchen. None of it is to Sian's taste, yet it seemed disrespectful to remove it.

It had been several hours since Sian last glanced at the black and white photograph of the Fields, hidden behind the handkerchief. She was reluctant to look at it for fear that her hunch was right. Once again, she had to take a couple of deep breaths to calm her nerves before she lifted the white handkerchief. It was rather creepy, and if she had it her way, she'd pull that thing off the wall and throw it out the window. But for some reason, the frame is glued to the wall with some sort of super glue, and she can't for the life of her prise it off.

They've moved again. The young man had lowered his scythe slightly, his shoulders were twisted to the right. He was changing poses, it seemed. She peered more closely at his face. Was he Ben Stokes? It was hard to tell, because his head was turned slightly, and he was several years older than the Ben Stokes Sian saw in the Museum.

Sian dropped her eyes down to May's parents. Both were now sitting, the stoicism on their faces from that generation of farmers still there, but they were now showing a hint of fear.

'Fear from what? What are you afraid of?' Sian whispered. Her heart raced when she took in the entire image. She may have been mistaken, but it looked to her like the young man was preparing to swipe something with the blade of his scythe. 'No!' Sian called out, letting the handkerchief fall back over the photograph. Was the young man about to kill May's parents? Was the photograph showing Sian a slowed down visual of how May's parents' died?

There were only two people who could possibly know the answer to this; Mavis, and Sian's mother, Bev. Perhaps it was time to give her mother a call, just to let her know that she's doing fine. She'll have to buy a new cell phone. Maybe take a drive down to Wellington to buy one, and have lunch there. It's only a two hour drive, and in the opposite direction to Lakesford, so the chances of bumping into *him* were very slim.

***

Rosie had been up all night fixing damaged canvases, and painting more river rocks, so she had some on standby in case she sold out. She had taken the rocks from the bed of the Manawatu River that ran along the edge of Woodville. The stream that ran through McCrae's Forest trickled into the Manawatu River as it flowed on its way to the Pacific Ocean. When Sian turned up ready for another busy day of crowds and bargaining with city folk, Rosie looked as perky as ever, even though she hadn't slept a wink.

'Mascara,' Rosie joked. 'I feel like death warmed up on the inside, but with a little help from my friends, mascara and foundation, I can look decent on the outside.'

'Where are Chloe and your mum?' Sian asked.

Rosie flung her head back and yelled, 'MUM!' Moments later a smiling woman with short blonde hair, wearing a turquoise and navy wrap appeared at the front door. 'Where are my manners?' Rosie said, 'This is my mum, Theresa.' Theresa stepped out of the front door, holding her arms out to hug Sian. Sian froze. Being hugged was not something she was used to. Her mother rarely hugged her brother and herself, her grandparents died when she was young, and past boyfriends seemed to go in for a hug only to trigger foreplay. The only person she let hug her was Nigel, and even then it took her a while to relax into it. But there was no time to escape, before the warm embrace of a mother hug was crushing her.

'It's wonderful to finally meet my daughter's neighbour,' Theresa said, stepping back and inspecting Sian properly. 'What did you say your name was?'

'Sian,' she replied.

'Oh! I thought Rosie said another name.' Chloe appeared at the front door rubbing her tired eyes, and Theresa retreated toward the house to pick her up.

Rosie cocked her head at Sian and closed one eye, utterly confused. 'Have you forgotten something?' she whispered, out of earshot of her mother, who was proudly holding the apple of her eye on her hip at the front door. 'I thought you were going incognito as Ingrid Bone?'

'Oh yeah!' Sian said. 'The copper said I should be careful about doing that, you know, signing forms etcetera. It can come across as being deceitful. Either I change it legally, or keep my given name. So I've decided to be me.'

'Ah!' Rosie said, rolling her eyes. 'No more Ingrid. I guess you could always use the name Ingrid when you're meeting people you don't trust. I mean, people use their middle names and nick names all the time.'

'True.' This was a good point. It was never Sian's intention to start off on the wrong foot with people here in Woodville, though.

'Will you be coming over for Christmas?' Theresa called from the front door.

Sian shrugged.

'Of course she'll be coming,' Rosie answered for Sian. 'It wouldn't be right for you to be in that old shack on your own.' Rosie leaned in and whispered, 'Besides, I need someone to keep me sane.'

Sian laughed.

'You'll finally get to meet Nate my husband, in case you're wondering if he's only a fragment of my imagination,' Rosie added. 'He gets two weeks off over the Christmas break. We usually head down to his parents in Nelson, but this year we've decided to stay home, and most of our families will be coming here.' She pretended to wipe sweat off her brow. 'The stress of it all!'

They loaded the last of the canvases, painted rocks, and hand-crafted jewellery into the cars, then set off into town.

TWENTY FIVE

The Therapist

'I wasn't lying before,' Alice said to Dave the next morning at Sunday breakfast. The pink bags under his eyes were puffy from a sleepless night, and he had been staring at his bowl of cornflakes for over half an hour, without taking a mouthful.

'Huh?' he grunted, barely listening.

'I had hired a hitman.'

This made Dave look up to analyse the expression on her face. 'This is no time to joke, Alice,' he said, pushing his chair out from the table to leave.

She watched him walk away from her, wondering whether or not to say any more. 'I'm not joking. I've done it twice before.' She had decided in that instant to tell Dave everything, and deal with the consequences now. For it all to come out later, without giving him any warning about the incriminating evidence Brendon Durie has, would most certainly ruin both their lives.

Dave stopped at the doorway that led into the hall. His back was to her, she couldn't read his face. He was wearing those baggy jeans that she hated. They were too long in the leg, scuffing the ground as he walked, and too loose around the waist, slipping down his backside when he bent over. 'Twice before?' he asked, shocked.

'Sit down,' she said, pushing the dining chair opposite her with her foot. Defying her, he took another chair, sat down and crossed his arms, staring straight ahead and avoiding eye contact.

'I've hired a hitman twice before,' Alice began, 'and I hired the same man to kill Brendon Durie.'

Dave held up three podgy fingers. 'Three times, are you having me on?' He looked at her like she was a stranger. 'Why?'

'It doesn't matter.'

'I think it does matter. It matters that I'm sleeping with a...with a man killer.'

'You're not...I'm not the one who killed them, that's the job of the hitman.'

'But you paid the hitman?'

'Yes.'

'With our money?'

'My money, I used my money.'

'Why?'

'You have to understand they are...were, very bad people. Just like Brendon Durie.'

Dave rolled his eyes. 'So when is he supposed to be knocked off then?'

Alice cleared her throat. 'Something hasn't quite gone to plan, I'm afraid.'

'What do you mean?'

'He was supposed to have died last night.'

'Last night? Last night? Fat lot of good this hitman was then. How much did you pay him for doing nothing?'

'I only pay a down-payment-'

'A down-payment, a down-payment? Like when you're buying a bed, or a car?'

'Will you stop repeating everything I say?'

'No, I won't.'

'What I'm trying to say is, I put down a payment before the job, then pay him the rest afterwards. He's very efficient-'

'Oh good, I'm glad to hear your personal hitman is very efficient.' On the very rare occasion that Dave gets stressed, he turns inadvertently comical. He can't help it, it's not intentional, but it can be very funny to watch. If there wasn't a deadly serious undertow, Alice would've burst out laughing. 'I can't believe I'm hearing this. My own wife hires hitmen!' He got up from his chair and began pacing back and forth, waving his short, fat arms about and muttering like a madman. 'Wait a minute,' he stopped, placing his hands on his hips. 'The other night with that phone, you said it was a patient's phone left in your office. Who's was it really?'

'It's the cell I use to contact Birdie.'

'Birdie?' His face was the colour of beetroot, ready to burst.

'He's the contract killer,' she said, far too casually.

'Oh! Thank God!' sliding to his knees on the carpet and dropping his face into his hands. 'I thought you were having an affair.'

Alice's mouth dropped open in wonder. Of all the despicable things she had just spoken about, it was the thought that she was having an affair that upset him. Stifling laughter, Alice brought the conversation back to the crux of the matter. 'No! No! No!' she said. 'But we...I, have a problem.'

He dropped his hands down from his face, and unsteadily got to his feet. He stood opposite her, hands on hips, breathing hard. 'I'm not going to like what you're about to say, am I?'

'I don't think so.' Alice bit her thumb nail, a pause to find the right words. 'Brendon Durie is trying to bribe me.'

'Why? What has he got on you?'

'He's got footage of me talking to someone before they disappeared.'

Dave cringed. 'And so?' knowing she was telling only part of the story.

'The person I was talking to was a target. I lured him to the location where Birdie was to take over, to do his part of the deal.'

'Brendon Durie has footage of you and Birdie killing someone?'

'I didn't kill him. Birdie did. But I stayed to make sure he was dead, and my face was all over it... I don't know how he did it. We made sure that no one was there, and it was dark, pitch black. But whoever took the pics, had an infrared camera.'

'But it showed this Birdie character stabbing...shooting...whatever, the victim, and not you. So you're a big fat not guilty.'

'I'm still an accomplice.' Alice sighed.

'There's more, isn't there?'

'Birdie was wearing a balaclava the whole time, and he never takes his car to his hits, so he can't be identified. No licence plate number, nothing.'

'Right, but *your* face is as clear as day, I take it.'

Alice found the images on her cell to show him.

Dave hissed. 'What does that piece of shite want?'

'Who, Brendon Durie?'

'Who else do you think I'm talking about? Mickey Mouse? The Queen of Sheba? Of course I'm talking about Brendon bloody Durie!' he bellowed irately.

'Alright! Calm down. The neighbours will hear.'

'Calm down? Calm down?'

'You're repeating yourself, again.'

He got up from his chair and began pacing back and forth impatiently, blowing out hot air as he went, the bottom of his jeans scuffing along the carpet. 'He wants the location of his ex,' Alice said, finally.

'Easy. Get it and give it to him.' He rubbed his hands together as if washing them. 'Job done, over and out.'

'I told you before. I can't do that.'

'Yes, you can. Give the shite the girl's location, and in return he'll leave us and our daughter alone.'

'There's another thing,' Alice said.

'Of course, there is,' he answered, sarcastically.

'Birdie has just contacted me and wants to meet. It's unlike him to fail a job. I'm worried about what he's going to say.'

'Do you want me to talk to him?' Dave asked, puffing his chest out like a tough guy.

'No. I'll have to go on my own. But I feel I need support from afar.'

'Where and when?'

Alice looked at her watch. 'He wants to meet in one hour, at Calhoun Lagoon where they play water polo.'

'Fine.' he shrugged, and left the room.

TWENTY SIX

The Therapist

Under 18 water polo finals were underway, and the dirty lagoon was jam-packed with kayaks of all different colours. There were two games being played, side by side, while several other teams waited, or practised in the water nearby. On the sideline were proud parents, and ducks waddling about looking for food. It was early afternoon and becoming warm, which unleashed the stench of the duck poop-infested water.

Birdie had texted Alice to meet him at the park bench closest to the kayak shed. Alice and Dave decided to take two cars. The plan was for Dave to park further down the road so as not to raise suspicion, and Alice would text him the letter, *H,* if she needed his help.

The road that weaved alongside the lagoon was full of parked cars, so she had to park much further up from the kayak shed than she had intended. Looking in the rear vision mirror, she could see her loyal husband driving slowly in the shiny black land cruiser, while she was in the inconspicuous grey sedan. She hated the land cruiser and couldn't understand why Dave wanted to buy it. They never drive off-road, they're city people through and through, so why did Dave feel the need to buy an over-sized four wheel drive? It had only just occurred to her now as she watched the shiny, black beast curve around the bend behind her, that he must feel huge in that thing. The vehicle is set higher than most road vehicles, so the driver looks down on everyone. For a man of average height, average intelligence and average looks, that must feel grand.

Alice climbed out of her sedan, looking warily around for anyone suspicious who may be watching, or taking photographs. It was broad daylight, and she was about to meet her hitman. This was simply a ridiculous situation to be in. Her only hope was that Birdie didn't turn up wearing a balaclava, because there were many people about. How ridiculous that would look.

The park bench closest to the kayak shed already had someone sitting there, a child, feeding bread to the ducks. Nearby there's a sign that reads, PLEASE DON'T FEED BREAD TO THE DUCKS. The kid obviously can't read. Alice remembers a news item recently, about a large gaggle of geese living in a park in Auckland that have become ill from malnourishment, due to a diet mostly made up of bread fed to them by the public. As soon as Alice sat down, the kid ran off to his grandmother, who was watching the polo. There was a lot of noise, too much noise; crowds cheering, people chatting and ducks quacking - not quite how Alice imagined the atmosphere of her meeting.

Birdie was supposed to meet her there at 1.15pm. It was now 1.35pm, and Alice wondered if he had been surprised to find the mass of people gathered when he arrived, and so left again. She wouldn't blame him. She turned to look in the direction where Dave was parked, and saw the black shiny beast parked on the side of the road, jutting out further than the surrounding cars. When she turned back, she found someone was sitting next to her; a posh woman hiding under a wide brimmed, black hat with large sunglasses that swallowed most of her face. She was watching a kayaker paddle downstream.

1.45pm and still no Birdie. Alice's phone beeped. It was Dave.
How much longer?
Alice: *He hasn't turned up yet.*
Dave: *He might be lying on the bottom of the lagoon*

Alice got up to walk back to her car, when the woman next to her said, 'Shall we walk?'

'Pardon?' The posh woman continued to gaze out across the brown waters towards the million dollar homes on the other side. Alice assumed she was talking to herself, and proceeded to walk away.

The woman stood up. She wore large rings on her fingers and her lips were painted a blood red. She was thin, but strong and elegant, a trait rarely seen in younger women. 'Shall we walk?' she said, again.

'Do I know you?' Alice asked.

'Let's move away from the crowd, shall we,' the woman said.

'Have you got the right person?' Alice asked.

'Oh, I have the right person, alright. There's no question about that.'

'Who am I, then?' Alice asked.

But she failed to answer. Instead, they ambled along the side of the lagoon for ten minutes in silence, until she said; 'Your name is Alice Granger.'

Alice said nothing. She turned casually behind her to find her husband's vehicle. It was following slowly behind.

The woman continued, 'You hired my husband to kill Brendon Durie, among others.'

For fear that she may incriminate herself, Alice remained silent.

'My husband is lying in a coma in Middlemore Hospital.' The woman stopped, and turned to Alice. Alice could see her own reflection in the woman's sunglasses. 'Don't fret, I don't blame you,' she patted Alice on the arm.

Alice stumbled on her words, worrying about what to say next and where this conversation was going. Was this woman, who claimed to be Birdie's wife, recording this conversation? To be safe, Alice remained silent.

'The tables have turned,' she said, after a short pause. 'Now I want him dead as much as you do.'

'Who?'

The woman began to walk again with Alice following slightly behind her. She was attracting many stares due to the wide brimmed hat, and large sunglasses. This outfit she wore was a great disguise Alice thought, as she could barely see the woman's face, but it was hardly inconspicuous.

'The price has gone up,' the woman said. 'If you still want him dead, you'll have to pay double.'

'Want who dead?' Alice asked, acting dumb.

'Brendon Durie. He outsmarted you, and my husband bore the consequences of that.' The woman tensed up like a ball of suppressed rage. 'My husband was ambushed. It looked like a set-up to me, which can only mean that someone snitched.' She glanced at Alice's face to read her expression. 'There were only four people who knew about this meeting; one of them is lying in a hospital bed, another is enjoying his freedom with your daughter, and the other two are walking alongside this filthy duck pond.'

Alice was desperate to ask questions, but was still wary of this woman. How did she know so much?

'So who was it then? Who snitched?'

Alice shook her head, feeling her temperature rise. She was always careful how she communicated with Birdie. It was only ever on a cheap cell phone, which she always discarded after the deed was done. Then it dawned on her. How could she forget? There was a third party; the person who took those infrared photographs of Birdie knocking out, and then drowning Damon Ridge. This occurred over two years ago. About the same time that Sian Tanner started seeing Alice to help deal with her "unpredictable and obsessive" partner, Brendon Durie. Her visits were kept quiet from Brendon. He only found out later on that she was seeing a therapist, when he was arrested for kidnapping and assault. That's the day he sent a man to Sian's mother's house, dressed in a police uniform. He's got people working for him. He comes from an influential family. This is a big problem.

'Someone took photos,' Alice said, finally.

'What photos?'

'Birdie killing Damon Ridge at Stanley Stadium.'

The woman fell quiet.

'Brendon has them in his possession.'

'How did he get them?'

'I don't know.'

The woman paused for a moment to collect her thoughts, then said, 'He's not a nice man this Brendon Durie, is he?'

'No. He's the worst of the worst,' Alice answered, realising now that if this was a set-up by the police, and this woman pretending to be Birdie's wife was wearing a wire, she'd just got herself into a lot of hot water.

'I know of his father and uncles.' she said, lowering her sunglasses to peer over them at Alice. Her eyes were a vivid blue with laughter lines surrounding them, indicating she had a good sense of humour. Alice thought she was probably pushing sixty, a similar age to Birdie. 'One of them even hired my husband, a few months back,' she said, then pushed her sunglasses back over her eyes again.

'How long have you known what your husband does on the side?' Alice asked, curiously.

The woman scoffed. 'My dear, I was the one who persuaded him to do it. But that's getting off the subject. Can you show me these pictures you have?'

Alice found the images sent from Brendon Durie on her personal smart-phone, and showed the woman claiming to be Birdie's wife. The woman let out a deep, despairing sigh when she saw them. 'This has gotten personal,' she said. 'Luckily for my husband, the only people in these images that can be identified are you, and the target. Do you still want the Durie dead?'

'Now, more than ever,' Alice said swiftly, meaning it. 'But I'm afraid it may be too late. I was supposed to come through with my end of the bargain the night your husband... I didn't, so those pictures are probably sitting in a local journalist's inbox as we speak.'

The woman opened her black handbag and took out something small, holding it tightly in her clenched fist. 'It's never too late to bargain with the devil, especially when one's own child is involved,' she said, handing Alice a small piece of folded paper. 'This is the new going rate if you want him dead. Use the number you contacted him on, to contact me if you want to move forward.'

Alice gasped at the number written on the paper. This would almost wipe out both hers and Dave's savings accounts, if they went ahead. When Alice looked up again, the woman was already several feet away, walking at a measured pace.

'Who will do this?' she called, then immediately clammed up when a couple of teenagers carrying their kayaks walked by.

TWENTY SEVEN

The Therapist

Alice clambered into Dave's land cruiser, and quickly relayed the conversation to him. She was breathless, and her heart was fluttering about in her chest like a butterfly, desperate to break out of its cage.

'How much?' Dave asked.

She handed him the piece of paper, and he swore ferociously when he read it. 'That's everything we have!' he yelled, screwing the piece of paper up in his hand. 'This whole problem would be solved if you just told that shite where his ex is. We won't have to spend any money. We won't have to lose our jobs, or hide our heads in shame, or go to prison. Most importantly, our daughter won't end up dead.'

'I'll be going to prison, if all of this comes out,' Alice assured him.

'I'm an accomplice now though, aren't I,' he blurted, then calmed down by blowing out hot air. Every time he did this, it reminded Alice of one of those body builders you see at the gym, blowing out air as they're lifting heavy dumbbells. Perhaps the weight of all of this was too much for Dave to bear.

'You've forgotten one important detail, Dave. The deal with Brendon Durie was, if I gave him Sian's location, he wouldn't send those pictures to the press. He never mentioned anything about

Sarah. He may choose to keep dating her, for whatever devious reason he has, and she may have to learn a hard lesson, unless we knock him off.'

Dave growled angrily, slamming his fist on the steering wheel. 'A hard lesson, a hard lesson?'

'We warned her, and she refused to believe us.'

'Make a deal with the shite. If you don't, I will.'

Alice shook her head. 'It's too late now. Time's up. I didn't go through with my end of the bargain. Instead, I sent a contract killer in my place. He's bound to have already sent those pictures to the press. I've probably made him even angrier.'

Dave snatched Alice's phone from her hand, and found the pictures sent from Brendon Durie.

'What are you doing?' Alice screeched, trying to grab the phone back off him.

To get away from her thrashing arms and sharp fingernails, Dave opened the door and slid out of the vehicle, running as fast as his porky legs could go, to a nearby park bench. Alice jumped out of the land cruiser and ran after him, but it was too late. By the time she'd caught up with Dave, he had sent a text to Brendon Durie. The message read, *Make a deal? I'll give you your ex's location, if you don't send the pics and leave our daughter alone.*

Alice grabbed her phone off Dave, and stormed back to her sedan. She was far too angry to say anything to him, and conscious of the many people looking on at this middle-aged couple, having a tiff.

It took Alice several minutes before she got back to her sedan, and there was a reply from Brendon Durie. *Too late*

Tears formed in Alice's eyes. How could she be so stupid? Her career, marriage, and relationship with her daughter were in ruins. Not only that, but Birdie was lying in a coma, according to that mysterious woman claiming to be his wife, and all of this was because of her. Dave was right; all of this heartache could have been avoided if she had given Sian's location to Brendon Durie. Sergeant Louise Ratahi said Sian was residing in a rural town called

Woodville. It wouldn't take much to find which house she was living in. All Alice had to do was contact Louise with a legitimate reason, and she'd probably give it to her, she hoped. Although, Alice was quick to remember Louise's words, "If Sian wants to make contact, she will."

Alice wiped her blurry eyes and Googled Woodville. Immediately, colourful pictures came up of the Woodville Spring Market on this weekend, a great excuse to visit a town she's never bothered to visit before. But it was after 2pm. It would take approximately four hours to drive there, and the market would be over by then. She scrolled down, looking at scenes of farmland, old farm houses, McCrae's Forest where sixteen year old Ben Stokes disappeared in 1956. Apart from an unsolved mystery, and the annual Spring Market, there's not a lot going on there. Besides, her knowledge of small towns was that everyone knows everyone else's business. All she had to do was ask the person who ran the local dairy, or hair salon, and they'd send her in the right direction.

Alice texted Brendon. *Why is it too late?*

Several minutes later a reply came through: *You lied. We had a deal. The pics have been sent to your friend in the police force.*

'Damn it!' she cried.

The passenger door swung open, and Alice screamed. It was Dave checking to see if she was okay, but the red eyes and pained expression said it all.

'What's happened?' he asked.

She handed him the phone to read the messages. He swore under his breath. 'What friend is he talking about?'

'It'll be Louise,' she said, sniffing.

'Does Louise work the weekends?'

'Sometimes. Her hours change.'

'Is there a chance that she hasn't seen them yet?'

'What are you suggesting, Dave? Break into the police station, and wipe Louise's inbox before she arrives for work on Monday?'

'Yes, actually, I am suggesting that.'

Alice rolled her eyes.

'Well I don't hear any suggestions from you.' he bit.

'I have no suggestions. I'm all out. I have nothing left,' she wept, desperate for a hand of support from her usually loving husband.

She was broken and awash with grief. Dave wanted nothing more than to wrap his arms around her as he had done so many times before, but on this occasion, he held back. He needed her to suffer. She was prepared to put their daughter in danger, and that crossed the line.

He replied to Brendon's text, *Let's make another deal. We'll give you your ex's location if you leave our daughter alone.*

Brendon: *Give it to me now!*

Dave: *Break up with our daughter first*

Brendon: *No deal. You fooled me once...*

Alice was gazing out the window, her mind a million miles away. Dave was wary of what this Brendon character was capable of. He ambushed a hitman, for goodness sake. Who does that? But this also raised the fact that Brendon knew he was going to be set up, so there must be someone working for him. Someone, who knew where the other target, the Ridge man, was going to be killed. In Dave's naivety, he figured the only option was to be honest, which was Dave's answer to everything. "Be honest and people will respect you for it."

'So where is the ex hiding out?' he asked Alice, softly.

Alice shook her head. After all that had happened she still had an unbending loyalty towards Sian Tanner. It wasn't just the therapist/patient relationship, the code of conduct, but the knowledge of what Sian had suffered, and was brave enough to escape from. Mostly, it was the innate fear that this psychopath, who had already gotten away with so much, will hunt Sian down and kill her, but not before torturing her first. This was a fact.

Dave suppressed an angry growl, when she didn't answer. He tossed Alice's phone between each hand, as he tried to think of how to get this information out of her. Yes, he was aware that today may be the last day of his beloved wife's freedom, but his daughter may also be hanging upside-down somewhere, naked and beaten. The image of the naked, half buried woman with Sarah's face kept appearing in his imagination. This shite was sick. Sick as sick can be.

He was aware he still had Brendon Durie hanging on the line, and started to Google, *How to extract important information out of a wife,* when he noticed Alice's last search, *Woodville.* He read about Woodville for a few moments, and once he realised there was absolutely nothing in Woodville that would interest his wife, he came to the conclusion that this must be the location of the shite's ex.

Dave: *Woodville, Lower North Island. Now break up with my daughter!*

Brendon: *Once I've found out this is the accurate location, I'll break up with her. For yours and your daughter's sakes, this better not be a stitch up.*

Dave shut his eyes tightly as a cloud of panic came over him.

'Love,' he said to Alice, who was still a million miles away, and looking as miserable as ever, 'is the shite's ex in Woodville?'

Alice started, and turned towards Dave. 'I said I don't know where she is.'

There were two things Dave noticed: One. Alice refused to make eye contact when she denied knowledge of Sian's location. And two. As soon as he said 'Woodville', she jumped like a startled rabbit. She was lying, and Dave rested in the knowledge that the location of Brendon Durie's ex was indeed, Woodville. Everything was going to be fine. Well...maybe not for Sian Tanner, or for Alice when Sergeant Louise Ratahi opens her emails tomorrow morning, but at least his daughter would now have a future.

179

TWENTY EIGHT

I t was a much thinner crowd on the Sunday at the Spring Market. The balmy weather they were lucky to have yesterday, didn't spill over into today. Instead it was cooler and cloudy, with the hint that rain was about to fall. This didn't worry Rosie too much, as her best artwork had sold the day before, and she had a couple of commissions for city folk in Wellington as well.

Determined to get to the bottom of the mystery of Ben Stokes, Sian left Rosie's stall to find Fred, which wasn't too difficult. He was where everyone expected him to be, at the front counter of the Woodville Information Centre and Museum.

'You again,' he said, as soon as she walked in.

Cutting to the chase, 'What did you mean yesterday? You said my Aunt said I played with the ghost of Ben Stokes.'

He scoffed. 'She was mad, that woman.'

'You said that yesterday. But I just want to know more about her.'

'Then you're best to ask the other mad one. She's still alive, only just. I never had much to do with either. They were too...' he shook his head searching for the right words, 'too strange for my taste.'

'What do you mean by strange?'

'Look it up in the dictionary.'

Time for a change of subject, this old man has the patience of a hissing rattle snake. 'Were you here when Ben Stokes disappeared?'

His expression softened.

'Yep. I helped search for him. I went out every day. Even when everyone else lost hope, I still kept trying to find him.'

'And nothing was found?'

'Not a dickey bird. It never made any sense to me how a kid like that, who practically lived in the bush, could disappear. He had all the skills to find water and hunt, and that forest wasn't even that big. He could walk himself out of it in a day or so.'

'Maybe he didn't disappear in the forest.'

'That's what I thought.' He was about to add to that comment, when he stopped. 'Why are you asking all these questions?'

'With Sergeant Lee's permission, I've begun my own investigation into his disappearance.'

Fred chuckled. 'You're not going to get far.'

'Did you know Ben Stokes well?'

'Yeah, we were friends. There was an age gap between us. He was five or so years younger than me, but we liked to hunt and fish. He was good company for a young lad. He wasn't stupid, either. He was a real smart kid up here,' tapping his temple, 'as well as with his hands. He was good with engines, built a motorbike from scratch. I remember him racing along the paddock on it,' a twinkle in his eye flickered at the memory. 'And he was only eleven or twelve at the time. But that's a different generation, and a different time.'

'What was his family like?'

'The Stokes? Long gone. Sold their farm after he disappeared, and no one heard from them again.'

'Do you know where they moved to?'

'No. They just dropped contact. Ben's mother was distraught. He was her only child. I think she wanted to leave, 'cos being here brought up too many bad memories.' He began tapping his stick on the wooden floor, irritably. 'Between you and me, something wasn't right there, I mean, with his father. I never liked the look of him.' He pointed his crooked finger at Sian as another memory appeared in his mind, 'I'll tell you what else. The day after they left, someone

181

burned their house down. Now, back in those days, there were two reasons why someone would burn a house down. To get rid of the living, or to get rid of the dead. It was a good way to drive out unwanted people from a community.'

'But the Stokes' house was burned down after they left?'

'Yep, the day after.'

'So someone didn't want them to return?'

He shook his head. 'I never said this to anyone, but I reckon they came back, and burned that house down themselves.'

'Why?'

'To hide something. No-one else had any reason to burn it. No one here in Woodville admitted to burning it down, and this was an even smaller community back then. Someone would've known something. But when the police investigated, they came up blank, just like with poor Ben Stokes. As far as I can remember, it was a perfectly nice house, and the people who bought their farm would've been pretty upset about that.'

'What was Ben's father's name?' Sian asked.

'Too long ago to remember,' he said, waving the question away impatiently, because he had something more important to say. 'Ask me the question you should be asking me. Come on! If you think you're a bit of a sleuth, ask me the most important question,' tapping his stick with each syllable he spoke.

Sian felt flutters of anxiety rise in her stomach at the pressure of figuring out what the 'most important question' was.

Fred lost patience with Sian and said, 'Ask me where their house was?'

'Okay. Where was their house before it was burned to the ground?'

'Right under your nose,' he said, pointing his crooked finger again.

'Here, the museum?'

'Nope, across the road from your house which was the Fields' house. How do I know this? 'Cos me father bought the land off the Stokes. It's still in the family, now.'

'So the Fields and Stokes were neighbours?'

'Yep!'

Sian's mind raced. The buried bones and shallow grave. *It's a secret.*

Fred continued, 'I have nothing against them. The Fields were very nice, hard-working people. Mr Fields was a good man, had a few laughs down at the pub on Fridays, and he even joined the local rugby team. Not that we ever had a full team, 'cos there weren't enough men. But they died old and happy in that house some time ago.'

'How did they die?' Sian asked.

Fred shrugged. 'Old age, probably. It takes us all.' His eyes widened in wonder. 'And then she turned up from boarding school.'

Sian felt her hands tremble. 'Who did?'

'Her! Your Aunt. You coming here out of the blue was a repeat of then, when *she* arrived here with her leather suitcase, and shifty eyes. The Fields had been living in Woodville for years, yet you hardly ever saw their daughter. Then one day, she turned up from boarding school and never went back.' He broke into a cackle when he saw the look of horror on Sian's face. 'You never saw that one coming did ya? And then *you* turn up all shifty-like, and keep to yourself as well. And I think you're just another one, like her.'

'How old was she when she left boarding school?' Sian asked.

'I don't know. Like I said, I never liked her much. And she was a tad younger than me.'

'So Aunt May must've known Ben Stokes, if they lived across the road from each other.'

'I guess so.' Then he laughed. 'It was probably her that burned the house down, doing one of her witch spells.'

Sian's throat began to tickle, and she coughed. The single cough turned into a coughing fit, and Fred fetched a glass of water from the kitchen out the back of the museum.

'You're not choking on something, are ya?' he asked, handing her the grimy glass of water.

Sian shook her head. 'I'm just a little surprised,' she gasped, in between coughs. 'And just to clarify, I swear Aunt May left me the house and land in her will. I have the paper work, if you don't believe me.'

'I believe you, alright. I just got my heckles up when you turned up using a false name. The Fields were good people even though their daughter left much to be desired.'

Sian frowned. 'I used a pseudonym because I'm hiding from someone. I've changed my mind about that, now.'

'Oh good! As long as it's not the law you're hiding from.'

'No, it's not. How did you know I was using a false name, anyway?'

'Everyone knew. It was obvious. It's a small town.'

Sian was about to take another sip of water, when she noticed a ladybird floating on the surface. She scooped it out, and lay it down on the counter to dry off. Fred was watching her every move. Aunt May was always kind to all creatures great and small, that's where Sian believed she got her softness for the little things from. Regardless of who her Great Aunt May was, she was a powerful influence in Sian's life. Her mother couldn't care less about birds and insects, although she once had a soft spot for a neighbour's cat.

'Do you have a photograph of Ben Stokes closer to the age that he disappeared?'

He screwed up his face. 'Maybe in the old newspaper clippings you'll find something. People weren't like they are today, where they take a selfie, or whatever you call them, every five seconds to post on whatsit. Vanity it is, pure vanity. Back in my day, not many people even owned a camera.'

A small amount of drool ran from the side of his mouth. Sian watched it slide down his chin then drop onto the floor. He hesitated before he said, 'We were starting to wonder if that house was cursed. It sat empty for a while after that mad woman died in it.' grasping a memory, that made him shudder slightly, 'No-one went near it, apart from a couple of Sorenson boys, who'd use it to kip in after they'd been hunting possums. They sell the fur to the Fairbrothers in Norsewood, who make socks and other bits and pieces out of it.'

'Sorenson boys? Do you mean Angus and Sam?'

He scoffed. 'There's more than that. They all look the same to me, anyway. Some of them came out good, some of them are bad eggs. They used to say the Sorensons' were born with lice in their hair, and boils on their butts. Grimy kids, they were. Probably still are. Always had dirty faces and hands, never pulled their socks up, if they had any socks to pull up. Yet they keep multiplying. I grew up with the Sorensons, as did the generation before and the generation after. When we come to the end of the world, all that will be left will be cockroaches, bacteria and Sorensons.'

'Do you know about another boy called Benny Sorenson?'

He shook his head. 'You're wasting your time asking me about them Sorensons. I get them all mixed up.'

'He died about fourteen or fifteen years ago,' Sian said, trying to trigger a memory.

Fred's eyebrows shot up. 'Oh yes, how could I forget? He was a teenage drunk like his father, and they found him in the river. Must've slipped in and drowned. Was his name Ben too? I forget now. Funny coincidence. If you want to know more about a Sorenson, the best people to talk to are the Sorensons. Although they might pull the wool over your eyes, bunch of scallywags. There were about ten kids running amuck in that family. One of them was probably called Ben. It's an easy name to pronounce, and they weren't the smartest of people, so they could've called a son Ben.' He gave Sian a suspicious, little glare that caught her by surprise.

'I played with a boy here called Benny when I was a kid,' she said. 'He looks so much like Ben Stokes. The Ben Stokes in that photo,' nodding towards the Museum entrance. 'Then you say, my Aunt said I played with the ghost of Ben Stokes.'

Fred wore an expression of bemusement. He liked Sian, which was good as it meant he might help her in the future, but he was still a little suspicious of outsiders coming in and settling down, especially outsiders related to May Fields.

'I hope you find out what happened to Ben Stokes,' he said 'and when you do, I hope we can give him a proper burial, like he deserved.'

TWENTY NINE

Sian caught sight of Angus hovering by Rosie's stall. He was a tall, good looking guy and he had a nice smile with a hint of charm which just made her distrustful of him. Men who have the ability to lure woman easily, are not the kind of men she'd like to become friends with. And being a friend was all she could manage right now, anyway.

'If it ain't Irish,' he said, as she walked up to him.

Sam appeared carrying two hotdogs covered in tomato sauce, wafting them dangerously close to Rosie's canvases. Rosie was watching, glowering. She was having a slow day, all the action had taken place the day before. The last thing she needed was a clumsy fool dropping his greasy hotdog on a beautiful painting of Mount Ruapehu.

'Want your knife back?' Sam asked, with a crooked smile. Half of his front tooth had been knocked out. Sian didn't bother asking why, she wasn't interested.

'No, thank you.'

'You never quite told us why you were in the forest with it, anyway,' Sam said, looking Sian up and down, which made her feel uncomfortable.

'It's none of your business.'

'You could've done yourself some harm,' Sam added.

'Come on, let's go,' Angus said to Sam, who was still deliberately waving his hotdog over one of Rosie's canvases.

Rosie rolled her eyes as they left. 'Have any luck with Fred?'

'Yeah, he gave me quite a lot of information. But he hasn't got anything nice to say about my Great Aunt May.'

Rosie chuckled. 'Before you moved into May's house, he'd say that nothing good would ever come from that house and land.'

'He thinks I'm May Fields all over again,' Sian said, noticing Rosie looking past her to where Sam was striding over to them.

Rosie waved Sian closer, just as a pumped up Sam arrived, wearing a face like thunder. 'Why do you keep asking about our brother?' he asked heatedly, his hands clenched into fists.

Where was this coming from? Sian wondered. He was fine moments ago.

'I was told you were just asking the old man in the museum about him?' he said, irately.

'I was asking about the other Ben, Ben Stokes.' It was a lie.

'Everyone likes to knock us Sorensons, put us down because we're poor, and our old man was a drunk. I get sick of it!' He swung round searching for his brother. When he couldn't see him, he dragged his phone out of his pocket to text him.

'I played with Benny when I was a kid. I just don't remember him being a drunk.'

'He wasn't a drunk,' Sam barked back. 'That day I'll never forget for as long as I live. The old man smashed a beer bottle over his head.' His voice was raised, and people nearby were listening in.

'Can't we take this conversation somewhere else?' Rosie demanded, finding this discussion inappropriate, especially since it was taking place in her stall.

'What?' Sian was stunned. But anyone who knew Sam Sorenson knew he loved to exaggerate, to create waves, to twist the knife.

Sam laughed at the look of horror upon Sian's face. 'He didn't kill him,' Sam said, although no one else was laughing. 'He just knocked him out. Our old man,' Sam continued, 'all of us kids were afraid of that drunken bastard. Benny would go to your Aunt's house to hide from him. Should've been the old man that carked it, not our Ben.'

'Where was your mother?' Rosie asked, the question everyone asks when someone describes a household of upheaval.

'Feeding our father the alcohol, so he'd finally pass out drunk. That's the only time he left us alone, when he was asleep or passed out. It was the booze that finally killed him, and not soon enough.' Sam seemed to enjoy relaying his awful childhood. He spoke with a detachment, as if talking about a movie he went to see last night. He beamed his toothless grin when Sian and Rosie gasped. Clearly he liked to shock people, and his childhood stories were enough to trigger cries of horror. 'Ben was woozy when he woke from being unconscious, and took off. We found him drowned in the river. And they said he had a high blood alcohol level. They obviously never checked to see if he was concussed.'

Angus had turned up again. He looked annoyed that his brother was at it again, raving like a lunatic.

'We buried him in the backyard,' Sam added, hoping for more howls of disgust.

'Come on!' Rosie yelled. 'This is bull crap!'

Angus cringed. 'I already told her he was at the cemetery.' Turning to Sian he said, 'Ignore him, he's spinning a yarn.'

'Why weren't the police called?' Rosie argued, not believing a word of it.

Angus's patience had dried up, but just as he turned his back to walk away, Sam said, 'Cos the old man *was* the damn police!'

THIRTY

The Therapist

'W'hat have you done?' Alice cried, snatching her phone off Dave, and reading the conversation between him and Brendon Durie.

'We made a new pact,' he said casually, like it was no big deal. 'I sent him the location of this client of yours, and he will stop dating Sarah.'

Alice fumed. 'You stupid, stupid man!'

'Steady on. You're hurting my feelings.'

'You really have no idea what you're dealing with here. He's capable of murder! You've just written Sian Tanner's death warrant.'

Dave shrugged. 'It doesn't matter, as long as he leaves our daughter alone.'

'Do you honestly believe he will do that just because you asked him to?' her voice becoming shrilled. Teens walking by carrying their kayaks, turned to see where the yelling was coming from.

'Like I said, we made a deal.'

Alice was so angry she was incapable of words, and growled instead.

'Think logically,' she thought aloud.

'What?' Dave asked.

'Just shut up for a moment, so I can figure this out in my head.' She took long, deep breaths, a technique she taught her clients to calm their anxiety. At this point her only option was to contact Sergeant Louise to confide in her. If an arrest was going to be made, then so be it. The main concern now was that Sian and Sarah were rescued from Brendon Durie. It's a four hour drive to Woodville. He's not rich enough to take a helicopter; therefore she can assume that he will reach Sian in four to five hours, if he was to leave straight away. There are police in Woodville, they need to be informed. She sighed, and scrolled through her contacts to find Louise's number. She was about to hit the call button, when her phone began to ring. An unknown number.

'Hello?' she answered.

'Is this Alice Granger?' a man's voice, one she doesn't recognise.

'Who is this?'

'My name is Wayne Myers from the Lakesford Standard. We've received some interesting, potentially incriminating images, and I was wondering if you'd like to comment on them.'

Playing dumb, 'What are the images of?'

'You mean you don't know?'

'No.'

'I'll send them through to you.'

The conversation was cut short.

'Who was that?' Dave asked.

'That was trouble, the beginning of the end.' Her phone beeped three times and she handed it to Dave. 'I don't want to look.'

Dave opened the first text, and at first thought it was the image he had seen before with Alice in the background, watching a balaclava - clad man, rock in hand, arm raised, in the throes of knocking out Damon Ridge. But something was off. He made the image larger, and froze when he saw the face of his daughter.

'That shite!' he bellowed, opening up the second text. The original image of Alice standing in the background once again, watching on as a balaclava clad man drowned Damon Ridge. Only this time the image had Sarah's face superimposed over hers. The third image was similar.

The phone rang. 'Would you like to comment?' the journalist asked.

'These images are fake!' Dave yelled.

'Sure they are,' Wayne said, sarcastically. 'And who am I speaking to?'

Alice snatched the phone off Dave. 'Listen to me, you jumped-up piece of shit!'

'Mrs Granger? So delighted to speak to you, again.'

'These images are fake! If you do your background work, you'll find that I am right. If you print these, the only person to look like a fool will be you.'

'Is this your daughter Sarah Granger in the photo, watching on as a man thrashes the skull of missing man, Damon Ridge?'

'No, it is not!'

As soon as she cut the call, a text came through indicating that someone had left a message. While Dave swore at the top of his lungs, bashing the dashboard with his fists, Alice retrieved the call. It was Sergeant Louise Ratahi. 'We need to talk. Please ring me ASAP.'

'Can you come in to the station?' Louise asked, sternly. This was not a social call.

'Are these about the images?' Alice asked.

'Yes. You know about them?'

'We just had a journalist send them to us. They're fake, Louise, you have to believe me.'

'We've already come to that conclusion. It's obvious that your daughter's head was superimposed over someone else's. The problem is why? What does your daughter have to do with the death of missing man, Damon Ridge?'

'Nothing!' Alice yelled, her voice louder than she intended. 'She's got nothing to do with it.'

'This is evidence that Damon Ridge was killed, which means it's been upgraded to a murder enquiry.'

Alice paused. 'We're coming down to the station now.'

Louise was at the front counter when they arrived, her hair pulled back into a tight ponytail. She looked unhappy. It was her day off; Alice knew she had planned a weekend of surfing with her partner. Surfing and barbequing. She took them into a pokey, windowless interview room where there was only a desk and two hard chairs opposite.

'Take a seat,' Louise said.

'We...I have quite a bit to confess,' Alice said, pulling out one of the chairs, while Louise leaned against the wall. 'Sian's in trouble.'

'Wait!' Louise left the room, and brought back a digital recording device. 'Alice Granger, please repeat what you just said.'

'I have to confess a few things,' Alice said, leaning forward so her voice was clearer on the recording device.

'Carry on,' Louise said, encouraging more talk.

'Sian Tanner is in trouble. This guy,' slapping Dave on the arm, 'made a deal with the devil and told Brendon Durie where she's been hiding.'

'Why are you communicating with Brendon Durie?'

'Because he's dating our daughter!' Dave shouted, tears of frustration welling in his eyes. He wiped his cheeks with the back of his hand.

'Ah!' Louise said, as a piece of the puzzle fit perfectly into place.

'Please, Louise. You have to contact the Woodville Police.'

'I'll do that. But first you have to tell me why you told Durie where Sian Tanner is.'

Alice and Dave exchanged glances. This was it. This was the end.
'He had information on me,' Alice said. 'Incriminating information.
It was me in those images. I don't know why he put my daughter's
face over mine, and then sent them to you and that journalist, but I'm
telling you now, that it was me who hired the hitman to kill Damon
Ridge. It was me who stood behind and watched the hitman do it.
And, somehow Brendon Durie obtained images of that moment.'

Alice's hands trembled. The weight of the secret had been released
and she found herself feeling greatly relieved. There was a long
silence. Louise, arms tightly crossed over her chest, stared at the two
people across the table from her. She couldn't quite believe it. These
good, hard-working folk, heading towards retirement age, had hired
a hitman to eliminate someone that they hardly knew. *She* knew who
Damon Ridge was - scum of the earth - gambler, wife beater, child
molester. Was she pleased to have a rooster like Damon Ridge wiped
off the planet? Of course. It made everyone's life a little easier, and
it made the planet a little safer. But unfortunately for Alice Granger,
she's committed a serious crime, and the law in New Zealand states
she must be punished for it.

'Give me the name of the man wearing the balaclava,' Louise
demanded.

'Come on, Louise! Let's face it, I did everyone a favour having
Damon Ridge targeted,' Alice replied.

'You committed a crime, Alice, and I don't think you understand
how serious that is.'

'Yes, I do understand. I just don't care. My daughter is in trouble.'
She scrambled to find her phone in her handbag. Her hands shook so
much, the phone kept slipping through her fingers. Seeing that she
was struggling, Dave took the phone from her and found what she
was looking for - the repulsive image Brendon had sent of the naked,
half-buried woman with Sarah's face superimposed over hers.

Louise's dark eyebrows shot up in surprise when she looked at the
pic, although the rest of her face remained severe. She spent a few
more seconds reading texts and looking at images...until...snap! She

found the images sent by an unknown number - of Alice standing by, while the balaclava-clad man did his work, - the same number the image of the half-buried woman was sent from. Silently, and avoiding eye-contact, she stepped over to the door, opened it, and called a constable to her. The phone was given to him, with instructions to get the Woodville police on the phone.

Alice breathed a sigh of relief. That was Sian sorted, now her daughter.

'The name of the man in the balaclava?' Louise repeated.

'I can't. I mean...I don't actually know his real name.' This was a lie. If she said his name, they'd find him lying in a coma in the ICU. It's easy to catch a killer, when he's half dead.

'What name do you call him by?' Louise asked, unsurprised by her answer.

'Birdie.'

'And you communicate with him using that phone,' she nodded towards the door.

Alice wasn't going to do this, but she had nothing to lose. Reaching into the inside pocket in her handbag, she brought out the cheap, throwaway phone she used to communicate with Birdie, and slapped it on the table.

'My, you have been busy, Alice Granger,' Louise said, still trying to grasp the fact that she had known Alice for years - they had worked together on numerous occasions, assisting victims of violence - and here she was with her own little vigilante organisation. Who would've guessed? Alice *Annie, get your gun* Granger.

'Are you going to do something about our daughter, Sarah? Sarah Granger?' Dave asked.

'Where is she staying?' Louise asked. 'We'll send a car round to check up on her.'

They gave details of the location of Sarah's flat, and her cell number. Louise was already aware of where Brendon Durie lived, and what he liked to get up to. She handed the information over to the unseen constable on the other side of the door.

'Why would Brendon Durie send these images of Sarah's face over the top of yours, and that deceased woman's?' Louise asked.

'We don't know,' Dave said, his legs jiggling up and down under the table. He was frustrated at the lack of urgency in finding out whether his daughter was okay. All this police woman seemed to be interested in, was who the balaclava-clad man was. Who cares about him? 'We made a deal with the shite - that if we told him where his ex girlfriend is, then he'd leave Sarah alone. And not send...' he bit his tongue.

'-and not send those images to the police and press?' Louise finished his sentence. She was no idiot. It was as clear as day what was going on.

'Yeah.'

'It seems he didn't keep to his side of the bargain,' Louise said, watching their body language closely. 'Why was that, do you think?'

'Because he's an arsehole,' Dave said.

Louise nodded, and picked up Alice's cheap cell that sat on the table. She read the short conversation that went back only a couple of weeks. 'Did you use this phone to converse with Birdie about Damon Ridge?' she said. '

'No,' Alice admitted. 'I destroy the phone after the deed is done, but keep the number.' There's no point hiding now. The evidence was there on both cells, as clear as day.

Louise shut the phone off and slipped it into her trouser pocket. Alice assumed she was going to have it analysed later. There was a knock at the door and Louise opened it. The constable, a plump, unshaven man with auburn hair, peered in to take a look at Alice. He whispered something to Louise. She thanked him and closed the door behind him.

'The Woodville Police Department has been contacted. We've got police out on the beat where Sian Tanner is at the moment. She's currently out in the open at the Spring Market, but they'll keep an eye out as the hours go by.'

'And Sarah?' Dave asked.

'We haven't been able to get hold of her, yet.'

***

Constable Kerryn Gillespie was given strict instructions from his superior, Sergeant Ratahi, to contact the Woodville Police Department. He was to inform them that a Brendon Durie, potentially armed and dangerous, now knew the location of his victim, Sian Tanner.

He picked up the phone, pretended to dial their number, and then proceeded to have a fake conversation. Once he put the phone down, he texted his old buddy Brendon to update him on what was going down. Kerryn and Brendon go back a long way. They had been tight mates for years, were even in the same rugby team together, until Kerryn got fat and lazy. Socially however, they're worlds apart. Brendon came from a wealthy, well-known family, and Kerryn from a state housing area. But Brendon relied on his great mate to assist in certain sensitive operations. In return, he'd pay him a healthy sum of money.

Over the years, Kerryn played the role of many characters - driver, policeman, electrician etc - so Brendon could live out his strange and violent fantasies. No questions asked. But no role was as important as his actual job, as constable. He worked closely with Sergeant Ratahi. As soon as he received the location where Sian was hiding, through Louise Ratahi, he passed that information on to Brendon. That evening a chunk of money was in his bank account. It was the perfect friendship.

What Louise didn't know was that Brendon Durie had known where Sian was hiding for two days now. What Louise also didn't know, was that Brendon Durie was already there in Woodville, and had spent the day at the local Spring Market, watching Sian Tanner, mostly from afar.

There was one occasion, a moment he was most proud of, when he walked past her so close he could smell her short hair. She was too deep in conversation with two toothless rednecks to notice, and he was too clever in disguise to get caught.

Let the games begin.

THIRTY ONE

The photograph of the Fields had changed again. The young man was preparing to slice the heads off May's parents with the scythe. That's what it looked like to Sian. May's parents, wearing expressions of fear, were in the process of turning their heads to see what was coming behind them. And what was coming, was the blade of the young man's scythe. The young man who Sian suspects was Ben Stokes. But why was she being shown this?

She was still in the dark as to what had happened to him. Just like she was still in the dark about what happened to the other Ben, Benny Sorenson. Rosie reckoned Sam Sorenson was making all of that stuff up, about their old man hitting Benny over the head with a beer bottle, and then burying him in the backyard.

'He's a pig of a man,' Rosie said, cringing in disgust.

Not long after Sian arrived home from the market in town, a police car arrived, and parked a few metres down the road from her house. She expected a knock on her door, only the officer remained inside the car for about thirty minutes, then drove down the road to Rosie's, where it stopped right outside her house. Sian could see the officer climb out of the vehicle and disappear behind the wall of trees that act as a wind block. The car was parked there for a good twenty minutes, before it left again. She hoped Rosie was okay, and without a cell phone to send a simple text, she'd have to walk or drive down the road to find out. She must get a phone to replace the one she smashed and buried in the backyard. She was going to order one online the other day, but got interrupted. She was using the computer at work in the library, when a customer came up and asked the whereabouts of a particular book. She forgot to continue on with the order after that.

Without a television or computer to keep her mind busy in the evenings, Sian would either do a bit of handy work, or read one of Aunt May's many books. She had an eclectic taste, Aunt May. An array of fiction authors from Bryce Courtney to Barbara Cartland, and non-fiction subjects varied from Helena Blavatsky and Edgar Cayce, to books on birds, herbs, and engines.

Sian lay in bed for what seemed like several hours, before she finally drifted into a much needed slumber. Thoughts in her mind of the day's events - the conversations had, and the police officer that visited Rosie, kept her awake, along with the constant feeling of apprehension. Apprehension was a normal post trauma feeling. It arrived like an unwanted friend, and it raised its ugly head with a vengeance whenever she thought of Brendon Durie. An awful feeling something bad was about to happen, a mistrust of the future that kept her on edge. It was always there, this monster, either hovering in the background or right in her face, breathing down her neck, putting her on the verge of a panic attack. These days, the feeling of apprehension was lessening, as her confidence grew and her mind was kept occupied. It was always important to keep her mind occupied.

The sun fell quickly over the west, casting shadows over the living room. In the end she didn't go down to Rosie's to check that everything was okay. Perhaps she was being just a little too busy - bodyish, a nosy neighbour wanting the latest gossip. Besides, Rosie's mum, Theresa, was there. She'd comfort Rosie if something was wrong. Instead, she'll go down first thing in the morning, on the way to work.

Rosie's house was empty of life when Sian stopped by on her way to work. It was Monday morning and both Rosie's and Theresa's cars were gone. Theresa was probably on her way home to Lakesford, and Rosie would be dropping Chloe off at the kindergarten.

Sian went to work at the library on Monday morning with a new purpose, and a slight spring in her step. She still had anxiety that at times made her afraid to leave the house, and was still mistrustful of people, but she was feeling stronger and healthier. Animals were easier. The shining cuckoos that began to call in early October, indicating Spring is here, the cottontail rabbits that hopped frantically about in the paddocks when she went on her runs, and let's not forget Popo, the oversized cat that brought a wonderful calmness, that so far no human had managed to achieve. No human apart from Alice, her ex-therapist.

As soon as Sian was able to, she cornered Mavis by the non-fiction House and Garden section, and asked her about the Sorensons.

Mavis screwed up her sharp nose, and peered over her glasses at Sian. 'A very unfortunate family,' she said.

'Do you remember a Benny Sorenson?' Sian asked, cutting to the chase.

'I didn't know all of their names. There were quite a few of them.'

'I played with a boy named Benny when I stayed with Aunt May. I was just wondering what happened to him.' Sian said.

'Yes, I remember him.'

'He looked a lot like Ben Stokes,' Sian said.

'If you say so,' Mavis said. 'I can't remember. I had several Sorensons in my classes at one time or another.'

'Fifteen years ago?'

'I've been retired for more than fifteen years. It's coming up twenty five years.'

'Was Mr Sorenson a police officer here, once?'

Mavis gazed up at the ceiling, collecting a memory. 'There's been a couple of Sorensons working as police officers over the decades. One was a drunk, and the other was actually pretty good. But that summed up the Sorensons. Some of them came out good, others not so much. ' A repeat of what Fred said. It amused Sian that two people that disliked each other so much, were so similar.

'The drunk officer was back when I stayed with Aunt May.'

'Yes. They tossed him out, then he drank himself to death.' She cringed. 'Not a nice character, that one. If alcoholism is a disease, which is what they say these days, then he was severely infected. His father was a drunk, and so was his father and so on. It's a miracle he managed to get through Police College.' She narrowed her eyes. 'A little bird told me you're investigating Ben Stokes' disappearance.'

'Yes, that's true,' Sian replied, wondering who this little bird was, as she had only informed Rosie, Fred and Sergeant Lee of her plans. So far she's had no resistance. She also wondered who it was that told Sam that she was asking about Benny. There were people hanging around in the information centre, maybe it was one of them. It's a small town. Everyone knows each other.

'It was a long time ago, Sian. You'd be lucky to find people who remember clearly.'

'I've spoken to Fred,' Sian said, expecting a comeback from Mavis, and was happy to notice an eye roll, 'He can remember quite a bit. He was friends with Ben Stokes back then.'

'Yes, so was your Aunt May.'

'I wondered if that was the case. They lived across the road from each other.'

'Yes,' Mavis said. She hesitated. There was more she wanted to say. 'I didn't know your aunt back then.'

Sian prompted her. 'Were they good friends, Ben and May?'

Mavis hesitated again. Then said, 'Your Aunt believed she could see some ghosts, and Ben was one of them. He'd visit her often. She only ever saw him in McCrae's Forest.' She watched Sian's face for a reaction, but Sian's expression remained steady and focussed. 'And before you ask, yes I did believe her. I couldn't see spirits, but sometimes I felt them, in McCrae's Forest,' she repeated. 'There's something about that forest, it unleashes the dead.'

'But were they friends when he was alive?' Sian asked, finding it odd that she avoided answering the question, and instead nattered on about the ghost of Ben Stokes.

'Sorry, I hope I don't scare you, since you live so close.'

'None of this surprises me. I just prefer not to think of that forest as a graveyard of restless spirits.'

'Have you seen any yourself?' Mavis asked, still watching Sian's face closely.

'No. I don't think so. But there are other things...in the house.' She swallowed a lump in her throat. 'Like a photograph of May's parents taken when they were pretty old. They move.'

'They move?'

Sian brushed it aside. 'It's silly.'

'The people in the photograph move?' Mavis asked, eager to pursue this line of conversation further.

'I mean, I don't see them move. One day they're looking forward, the next day they're looking to their right.'

'Oh, that's fascinating!'

'You think I'm nuts, don't you?'

'No. I think you're your Aunt's niece.'

'There's also a young man in the photograph who doesn't quite fit. He wasn't there to start off with. I wondered if he was Ben Stokes.'

A classroom of children from the local school flooded into the library, wearing blue sunhats and sweat shirts to match. They were there to have a book read to them by its author, a book about a hefty wood pigeon with a broken leg - a rare and special treat for the children of Woodville Primary School.

Mavis was gazing out the window, as she usually did in the staffroom at tea break. The crimson cherry blossom outside the window was humming with bees. An ominous black cloud was moving in their direction, bringing with it an unwanted chill.

As Sian took the seat next to her, Mavis suddenly said, 'I was only twenty two at the time, when I came to these parts to teach. It was my first job, fresh out of teacher's college. Back then, all the country kids in quite a large area travelled for miles to get to school. Her pale eyes glazed over.

'I heard the Stokes house was burned down,' Sian said.

Her eyes narrowed. 'So they say,' she said slowly, as the memories came crawling back. 'The wood was probably infested with Bora. Like I said, I wasn't here then. So you see, Sian, you're going to find it difficult getting clues of Ben Stokes' whereabouts, when all you have to rely on is that old bugger in the museum.'

Sian chuckled. 'I also have the police files. It's an unsolved cold case. They've welcomed me to give it a crack.'

'Probably because they expect little from you.'

Sian raised her eyebrows. She wasn't born yesterday. She knew that if there was plenty of evidence to go on, Ben's body would've already been found. It's likely to be a very thin file, and unless she can contact the ghost of Ben Stokes herself, like her eccentric Aunt, then she's probably going to come up with nothing.

When she left the staffroom to finish off the day's tasks, she spotted Sergeant Lee leaning against the front counter talking to the librarian. When he saw Sian, he waved her over. Her heart pounded against her ribcage. A loud burst of children's laughter sounded out from the reading room, where the author was reading a wood pigeon book to about thirty children. Sian was startled, and pressed her hand against her chest to help calm her breathing.

'Shall we go for a little walk,' Lee asked, opening the entrance door for Sian to step through. The large, ominous cloud Sian had seen moving closer to Woodville had settled over the small town and began to drop soft, cold rain. Lee pointed to the cafe across the road, and asked if she'd like anything to eat.

'No, thank you.'

He looked at her up and down. 'You need to keep your calorie intake up.'

'Oh! You're an expert on nutrition now?' she asked, sarcastically.

'No,' completely unfazed by her tone. 'But no-one gets strong by not eating.' His calm disposition never changed, no matter what was said, or what activities were going on around him. His eyes flickered this way and that, taking note of every car that drove past, and every person that smiled and said hello. You could quite easily describe Lee as a laid-back officer, but in truth it was a combination of his demeanour, and his training. If some kid were to hurl insults at him, he'd speak to him calmly and steadily, probably with a hint of bemusement but never getting riled up. It's been a long time since Sian has been in the company of a heterosexual man she felt safe with. Assuming he was heterosexual, you never know these days. 'You're doing okay?'

'I'm doing really well,' she said, and meant it. 'Which reminds me, can I get those files on Ben Stokes from you?'

He chuckled. 'You're really quite serious about this?'

'Yes. It's just the thought that he died alone, somewhere.'

Lee nodded his silver head, then chose a steak and cheese pie for lunch. In the corner of the cafe were four men, two of them were Angus and Sam. The other two were just as unruly looking with untamed hair, grimy hands, and wearing bush shirts. Hunters, bushmen. They were feasting on something greasy and low in nutrients. Angus was sitting with his back to Sian, but didn't turn his head when Sam signalled that they'd just walked in. Sam liked to stir the pot, create waves, and deliberately annoy the crap out of people.

Angus, on the other hand was reserved, thoughtful and more likable. Sian wondered where the rest of this infamous family hung out. If there were ten children, like Fred believed, they and their offspring would be crawling all over the place, you'd think. Perhaps the other two men were brothers, as well. The spotty-faced, gum-chewing girl who served Sian in the small supermarket the other day, could've been a Sorenson, or even the woman who just sold Lee a steak and cheese pie. They're probably everywhere, like fleas on a dog.

'How are you going, chaps?' Lee said to them, walking casually over to their table to strike up a short conversation about possums, deer and goats. The Sorenson boys were no strangers to the police, Sian suspected, no strangers to police cells either.

'I see you're friends with Benny's girl,' Sam said scornfully to Lee.

'Benny's girl?'

'You remember our brother who died?' Sam said, rather sharply. 'He was fixated on her.'

Tears welled up in Sian's eyes as she remembered her boy, her best friend, Benny.

'How did he die?' Sian asked Lee, when he walked back to her.

'Haven't we discussed this before?'

'Yes, but I've been told different things by different people.'

'A drowning. He was drunk.'

THIRTY TWO

'Do they suspect I had something to do with Ben's disappearance?' Sian asked, slightly miffed.

'I wouldn't be too concerned what Sam Sorenson thinks,' Lee said.

'Did he have a head trauma?' Sian asked, as they walked back out of the cafe onto the quiet street.

'Who, Ben Sorenson? According to the police reports, he took after his old man and started drinking from a young age, and later drowned in the river. He had injuries, but they were self-inflicted.'

'Impossible,' Sian said. 'I spent every day over the summer with him for years. He never touched alcohol. He was never drunk. I never once saw a bottle of liquor in his hand.'

Lee shrugged. 'Sometimes people aren't who you think they are. Listen. Stop by the station when you want the files on Ben Stokes. And don't forget if there's anything you need, like extra support, let us know. I mean, if you feel unsafe or threatened, it's important to inform us so we can protect you.'

Sian trembled at his words. 'Is Rosie alright?'

'Rosie?'

'She's my neighbour.'

'Yes, as far as I know. What makes you think she's not?'

'I saw a police car outside her house yesterday evening.'

He chuckled. 'Seeing the police isn't always a bad omen.'

'Has something happened?'

He paused. Sian could tell he was on the verge of saying something, but stopped himself. Sian assumed that it was confidential police business.

'Just make sure you look after yourself. Check windows and doors are securely fastened, and head over to your neighbours at the slightest moment that you feel afraid, the usual procedure.'

'The usual procedure,' Sian repeated. It was a nice feeling, having the local police watch out for her. They did this often - Sergeant Lee, Constables Jarrod and Rachel, the three people that make up the entire Woodville Police Department. They'd knock on her door now and again to check that she was okay, or pop in on her at the library. In small towns, even the police are on a first name basis, and are treated like part of the community, rather than on the edge of it.

Yes, Sian was finally settling into her new life. She even thought she might spread a lick of paint over the walls of Aunt May's house - no, it's her house now - change the interior to her liking, rather than living in the memory of her Great Aunt. Life's good she thought, and it can only get better.

On the way home, Sian dropped in at the police station to pick up the cold case files on Ben Stokes. Lee left them out for her to pick up, and, as she expected, the files were thin. She stopped by the local hardware store to pick up some test pots of paint. Aunt May's faded beige floral print was getting on Sian's nerves. It was obvious that May hadn't cared much for interior decorating. If there was a stain on the carpet or a gash in the floor boards, she covered it with a mat. If there was a hole in the wall, she covered it with art or bookshelves. Easy.

As soon as Sian got home, she opened the file. The file consisted of a brown manila folder, with a stack of about ten pages inside. There was a black and white photograph of Ben Stokes aged about twelve, standing in front of his parents, hand placed on a black and white border collie's head. His parents looked like nice people. His father didn't have horns growing out of his head, or a sinister appearance in any way. But she couldn't get past Fred's comment that he reckoned there was something amiss with Mr Stokes.

Time flew by as Sian read interviews and last sightings of Ben, all of them vague. His parents last saw him at home. He was planning on going trout fishing in the Manawatu River, which at the time flowed through McCrae's Forest. Now, the forest on the west side of the river is farmland. All that luscious forest burnt down, not long after Ben Stokes went missing. This in itself was a problem. If Ben went missing on that side of the river, then any ounce of evidence would be lost.

She searched through the faded leaves of paper to find who owned the land back in 1956, but couldn't find anything. Large amounts of land were rarely sold back then. Usually, the land was handed down to the children to carry on running the farms. So there was a strong likelihood that the land was still owned by the same people, only a generation older.

One detail that stood out like a sore thumb was that the local constable working on the case was none other than Constable John P. Sorenson. Another damn Sorenson! He had to have been Ben, Angus and Sam's grandfather. There were no photographs of him, but she only hoped that he was a good egg, not a bad one, unlike his son seemed to be.

Sian picked up the photograph of Ben Stokes, aged twelve, and peered closely at his face again. There were similarities in features to the Benny Sorenson in her mind, but she could now see many differences. Ben Stokes looked well built, well-fed and clean, with defined cheekbones. His hair was darker at this age, whereas Benny Sorenson had wheat coloured hair like his brother Angus, right through until his death at age fifteen.

It's a secret.

There was connection there between them, but Sian couldn't quite put her finger on it. Like the tide moving onto the shore, the memory returned of a shallow grave in the forest, the buried bones. *It's a secret.*

'What's a secret?' she whispered.

'I've seen them,' Benny Sorenson whispered to a young Sian.

A sudden thought smacked Sian across the cheek. She ran upstairs to compare the photograph of twelve year old Ben Stokes with the young man standing behind the Fields in the photograph on the wall. With shaking hands, she lifted the white lace handkerchief, and held twelve year old Ben Stokes up next to the young man.

He dropped the handkerchief back down, her legs collapsing beneath her in shock.

As clear as day, they were the same person.

***

'My house was broken into,' Rosie said, standing at Sian's door with a bottle of wine. Chloe was at her side sucking her thumb, her large blue eyes gazing up at Sian with that usual look of wonder.

'Is that why the police car was there last night?' Sian asked, opening the door wider so they could pile in. Popo, the oversized cat awoke to Chloe's little voice and raced over to her.

'I can't sleep,' Rosie said. 'I called Nathan and he's on his way here. But it'll take a couple of days' worth of transfers to get here. They would've done it when we were at the Spring Market on Sunday, and when mum and Chloe were at the supermarket. I got home before Mum did, and found the back door open. It might pay to check to see if your doors and windows haven't been tampered with.'

'I haven't noticed anything missing, or...' Sian thought about the bedroom window, the window that doesn't like to close. Even when she secures it down, it'll be open again the next time she goes in there. Strange house. This news shook Sian.

'The funny thing is... I can't find anything stolen. They just broke in, ramming the back door open, and that was it. Except...' she paused.

'What is it?' Sian asked, the nerves swimming in her belly.

'I told Constable Jarrod not to say anything to you, because of what you've been through. I'm sorry if I'm being selfish, wanting some support and company. I lied to mum, and said that I was doing fine so she didn't feel obliged to stay longer, 'cos Dad's pretty useless without her,' rolling her eyes.

'Not at all, I completely understand,' Sian said. This was about Rosie and Chloe now. Her fears and anxieties will have to be pushed aside. After all, this is what friends do, look after each other.

'I just didn't want you to get scared,' Rosie added, wrapping her hand around the wine bottle cap, and easily unscrewing it.

'I'm fine,' Sian said. 'I'm not a snowflake that melts at the slightest stress. Besides, this is about you.'

Rosie laughed and took a swig out of the bottle, then handed it to Sian. No glasses needed on this occasion. After a few gulps they were relaxed, and giggling about stupid things. Chloe was parked on the floor in the living room playing with Popo. Such a fascinating connection those two have. Sian wished the cat would love her as much as he loved Chloe. How ridiculous, competing for the love of a feline.

'A bag of pebbles,' Rosie said, giggling, watching Chloe and Popo play.

'What?' Sian asked, in case she wasn't hearing right.

Popo was crouching behind the curtain about to pounce on Chloe, when Chloe raced up to him, giggling hysterically. 'They took nothing, but left a bag of pebbles on the coffee table,' Rosie said, still watching her daughter and the big fluffy cat play. 'Honestly, it looked like they broke in through the back door, placed the bag of pebbles on the coffee table in the living room and sat on the couch for a while, 'cos their bum print was still there when I got home, and it was warm to the touch. I must've disturbed them. They're great entertainment aren't they,' turning back to Sian, whose face had gone a paler shade. She had stopped laughing, her mind elsewhere. 'I was meaning these two,' Rosie said, nodding towards Chloe and Popo, who together had fled up the hall. 'These two are entertaining, not the burglar. I'm not nuts.'

'A bag of pebbles?' Sian asked, covering her mouth with her hand.

'What's wrong?' Rosie asked.

'Nothing,' Sian lied. This was about Rosie and Chloe, she thought, so don't make this out to be about you. Brendon Durie has no idea where I am. This was a pure coincidence, nothing more and nothing less. Besides, he's moved on anyway. He's got a new girlfriend to torture.

THIRTY THREE

The Sergeant

Brendon Durie reportedly failed to show up for work on Monday. This concerned Sergeant Louise, as did the fact that no-one was home at his apartment on Sunday evening when she sent a patrol car around. On the Monday, Louise took it upon herself to pay him a visit, only no-one answered the door. It was a modern, two storey house with a sea view, probably worth a good two million plus dollars. Her sidekick Constable Kerryn Gillespie, fat and lazy, and too thick to pass the exams to get a sergeant's badge, waited in the car. Sharing a small space with Kerryn was like visiting a men's public toilet. He drowned himself in aftershave in attempts to disguise the rottenness underneath. His breath stunk as did his clothes, which Louise suspected were rarely washed. But he was reliable and followed her commands with little complaint. She suspected that he had a crush on her, and was probably loyal and obedient due to that, rather than her superiority.

She wanted to get inside the house, but couldn't do this without a warrant, which may take some time to achieve. The only option was to break inside on the sly, which meant Kerryn had to disappear. She walked back to the car and told Kerryn to talk to the neighbours, check if they had any idea of Brendon's whereabouts, and if they remember the last time they saw him and his girlfriend, Sarah Granger.

The story was the same with Sarah. A patrol car had gone to Sarah's flat yesterday, she wasn't home and her flatmates assumed she was with Brendon. Today, she's still unreachable. Her cell goes straight to answer phone when rung, and she hasn't returned any texts or messages on social media. Her flatmates were given strict instructions to contact Louise as soon as she turned up. So far they've been silent, and Louise is greatly concerned for her safety.

Kerryn made out he was reluctant to leave Louise on her own, considering how dangerous Brendon Durie was known to be towards women. But Louise felt his hesitancy came from laziness, he just couldn't be bothered getting his fat body out of the car, and taking a walk. Typical.

Once Kerryn had gone, she ran along the narrow stone path that led to the back of the house. An owner of a house like this was likely to have a burglar alarm. This was a problem, but only if it was set. And it would only be set if there was no-one inside. But Louise had a hunch that someone was in there.

The back entrance was a glass sliding door that led out onto a low maintenance rock garden. She peered through the window to an open plan living room and kitchen space, cold and minimalistic. She tried the sliding door handle, but it refused to budge. Then she heard a window open on the top floor, and she peered around the corner of the building. It looked to be a bathroom window. Her hunch had proved right. All she needed to do was, wait. Soon someone will walk down to the kitchen to fix themselves something to eat, and moments later, someone did.

But it wasn't who she was hoping. It was a girl, young, too young for Brendon Durie, dressed in nothing but his white shirt, long golden, blonde hair falling down her back. When Louise knocked on the glass, the girl took fright and was about to flee, but then she realised that she had been spotted. There was no point running.

'Who are you?' Louise asked, holding up her badge.

'A friend of Brendon's,' the girl answered with a smirk.

'Can I come in?' Louise asked.

'I suppose,' the girl said, opening the door wider.

'Where is Brendon Durie?' Louise asked.

'He's away on business.'

Sure he is, Louise thought. 'Do you know where?'

'Wellington. Why, what's this about?' she smirked.

'How old are you?' Louise asked.

'Twenty one.'

'That's a lie,' she said swiftly, looking about the living room and kitchen.

'He won't like you being here,' the girl said, panicked. 'He gets a hard time from you lot.'

'Does he?' Louise was amused. *Poor, little, rich Brendon.*

'It's not justified. He's never laid a hand on me,' the girl added.

Louise opened a drawer in the kitchen, and searched quickly through the contents. 'Really? You must be his favourite then,' Louise said.

'Favourite?' She smirked again. 'I guess I must be. You shouldn't be looking through his stuff. He'll sue you, you know.'

Louise paused. 'You did let me in.' Then she vanished down the hall to the ground floor bedroom and bathroom, the young blonde followed behind.

'I think you had better leave.'

'Have you heard the name, Sarah Granger?' Louise asked.

The young blonde, crossed her arms tightly over her chest. 'Yeah, I know all about her. How she accused Brendon of all these awful things with no proof, 'cos she was upset that he wanted to end the relationship.'

'No.' *You fool!* she wanted to say. 'That was Sian Tanner. And she wasn't making it up, because I worked on that case. She was tortured and mutilated by a psychopath called Brendon Durie.'

It was evident that these words unsettled the girl, but it was also clear that she had been brainwashed by a handsome, rich man who could buy his way out of a lie. 'If that was true, why didn't he go to prison then?'

That's the question that always cut like a sharpened dagger into her stomach, every time it got asked. Instead she ignored it, focussing her attention on articles in cupboards and drawers. 'What's upstairs?'

'Our bedroom and ensuite plus another bedroom.'

'Our? You live here with him?' Louise asked, stunned.

'He's asked me to move in with him when he returns from Wellington,' she said, proudly.

'The man sure moves fast.' Louise shook her head in disgust, and quickly ran up the stairs to the master bedroom, to search through the drawers and walk-in wardrobe. Alice Granger told her that he had a special place where he liked to perform his torture. An abandoned warehouse had been used once, but Sian had described a darkened room that she often woke up in, strung up and naked. She couldn't give the location of exactly where it was, but she suspected it was within the walls of his house. She came to this assumption because of the fact that he could appear and disappear easily and quickly, bringing food and other supplies. When his house was searched this room was never found, but both Alice and Louise suspected that it was nearby, and probably contained enough evidence to put him away for life. Not that life meant life in New Zealand, it usually meant about ten years.

'What is that supposed to mean?' the girl asked.

'What is your name?' Louise asked, looking at her square on. She'd be no older than 18.

'Britney.'

Louise laughed. 'Of course it is.' That generation of children were named after pop stars and sports stars. 'Listen to me Britney, I don't know how long you've known Brendon Durie, but he's a very dangerous man. If I was you, I'd run like hell.'

Britney curled her top lip. 'You're just jealous.'

Ignoring her youthful idiocy, 'Do you ever hear any noises at night?'

'Like what?'

'Banging, crying, screaming?'

'Sometimes we hear possums on the roof.'

'And nothing else?'

She shook her head. Her expression of smugness was beginning to fade and Louise could tell something was bothering her. Louise wanted to push it, but thought otherwise. Instead, she walked quickly out of the master bedroom back into the hall, and stopped at a closed door opposite.

'What's in here?'

'That's Brendon's office. I'm not allowed in there.'

'Why?'

'It's where all of his important business stuff is. I might mess something up.'

Expecting the door to be locked, she was surprised to find it swung open when she tried it. Inside was what one expected from an office - a desk which was tidy with no paper work, a laptop, and a couple of pens. Louise went to the desk and sat down. The window looked out onto the driveway. Kerryn had returned from the neighbours, and was sitting on the police car bonnet. She radioed him to say that she won't be long. 'I'm just talking to a potential witness.'

'Who?' Kerryn asked.

'A house guest.'

Britney hovered at the door. 'I don't think you should be doing this,' she said. 'besides I'm more than just a house guest.'

'If he is an innocent man, he's got nothing to hide, right?' Louise asked.

Britney shrugged. 'I guess so.'

'How long have you been dating Mr Durie?' Louise asked, as she turned on the laptop.

'Four months. We've kept it quiet.'

'Why?'

'We work together. I'm a receptionist at Hillocks.

'He's twice your age.'

'Look at what you get for dating an older man, a gorgeous house and a fast car. Guys in my age group are driving old hatchbacks, and flatting.'

'I guess you've got to start somewhere,' Louise said, looking at the apps on the start screen. She clicked on one titled *Finances*. 'Are you aware that he was also dating a young woman called Sarah Granger?'

'No,' Britney said solemnly, yet appeared unsurprised. 'I guess it's a free world. He can date whoever he likes until we make a commitment.' Louise wasn't buying this 'shrug it off' attitude. Youth of today try to make out that they're independent and open-minded, yet Brendon Durie was cheating on her. It's got to hurt.

'Which is when he gets back from Wellington, is it?' There was nothing interesting in the *Finances* file, only a spreadsheet of his financial incomings and outgoings, dating back years. He liked to keep a tight rein on his expenses, by the looks. She clicked on another app titled *Contracts*, which contained nothing but copies of contracts and receipts, from car maintenance to work done on the house. They were sorted into years, very well organised, but nothing suspicious, nothing of interest, in fact all somewhat boring. He was a control freak, without a doubt.

'Yeah,' Britney answered.

'Well...this young woman Sarah Granger, has gone missing, so I'd like to find her quick. If you have any idea where she may be, please contact me. That would be much appreciated.'

'Do you think Brendon is with her in Wellington?' The worry lines that appeared on Britney's flawless face made her look even younger, sweeter. Of everything Louise has told her today, the thought that Brendon is cheating on her, upsets her the most.

'No,' Louise said, swiftly, looking up Brendon's latest searches. She was hoping to find child pornography, videos containing torture or rape, anything that could incriminate him. But it was clean. His latest searches were real estate in Auckland and Sydney, and Porsches for sale in New Zealand. The life of the wealthy!

Britney breathed a sigh of relief.

'Without a doubt he is not in Wellington. I'd bet my bottom dollar he's somewhere else, searching for his long lost girlfriend, Sian Tanner.'

Britney screwed up her face. 'Is that the one who tried to put him in prison?'

'Yes, that's the one. He has unfinished business with her. Do you know if Mr Durie has another house or flat anywhere?'

'He has an apartment in Wellington, since he's down there on business often.'

'Have you been there?'

'No.'

'Do you know where it is?'

'It's somewhere on the waterfront.'

'Right. Where are your clothes?'

'Why?'

'Because I think it might be a good idea if you got dressed, and trotted back to your parents.'

THIRTY FOUR

The Sergeant

Louise was about to turn the laptop off, when something stopped her. If there was a secret room within the walls of this house, it wouldn't have been here when it was built. Therefore he would have hired builders, and made up some bull crap story about needing a dark room for photography, or something. She clicked on the *Contracts* file and found the paperwork for the purchase of his house. It was in 2015, four years ago. The house though, was built in 2011, but the kitchen and various other areas were upgraded and modernised over the years. The piece of land the new house was built on had previously had a grand old villa on it that was built in 1908. It burned down in 2009, the land sold and a striking, architecturally designed house built on top. The surrounding houses were mostly from that era, just as opulent as the old villa, perhaps updated with a contemporary twist. It was definitely a street for the rich.

Brendon Durie had all the records here as clear as day, a precise, accurate history of his house and land. But there were no contracts or permits to add a room on. Maybe he had hidden them.

Britney was still hovering by the door, too afraid to step across the boundary into Durie's office.

'Are you still here?' Louise asked.

'I'm not leaving.'

'Fine.'

The radio crackled, 'How much longer?' Kerryn asked.

'Give me another twenty.' she replied.

Louise turned to Britney. 'I'm really worried about Sarah Granger. If we don't find her fast, I'm worried he may kill her.'

Britney dropped her head and stared at the carpet.

'Do you hear what I'm saying, Britney?'

'Yes,' she answered like a snotty, pouty teenager, which is exactly what she was. She let out a loud sigh, which was enough for Louise to pull her eyes away from the screen.

'Is there something you want to tell me?' Louise asked.

Britney hesitated, and then said, 'He has a wine cellar.'

'Where is it?'

'It's under the garden shed.'

Louise pushed the chair out from the desk, and flew out the office door. Britney followed behind her, begging Louise not to tell Brendon.

'Your secret is safe with me,' Louise said hastily, then called Kerryn on the radio for back up. 'Stay inside the house!' Louise ordered Britney. But Britney was terrified of the consequences, and as soon as Louise's back was turned, she texted Brendon that police were in the house.

Louise and Kerryn raced to the garden shed - a standard kitset shed that you could buy from any garden store. Even though the house was exceptionally tidy, too tidy, the shed was in utter chaos, with empty beer crates and boxes stacked high, covering every inch of the concrete floor.

'Who tipped you off?' Kerryn asked Louise.

'His house guest did. She's a teenager half his age.'

Hastily, Louise and Kerryn shoved aside every box and crate, until they found a trapdoor cut into the concrete floor. It was bolted and locked closed, and there were no tools to be found to break the lock. Louise ordered Kerryn back to the car to retrieve the tool box from the boot.

Britney appeared at the shed door. She had put on some jeans and a jersey, but was shaking like a leaf.

'How did you know?' Louise asked.

'I saw him one night, when he thought I was asleep, coming down here with a bottle of wine in his hand. It was an expensive bottle of wine, a gift from a supplier. The next morning while he was in the shower, I came down to see where he had put it and saw the trapdoor, and then put two and two together. I was kind of hoping he was going to share the wine with me. But I guess he's keeping it for another day.'

'Funny place to put a wine cellar, though,' Louise said. 'Did you ever ask him about it?'

She shook her head.

Kerryn returned with the tool box, and when he acknowledged Britney, she looked slightly startled. Her expression flashed confusion, then panic.

With both Britney and Louise watching on, Kerryn cut the lock with a bolt cutter, and opened the trapdoor. Louise flicked her torch on and flashed the light down inside. All that could be seen was a cold, concrete floor. She called out, but no one replied.

'I'm going down. I suggest you call for backup.' she said to Kerryn, just as she caught an exchange of looks between Kerryn and Britney. 'Have you two met before?'

In an instant Kerryn lunged at Louise, striking her head with the bolt cutters. The world went black.

***

When Louise awoke, she thought she had gone blind. It was so dark she couldn't see her hand in front of her face. A dank smell of wet earth and urine permeated the space. Her head ached, and a wave of nausea crept up on her, forcing her to roll over and vomit. The clothes she wore were damp on the left side where she had been lying, and her left cheek was covered in dirt. She felt around in her jacket pocket for her cell, but it had been removed, as had her torch. In her trouser pocket was the throwaway cheap cell that Alice Granger had used to call the hitman. She turned it on. The light from the small screen shocked her eyes. She turned it off again, rubbed her eyes and then turned the light on again.

This time, she shone the light for as long as she possibly could before the stabbing pain behind her eyeballs forced her to turn it off. In that small moment of light she noticed three things.

One. The light from the small screen lit the entire space. This was no wine cellar. This was a bunker, the size of small bedroom, deliberately designed to hide things, to hide people.

Two. There was no reception on the cell phone, but the battery was almost full.

Three. There was an orange curtain that hung on the wall opposite, possibly hiding an entrance into another space.

She rose unsteadily to her feet, using the dirt wall to prop herself up. The room swayed as another wave of nausea came over her. As she vomited in the darkness, she saw in her mind Kerryn Gillespie's fat face, and the exchange she caught between him and that girl, Durie's latest, all of about 18 years of age. What has she missed?

Covering her eyes to prepare them for the sting of light, Louise switched the phone on again. Taking deep breaths to ease the throbbing pain in her head, she stepped shakily over to the curtain and pulled it aside.

Another bunker. On one side of the dark space was a large cage, one a circus lion might be unlucky enough to live in. It was empty of life, but chains and a strange swing-like contraption hung within. Opposite the cage was a dismal camp bed, no blankets. On the floor next to the bed was large ceramic bowl. Going by the smell, it was used as a toilet. Louise placed her hand on the bed to check if it was still warm from being recently occupied. It was warm, and movement in the corner of her eye made her jump and reach for her stun-gun. It wasn't there. Instead, she shone the light from the cheap cell over to where the movement had come from. Slouched in the corner was someone shivering, their hands shielding their face from the brightness.

'Sarah?' Louise asked, pointing the light towards her.

Silence.

'I'm Sergeant Louise from the Lakesford Police Department. I know your mother, Alice. I'm here to help you.'

Sarah lowered her trembling hands. Her right eye was contorted into an enormous swelling, and her bottom lip was bloody. Louise felt fury rise within her. Sarah's hands were in cuffs as were her ankles. She could still move but not easily. *Twenty minutes*, she thought. *Give me twenty minutes in a room with Brendon bloody Durie.*

'You're here to help me?' Sarah's voice was soft and croaky. It was the voice of someone who has been screaming for long periods.

'Well...'Louise started, feeling slightly foolish, 'that was the plan. But it seems I've been double-crossed.'

'By whom?'

'My constable.'

'He dropped you down here?'

'Yes.'

'He doesn't work alone. Brendon has people...' Sarah said.

'So I have just discovered.'

'I should've listened to my mother,' Sarah said, weakly.

Louise couldn't help but chuckle as she crouched next to Sarah, to take a closer look at what state she was in. 'We all should've listened to our mothers.'

'It's all superficial,' Sarah said huskily, referring to her wounds. 'There's no way out. I've tried.' she added, holding up her hands, dirt under the fingernails from digging, and dried blood from the fingernails that ripped off in her desperation to dig a way out.

Louise slid down onto the floor next to Sarah, and switched the light off on Alice's cell to save the battery. 'The trapdoor bolt has been cut. If you climb up onto my shoulders, do you think you could try to push the trapdoor open?'

'No,' Sarah said.

'You've only been down here a couple of days. You'll be stronger than you think.'

'No, I mean, I think he's replaced it, not long after you were pushed down here. You've been out cold for a while. I heard scraping sounds like something has been moved over the top.' She began to sob. 'It's hopeless.'

'Not quite. We do have a hope in the form of Britney.'

'Britney?'

'She was there when my fat shithead constable hit me over the head and threw me down here. She's not the sharpest tool in the shed, but she'll know the difference between right and wrong.'

'Unless something's happened to her, as well,' Sarah said.

'Yeah...well... that's always a possibility. But I'm a hundred percent sure Brendon Durie is in Woodville and - ah damn it!' An awful realisation struck her.

'What's the matter?' Sarah asked.

Louise rubbed her eyes with the palms of her hands, feeling completely and utterly miserable. 'It was Kerryn I ordered to contact the Woodville Police Department to warn them that Brendon Durie was coming their way. One of his victims lives there, in hiding. He has unfinished business with her. I swore I heard Kerryn ring them., but,' she growled angrily, 'I bet you he faked the call, and now Brendon bloody Durie is in Woodville, and no-one knows a damn thing about it. How did I miss this?'

'Is it Sian Tanner?' Sarah asked.

'Yes.'

'I hope she lives,' Sarah said, meaning it with all her heart.

'So do I,' Louise agreed.

THIRTY FIVE

W ho owned the land on the west side of the river back in 1956?' Sian asked Fred. She found him sitting on a park bench near Ben Stokes' remembrance oak tree, feeding the birds and ducks with rolled oats. The morning sun was a little too bright for her eyes today. She was still recovering from the wine she drank with Rosie last night. She didn't sleep well. Wine did that to her, made her head too busy, and her heart race.

The bag of pebbles left on Rosie's coffee table bothered her. Brendon Durie had a bag of pebbles. He kept them in his home office, and used them to toss at her when she did something wrong. Sometimes he'd make her strip down to her underwear, and tie her up in a confined space like a wardrobe that she couldn't escape from easily. He'd throw one pebble at a time, slowly, deliberately, a look of pure pleasure on his face.

When he was really mad, she'd find herself in the dungeon, where the most awful activities took place. She shuddered.

To rest her mind, Sian decided that the bag of pebbles found in Rosie's house was nothing but a coincidence. End of story.

Rosie and Chloe spent the night on the couch. It was a nice feeling, having a full house for once, but she doubted that they got any sleep, either. The old couch sagged in the middle, and at times faint cat pee smells rose in the air. Great Aunt May had many cats over the years. Even though she often preached that introduced predators will wipe out the entire population of native wildlife, she still loved her cats.

'Never feed them bread. It kills them,' Fred said, tossing another handful of oats, creating a flutter of wings and snapping bills. 'It would've been owned by the family who burned the forest down.'

'Which was who?'

He turned to give Sian a sly look. 'I thought it was you doing the sleuthing, not me.'

'Well...if you don't mind me saying, there are not many people left who lived here in 1956.'

'You've changed,' he said. 'When you first arrived in Woodville, you were as meek as a field mouse.'

'And now?'

'Now, you're quite pushy,' he said, giving her a crooked smile. 'But I can understand that you'd like to get to the bottom of it all. Just don't be disappointed, if all you come to is a dead end.'

'It just looks to me as if the police in charge at the time couldn't be bothered questioning people properly.'

'They did it differently back then. And you must remember that it was a small community. The policeman in charge was part of that community. In many ways, he had to watch his step.' He paused to throw another handful of rolled oats to the birds. 'Remind me, who was the policeman in charge back then?'

'John P Sorenson.'

'Ah yes,' he said, tapping his long, bony finger on his knee in deep contemplation. 'Funny that.'

'Why?'

'You've just answered your own question. Who owned the land on the west side of the river? All that forest burned down, and not long after, Ben Stokes goes missing.'

Sian recoiled. 'The Sorensons?'

Fred nodded. 'You should be paying me for this information.'

'Do they still own it?'

He shook his head. 'We have it now. We bought it a long time ago.'

'I thought the Sorensons were poor?' Sian asked.

'They are. The money they received from the land flittered away. By the time the son got it, the drunk, the money was all gone and they rented the house from us.'

'I've been to the Sorensons' house.'

Fred shook his head. 'It should be pulled down.'

'How many of them live there?'

'I'm not sure. I don't keep tabs on them. I don't have anything to do with that side of things, anymore. My son and daughter in law run the farms now.'

'Do you mind if I take a look around the land?' Sian asked.

'You honestly think you're going to find a grave?'

'I don't know.'

'I give you permission. But it's a lot of land and it's been worked for years. Personally, I think you'll be wasting your time.'

'I can't help thinking the two Bens are related in some way. I mean, in life and death.'

Fred glanced over at the Woodville Museum and Information Centre across the road. A camper van pulled up, and a couple of people jumped out to head to the entrance, only to find the door still locked. It was after opening hours and Fred, the sly, old dog, would rather feed the birds than be bothered talking to strangers today. He paused, hoping they'd walk away. Instead they checked their watches, and impatiently knocked on the door.

'I suppose I'd better go and assist these people,' he said begrudgingly, then used his walking stick to help get him up. 'Don't get old. It's not much fun.'

As if she had any choice. Sian chuckled to herself as she watched Fred yell out to the tourists, 'Alright! I'm coming!' He waved his stick about, almost threateningly, which made them back away from the locked door.

Sian was about to get up to leave for work at the Woodville Library, when she could feel the presence of someone standing right behind her. After everything she had been through, it didn't take much for Sian to feel unsafe. Right now, her skin was prickling and nerves were swelling in her belly. She began to rise from the park bench, preparing to run or scream, just as the individual came around to her side, and sat down next to her. It was Angus, Angus Sorenson.

'Stay,' he said, not meeting her eyes. Instead he watched Fred open the Museum entrance, with his usual abruptness. He chuckled, shaking his head and muttered, 'Bloody old bugger.'

'I've got to go to work,' Sian said.

'We need to talk,' Angus said forcefully, still watching Fred's little display of insolence in the distance.

'Talk about what?'

Angus pulled his eyes away from watching Fred, and turned his head towards the oak tree planted in honour of Ben Stokes. 'Benny boy was obsessed with finding Ben Stokes. I remember the day our ma told us the story, when we were kids. Benny would've been no older than seven or eight. He always loved a good mystery, our Benny, but this one got him in the heart. I reckon it was because they shared the same name. Anyway, ma told us how Ben disappeared without a trace, and a search party of hundreds of local people, mostly farmers, came from far and wide to help find him. The following day, after being told the story, Benny went to the Museum to read more about him, and that old codger.' nodding towards Fred in the Museum,' told him how much he looked like him.' He paused and smiled, his blue eyes softening as warm memories of his little brother came flooding in. 'I even caught him a couple of times sitting under this tree. I asked him once if he was trying to get a clue about Ben's whereabouts from the ghost of Ben Stokes. And he said that Ben wasn't buried here.'

It's a secret.

Angus continued talking but the world closed in on Sian, drowning out Angus's voice. *Ben wasn't buried here.*

'He was fixated with him,' she heard Angus say, 'and now here you are, doing the same thing, searching for Ben Stokes.'

Sian desperately tried to remember her Benny talking about Ben Stokes when they were kids. He was always looking for someone or something, always searching, his eyes flickering this way and that continuously. That's why he was so good at hunting rabbits and catching fish. Because he was always on the look-out, and noticed movement in the grass, or the shape of water change when a trout swam through the stream

'Was your brother an alcoholic?' Sian asked, then immediately regretted it. The question seemed to desecrate the memory of her lovely Benny, and Sian felt bad for asking it.

'He said he found out where Ben was buried,' Angus said, ignoring her question, which she was pleased about.

Sian turned her body to face him. 'Where was he buried?' she asked.

His blue eyes met hers. 'He said he only told one person...and that person was you.' He gave her a lovely, warm smile, stood up ready to leave, and then added, 'So it looks like you always had the answer. You've just forgotten it.'

THIRTY SIX

Sian couldn't move. The seat beneath her seemed to sink into the ground. Her mind was gone, lost in the memories of when she and Benny Sorenson played in McCrae's Forest. She remembered her face carved into the trunk of the kauri tree. She remembered the kisses, the laughter and the stories told. They were always playing make-believe at finding treasure maps, gold coins, trolls, shipwrecks from the river... and a body.

'Let's look for the dead boy,' Benny said one morning, full of excitement for a new adventure. He would've been about eight or nine, so it was probably not long after he was told the story of Ben Stokes by his mother.

Another game of make-believe Sian assumed at the time, but was happy to go along with it. Why not? In their imaginations, they had already found a treasure chest, a family of fairies and a taniwhai - a water monster, in the Manawatu River. Why not find the body of a boy who died long ago? 'He was murdered,' he whispered.

'How do you know?' Sian asked, grasping the hem of her skirt and rolling the fabric in her fingers. Something she did a lot as a child when she was nervous. Along with biting the skin around her fingernails, and scratching a mysterious spot on her left ankle. All those little habits she still has today.

'Just because,' he said. 'Shall we look for him?'

'No,' Sian said.

'He's dead, he won't hurt you. He's a very nice person.'

'How do you know?'

'I just know.'

'Who murdered him?' Sian asked.

'It's a secret,' Benny said. Sian doubted that he had any valid information at all at this point, but he was determined to find out.

A siren bled out, which pulled Sian back into the present. The Woodville Fire Station siren was signalling for all volunteers to convene, immediately. She glanced at her watch. She was thirty minutes late for work. A bearded man with a crutch stood nearby watching the proceedings down the road, along with a few other people. Sian couldn't stay. She got up to leave for work, her mind whirling with memories. Or was she making it all up? *It's a secret.*

Mavis glanced up at the clock on the wall when Sian finally arrived, an expression of disapproval upon her face. 'It's alright, there's not much to do, anyway. Just tidy up the kids' section, and these returned books need to be put away.' She walked away, then came back again. 'According to the Neighbourhood Watch, your neighbour's house got broken into on Sunday,' Mavis said.

'I guess we're too far out for a Neighbourhood Watch to watch,' Sian said.

'Sometimes outsiders drive into town and just take whatever they like, then disappear back to the dives they came from,' Mavis said, bitterly. 'When I had my house broken into...' Sian gasped. Mavis waved it away like it was no big deal, and said, 'It was years ago. But I still remember that feeling of invasion of privacy. You want your home to feel safe. Did they take anything?'

'No,' Sian's stomach turned involuntarily at the thought of a bag of stones, left on Rosie's coffee table. 'It was a strange one.'

'Ah! It was the same with my house. Someone broke the window, climbed in, went through my drawers and cupboards, and took nothing. But they did leave something.'

'What was that?'

'There were dirty footprints on my carpet and wooden floor. I could tell by the size of the shoe print that it was a kid, and it was a sneaker mark. So I just put two and two together, and assumed it was a Sorenson looking for money. It's a shame, but those Sorenson kids were to blame for quite a lot of petty crime.'

'Maybe they were hungry,' Sian said.

'More than likely. I never bothered to report it. I feared too much for the consequences of those kids, since their father was part of the police force at the time. He could be brutal.'

The bearded man on a crutch came into the library and called out, 'False alarm!' so everyone could hear.

'What was?' Mavis asked.

'At the fire station. No fire. They were merely practising,' he said.

Mavis shook her head. 'They practise so often, I barely hear the fire siren anymore. I think they just like to play with the fire truck and hose,' she said mischievously, giving Sian a wink. Sian couldn't help but laugh.

By this time the bearded man was a couple of feet away from Sian, and was waiting for some assistance.

'I was wondering if you could help me find a book on knots,' he said.

'Knots?' Sian asked.

'Yes, different types of tying knots, like for sailing and climbing and various other exercises. I like to practise.'

Sian felt an icy chill at the base of her spine. This man gave her the creeps. Mavis had walked away, so she had no other option but to help him.

'I'll have a look in our online catalogue.' She punched in 'knots', and to her surprise there were self-help books on how to tie a variety of knots, for an array of activities. However, none of those books were in the Woodville Library. She showed the bearded man the books available, and said that she could order them for him from the Wellington Central Library.

'No need. I won't be here long enough.' He stared at her for a little longer than was necessary, then turned to leave. She stood at the window and watched him limp all the way across the road to the park, then disappear into the Wild Oats Cafe.

'You look like you've just seen a ghost,' Mavis said.

'I just found that man creepy,' Sian said, her eyes still fixed on the cafe he had disappeared into.

'I know you've been through quite a bit in your young life, but you can't be suspicious of every man that walks the earth. It will cut your chances of a relationship. I'm sure you would like to marry and have children one day.'

'Not really,' Sian said, honestly. 'Not all women have that ambition.'

Sian worked the extra 30 minutes she owed then fled home. She was going to stop off at Rosie's to make sure she was okay, but Nathan's car was up the drive, so she thought she'd leave the family be.

What Sian wanted to do more than anything, was to take her mind back to when she and Benny Sorenson played in the forest, amongst the trees. The best way to remember, she thought, was to go back into the forest. But first, the elephant in the room was that photograph hidden under a cotton handkerchief. She was curious to see if the young man, whom she now believed was Ben Stokes, had indeed swiped the heads off May's parents. She'd come to the conclusion that this photograph must simply be trickery, an old motion picture used for entertainment.

When she lifted the handkerchief, what she saw was quite different to what she was expecting. What she expected was the blade of the scythe to be almost at the necks of the two elderly people sitting on chairs in front of Ben. There were too many things about this town that raised the hairs on Sian's arms, and this was one of them.

Ben's position had changed. He had moved to the left of the photograph; his scythe was now angling away from the elderly couple. The elderly couple were looking off to the left, as if something had caught their eye, something or someone not shown in the photograph, and Ben was now in the throes of attacking this impending, unseen visitor.

A tui sang in the McCrae's Forest nearby, and Sian dropped the handkerchief back over the photograph. It really did frighten her, this picture. Yet, she couldn't help but look at it. It was like her own little horror scene in slow motion. She still had to check it every so often to see what doom was waiting underneath.

Sian slipped on her running shoes, filled a bottle with water, grabbed her backpack and ran into the forest. She figured that if she sat under the kauri tree where her face had been carved into the wood, memories may return of where Benny said the grave was. It was a long shot, but right now that was all she had.

The chorus of bird call was a joyous wonder as they flew from branch to branch drinking the sweet nectar from the native flowers. The coolness of the forest under the tree canopy was welcome on this day. It had been a strange day, and she was feeling hot and flustered. The conversation with Fred Anderson was a revelation, but then Angus Sorenson dropped his bombshell. She was late for work, and there was that creepy man in the library. Luckily he's not staying in Woodville for long. She didn't like the way he looked at her, or the way he lingered.

She found the large kauri easily enough, as it has the thickest trunk there by miles. She sat at the base, beneath her own face carved by lovely Benny, and closed her eyes. It came to her like the snap of a branch. Benny Sorenson had not only told her where the gravesite of Ben Stokes was, but he had shown her. She remembered so clearly, now. He had made a cross out of twigs, and placed a rock at the head of where he believed Ben Stokes' head would be. They were older at this point, eleven or twelve. It took him years to find where Ben Stokes lay, and it was only by chance that he did.

'How do you know a dead person is in there?' Sian asked. She was looking at flat, compacted earth, no sign that something had been buried there. But then the burial was in 1956, which was decades ago. Nature kept growing around his still bones.

'Because they come back to visit,' he whispered. 'I saw them the other day.'

'Saw who?'

'The murderer,' he mouthed, even whispering the word was too loud.

Sian shuddered. Was he having her on? Was this just another game of make-believe? She didn't think so this time. She knew him well enough to know the difference.

'What did they look like?'

'They wore a green jacket and a hood over their head,' he whispered.

'So you couldn't see their face?'

He shook his head. 'I listened to them talk to Ben.' His forehead creased into worry lines, which only made him look sweeter. 'I was hiding nearby. I heard them say they were sorry to shorten his life. Then they cried.'

'I don't think you should put those things on the grave,' Sian said to Benny. 'They'll come back and see that someone knows.'

Benny agreed, and took the stone and cross made of twigs off, to leave it bare.

'Do you think we should tell the police?' Sian asked.

'No way!' he said. 'I'll get a hiding.'

At the time Sian couldn't understand why Benny would get a hiding for informing the police about a dead body and a visiting murderer. But she knows now, as she sat in a daze under the great kauri, that his father *was* the police, and he was also a mean drunk.

Sian tried to picture the place where Benny believed Ben Stokes was buried. *It's a secret.* But all she could see were gnarled tree roots, dark earth and lichen inching up the trunks and branches. This was hopeless. If only Benny was here. He knew this forest inside out, just like Ben Stokes did. She shut her eyes even tighter, and breathed like her therapist, Alice Granger, had taught her. Deep, slow breaths to calm her nerves. Then she heard it. Her eyes snapped open. The river, she remembered he was by the river.

There was something else. A ribbon, a yellow ribbon.

THIRTY SEVEN

It may be a revelation of sorts, that the place Benny Sorenson believed Ben Stokes was buried, was near the river. The Manawatu River curls past McCrae's Forest, which meant that many acres of forest are near the river. This did not narrow his position down much, but it was better than nothing. The rock that Benny placed on Ben Stokes grave was one he had taken from the riverbed nearby.

Sian shut her eyes tightly again. There had to be a redeeming feature about the gravesite, or else both the alleged murderer who visited the grave, and Benny Sorenson, wouldn't be able to find it every time. The forest is dense and forever changing. All it took was a torrential rain or fierce wind to change the landscape of the forest, to break a limb, scatter leaves, crack open the earth.

Then another image came to her. This time she's not sure if it's her imagination, or the truth. But two ferns grew a foot apart at the head of Ben Stokes' grave. The two ferns that Benny boy had placed his river rock between. She remembered Benny looking upwards, and then pointing. A yellow ribbon was tied to the branch of a totara tree that grew next to Ben Stokes' alleged gravesite. The branch was a good six metres above the ground, and directly above the two ferns. If you weren't looking for it, you'd miss it for sure.

It was not unusual to see a rope tied around the trunk of a tree, or a brightly coloured bottle left on the ground. Hunters and trampers place these indicators to guide themselves back home. But a ribbon so far up? He or she would've had to climb up the tree to tie it, or use a ladder.

Benny was debating whether he should climb up and take it down, to fool the alleged murderer. But young Sian was feeling nervous at this point, in case the murderer were to appear now, or even worse, stood watching behind a tree ready to pounce. This was an unforgiving forest. Even in a small New Zealand forest, people can vanish without a trace; the ground can give way beneath them, or they can slip down a cliff into a swamp. Gone.

Sian got up from her perch under the large kauri tree where her face had been carved into the pale bark, and headed in the direction of the river. She was well aware that the chances of finding the exact location and for the ribbon to still be tied around the branch of the totara, were slim, very slim.

She walked some way over tree roots, and up ridges, down slopes, until she could hear the sound of the river. The Manawatu River is shallow and stony. The sound it makes is chatty and upbeat, a welcome sound for anyone lost in the bush. She figured that once she found the river, she'd use it as her guide. It flowed downstream, past Aunt May's house - correction, her house - through the gorge, carved out between the sharp, forest-covered hills millions of years ago and then ploughing into the Pacific Ocean.

Sian stood on a steep bank, looking down at the deep gash in the earth, probably created by an earthquake. There were a couple of inches of muddy water sitting in the bottom of the gash, and the black earth surrounding it looked damp and unstable. Through the greenery of ferns and tall trunks, she could see the glistening, silver river flowing past. To get to the river, she had to climb down the bank. It was a vertical drop, about four metres with some ferns and vines to hold on to. Not safe, but she had walked so far into the forest, she knew she'd never find her way back out again, unless she followed the river.

Taking hold of a bunch of fern leaves, she tried to climb down the damp bank, but her shoes kept slipping, and the earth crumbled away. In the end she sat down on the edge of the bank, and then jumped, landing in black mud, only for her balance to betray her, as she toppled over into the mud.

Brushing the black mud off her clothes, she climbed back up the other side which was much lower, and then in another ten steps or so she was out into the light on the river's edge. On the other side of the river was the land owned by the Anderson family, the forest burned down by the previous owners shortly after Ben Stokes vanished, to create more farmland. Further up river, Sian could see black cattle grazing, and downstream the river curved round a bend.

'Ben Stokes, where are you?' she whispered.

She decided to walk upriver up on the grey rock towards the cattle on the other side. The further upriver she went, the lower the bank on the other side became. Eventually the land was almost even with the river and she could see an old, white homestead floating on the green paddocks. Even at that distance, she could tell it was the Sorenson's homestead. A couple of the windows were smashed, the paint was cracked and flaking to show the pink undercoat underneath. It didn't fare much better fourteen years ago either, when Benny first pointed it out to her. Back then though, the homestead was a bustle of children coming and going. Yelling, screaming, and then silence when the old man came home, as the children scattered out of harm's way.

He forbade Sian from ever going there. He never gave a reason why, Sian only assumed that he was embarrassed by the state of the place, or perhaps it had something to do with his father. They never came this way again.

She would have liked to cross the river and take a closer look at the house, but the rapids were far too dangerous, and having drenched clothes wasn't a good idea. They were already muddy from falling in the ditch; she didn't want to add to that. There was a bridge a few miles away. She'd have to drive back through town, take a left over the one-way bridge and head up the gravel road, Moffat's Road, where she'd see a scattering of farmhouses rising up from green pastures.

Towards the end of Moffat's Road was where the Sorensons lived. Alas they were the only ones not owning the land they lived on. Instead they rented the land and house off the Andersons, Fred's family. Sian wondered where they all lived now - ten children, who had grown into ten adults, who then would've had children of their own.

Sian turned around and walked downstream, searching the thick foliage for a gap back into the forest. She had noticed a path, probably trodden by hunters, further downstream, and when she found it again, she turned back into the forest.

A bellbird sang. Its song echoed so eerily, Sian could feel her spine tingle. 'I'm dreaming,' she mumbled. 'There's no way I'm going to find the gravesite.' The sun was beginning to fall in the west; she had only another hour of good light.

Focussing only on totaras growing close to the river, she kept searching. The forest floor was a sea of ferns, and the totara were pretty common as well, but still she persisted. She owed it to Benny Sorenson. She owed it to Ben Stokes.

And with her persistence and sheer determination, two attributes she thought were lost forever in recent years, she came across *the* totara. She couldn't believe her luck. The yellow ribbon was still tied to the limb of the tree, four to five meters up. Benny was right; someone would've had to climb up the tree to tie it there. Then she dropped her eyes to the forest floor. Twin ferns grew a foot apart. Between them, Benny had placed a river rock as a headstone for Ben Stokes, and then made a cross from twigs. But Sian had warned him that if the murderer were to return, he'd find them there and know he had been found out. Benny removed the rock and threw it into a

241

manuka bush. The cross was snapped across his knee and tossed aside as well.

Sian stood at the alleged gravesite of Ben Stokes, realising that she hadn't really thought this through properly. She couldn't take a photograph of the spot, as she still hadn't replaced her last cell which she had smashed and buried in the backyard, and she didn't own a camera. Worst of all, she wasn't completely sure if she could find this spot again. And now that she had found it, she'd have to dig the earth to see if Benny was right, before she told anyone about it. She had neglected to bring a spade or a trowel. Aunt May had some in her garden shed. Why didn't she think to bring something to dig the ground with?

Scoping the forest floor for something that could be used to dig the rather solid earth, she found a thick branch and began to puncture the dirt with it. But she scarcely got far. She's going to need help and she knew exactly who to ask.

THIRTY EIGHT

The Sergeant

Sarah Granger used the heel of her hand to hit the trapdoor as hard as she possibly could. She was sitting up on Louise's shoulders, and could tell Louise was struggling to balance. The door wasn't budging, not even with the steadiest of thumps.

'We're going to die down here,' Sarah sobbed. 'Unless Britney is brave enough to defy that *piece of shite* and tell the police, we're doomed.'

Louise dropped to her knees so Sarah could climb off her shoulders. There was no food or fresh water. They could live several days without food, but without water they had four days, tops. Even then, they may have to resort to drastic measures and drink their own urine.

The glaringly obvious problem was that no-one knows that this bunker even exists, and even when Louise fails to show up for work in the morning, her colleagues are not going to know where she is. And what is Kerryn Gillespie going to do? Turn up for work and act dumb?

'How did I not see him for what he is?' Louise mumbled, with her face in her hands. Then a thought occurred to her. 'Was it Kerryn who tampered with the evidence?'

'What are you talking about?' Sarah asked.

'The case against Brendon Durie was thrown out due to an oversight. He was set free. The oversight was a mistake, allegedly made by the police. The evidence was deemed contaminated. Someone had planted hair belonging to one of our police officers on the scene, into the evidence bag. The judge threw the case out.'

'Because of that?' Sarah asked. 'Surely there was plenty of other evidence?'

Louise had fallen silent.

Sarah could not see her face in the pitch dark, but she could tell by the way Louise was tapping her boot on the concrete, that there was something on her mind.

'The judge,' Louise said finally, after several cold minutes of silence. 'We never looked more closely at that judge. It was mostly Sian's word against Durie's. But Sian Tanner had wounds that corresponded with someone who had been abused, specifically in the way Durie liked to abuse his victims. The judge wasn't interested, and threw the whole case out once the contamination came to light. We could've started again and taken it to the High Court, but Sian was done with it all. Living through all that again would've killed her.' Louise paused again. 'I'm wondering if that fathead Kerryn placed the hair in the bag. He had access to it. He was after all, my right hand constable, and worked on the case next to me.'

'What about the judge?' Sarah asked. 'You suspect the judge of foul play?'

Louise groaned. 'Maybe I'm over-thinking it all, sitting in here. But if I do get out alive, I'd like to quietly investigate that judge, just to put my mind at rest.'

'Do you think the judge favoured *him* over Sian?' Sarah's voice was higher pitched than she intended, but she was aghast.

'You just never know,' Louise said, tapping her boot even more rapidly on the concrete. 'He may have been paid off. The Durie family are not short of a few dollars, and apart from their wealth, they have friends in high places. Surely that's one of the reasons you were attracted to him?' There was a hint of bitterness in Louise's voice that Sarah ignored. Louise probably hated girls like her, who tried to get a free ride on the back of a rich man.

'I hate to admit it,' Sarah said, sighing. 'His looks were striking, his portfolio impressive. But I always knew it wasn't going to last. He was always too distracted, his mind never in the present when he was in my company. I always felt he had someone else on his mind.'

'I guess we have to be pricked by a few arseholes before we come to the roses. Or, however that saying goes,' Louise said.

Sarah laughed. *Isn't it, pricked by a few thorns*? But Louise's version was much better. 'Paying off judges only happens overseas in countries drowning in corruption, doesn't it?' Sarah asked.

'I don't know. But it's worth finding out. It would be interesting to find out the name of the judge who let Durie's uncle off the hook. The one who pushed his wife down the stairs, and liked to put her in a choke hold now and again.'

'Oh yeah, I remember that. Mum was furious,' Sarah said. 'He's that sports broadcaster. He didn't even lose his job over it. And now time has gone on, everyone's forgotten about it, and he's probably moved on to his next wife, rubbing his hands together in glee.'

'Until the next woman is murdered,' Louise said. 'Nothing seems to change.'

They fell silent again, caught up in their own thoughts. No outside noises could be heard. It was pitch black and eerie, and the air was thick.

Louise thought about the builders who had come to dig the hole, pour the concrete floor and build the walls to make this 'wine cellar.' *Surely, they must've been even a little suspicious. I mean, who wants a wine cellar under the garden shed, where it's grimy, and so*

impractical? Maybe he paid them off too, like he paid the judge.
Wait! I have no proof he paid the judge off, yet.

Coming to Brendon Durie's house was just a routine visit. They knew he was unlikely to be home. Louise won't admit it, but she was planning on breaking and entering to take a look around. Distract Kerryn, by sending him to all the neighbours down the street to ask if they'd seen anything suspicious. He's fat and slow, he'll take an age to get around all the houses. While he's doing that, she'll break in and take a look through Brendon Durie's drawers. That was the original plan. Turns out she didn't need to break in at all, thanks to Britney, the teenager, who was very compliant.

Turns out she was also double-crossed by her own constable.

In her mind, she had a list to motivate her to survive the oppressiveness of the darkness.

Find Brendon Durie. Make him pay.

Find Kerryn Gillespie. Make him pay.

Investigate the judge assigned to the Brendon Durie vs Sian Tanner case. Make him pay.

All within the law? I doubt it. I might have to quit the police and become a vigilante.

Then she thought about the cell in her trouser pocket, the cell that Alice Granger had used to call her hitman. She flicked it on, her eyes shocked into momentary blindness from the light. Once her eyes had adjusted, she clicked into the contacts. There was only one number, one name, *Birdie.*

Unfortunately, there was still no reception which made the phone virtually useless. But reading the texts was a good source of entertainment.

'If you were given just one phone call, who would you ring?' Sarah's voice bled out into the darkness. The trickery of sound in that underground bunker made her voice seem soft and distant.

Louise pondered in silence for a moment.

'I would ring mum and apologise,' Sarah said. 'I was such a fool.'

Louise remained quiet for a few more seconds, and then said, 'I would call your mum's hitman Birdie, and have Brendon Durie killed off.'

Sarah broke into laughter - then stopped suddenly when Louise didn't join in.

'Are you serious?' Sarah asked.

'Yes.'

'My mum used a hitman?' Sarah asked.

'Yes. Your mum is currently in custody for that very thing.'

'She hired a hitman called Birdie to kill Brendon Durie, and now she's in prison for it?'

'No. She's in prison for hiring a hitman to kill off another scumbag, called Damon Ridge.'

'What?' She moaned as if in pain. 'Does dad know this?'

'Yes.'

She moaned again. 'I do not know my parents at all. A hitman?'

This made Louise chuckle. She didn't know the half of it. *Could the real Alice Granger please stand up?*

'So, is that my mum's phone?'

'Yes, the phone I confiscated from her. The phone she used to call *Birdie.*'

'And if you were given just one phone call, that's who you would call, Birdie the hitman?' Sarah wanted clarification.

'Yes. He seems very good at his job.'

'Pity there's no phone reception down here,' Sarah said.

'Pity,' Louise agreed.

THIRTY NINE

Sian Tanner walked along the river's edge heading downstream, until the forest took over, and left no land to stand on. At this point, she turned back into the forest, but as much as possible kept sight of the river. Already she had lost her bearings as to where Ben Stokes' grave lay, but she felt reasonably confident that Angus Sorenson would obligingly help.

It was Monday evening. If she were Angus Sorenson, where would she be now? The only answer that came to her was the pub. She knew so little of Angus, except that his father was a drunken policeman. So the liking of liquor was in his veins. Even if he wasn't in one of the local pubs, maybe someone who worked there could tell her.

It was a miracle that Sian made it back to her house. She felt rather proud of herself for getting back, using only nature to guide her. Benny Sorenson would be proud.

She unlocked the back door, berating herself when she looked at the garden shed. All those garden tools stacked inside that she could've used today. Tomorrow when she heads back in, hopefully with help, she'll remember to take a shovel.

Expecting Popo at the door demanding food, she was surprised to find the house empty. She wondered if he was next door with the family, hanging out with Chloe. Not giving the missing cat a second thought, Sian ran up the stairs and into her bedroom to change her clothes. Just as she was about to leave again, she noticed something strange. The bedroom window was closed. No matter how many times she shut that window, moments later it would be open again. She wondered if it was crooked house foundations that made it do that. To be honest, she didn't really want to think too deeply about it. But she suspected Aunt May always had it open, and open it liked to stay.

Right at this very moment the window was not only closed, but stuck. She tried to open it again with all of her strength, yet it wouldn't budge. There was also a scent lingering in her bedroom of fresh soap, and another scent she couldn't rationalise in her mind, yet her nerves reacted to it by prickling her skin.

She turned to the photograph and lifted the handkerchief that covered it. There was a definite fourth person in the photograph, a dark figure. Aunt May's parents were looking up at him, that fearful look in their eyes, just as Ben Stokes was swinging his scythe. Sian leaned in closer to take a look at the fourth person. He wore a black hood, only his chin and mouth could be seen. He also wore a smile, a smirk. Sian had seen that smile before.

A door downstairs slammed, just as the bedroom window blew open. She could hear creaking floor boards. Someone was in the house.

Quickly, Sian shut the bedroom door and locked it, then made her way out of the window, climbing out onto unsteady roof tiles. Once she got to the edge she jumped, landing on soft grass. Keeping low, she ran to the front drive and tried to open the door to her car. Locked! Damn it! She didn't have the keys. She could see someone moving about in her house, and decided to make a run for it to Rosie's. As she ran, she spotted a white car parked across the road. She ran to it and tried to open the door. It was locked. She peered inside. The interior had the appearance of being recently groomed, and a travel insurance brochure was on the passenger seat. A rental car.

Sian kept running. Once she'd passed the windbreaker of trees that ran alongside Rosie's house, she noticed the driveway was empty of cars. No one was home. She ran around the back of their house to try the back door. It was locked. Of course it was locked. It was only yesterday that they were broken into.

She slid down against their door. She'd wait there until they got home. Her heart was beating a thousand times per minute, and she was having difficulty getting air into her lungs. She remembered what Alice Granger said, *Slow, deep breaths*, s*low, deep breaths.*

She could hear tyres driving along the unsealed road. From where she was sitting, she couldn't tell in what direction they were going, but only hoped it was Rosie coming home. She ran to the side of the house and saw a black sedan drive by slowly, heading towards her house. The view between her house and Rosie's was blocked by the line of windbreak trees. She couldn't see what was going on.

Sian crouched down again by the back door. She could hear a dog barking in the distance, probably herding sheep. The wind rose and shook the windbreak trees, and they rustled and swayed eerily, like elongated ghosts.

A shot rang out, quickly followed by another. Sian ran to the side of the house to look out onto the road. Two more shots followed, shortly after.

A few seconds after that, the black sedan sped back down the road.

Sian ran back to the back door and stayed there, too frightened to move.

***

It was dark by the time Rosie, Nathan and Chloe arrived home to find a terrified and cold Sian, leaning up against their door. As soon as she told them what had happened, Nathan called the police, while Rosie made a hot cup of chocolate.

Sergeant Lee and Constable Rachel went down to take a look at the scene, while Constable Jarrod stayed with Sian.

A while later, several police vehicles drove by. 'Forensics and Armed Offenders Squad from Wellington,' fresh-faced Jarrod said. He couldn't hide his excitement, his adrenaline pumping. It must be awful for him to be here as a support for Sian, rather than be down at the scene.

His phone rang, which made Sian jump. He barely said two words, the person on the other end doing all the talking. The call ended, and Jarrod gave Sian a sombre look.

'Have you ever worked a gun before?' he asked.

Sian shook her head.

'Do you own a gun, or any other weapon?' he asked.

'No. Ah! I have knives.'

'What sort of knives?'

'For cutting cheese and...'

'Your house is being searched for the offending weapon.'

'What have they found?' she asked.

'Someone's been shot.'

'Shot in my house?'

He nodded, still solemn. 'It looks like he was trying to get out of your house, away from the shooter.'

'Who is he?'

'We don't have an ID yet.' He kept looking down at his phone, expectantly. 'It will be good to get this sorted.'

'Someone was in my house when I came home. So I came here, and waited until Rosie came home.'

'A good move.'

'Then I saw a black sedan go by.'

'Towards your house?'

'Yes. Then a little while later, I heard gun shots.'

'How many?'

'About four.'

'You didn't have anyone living with you at the time, or a boyfriend visiting?'

'I don't have a boyfriend,' she said. Her lips were dry and she was having difficulties getting her words out.

His phone chimed and he opened up a text. 'Do you recognise this man?' Jarrod asked, showing Sian a pic sent on his phone. It was of a man dressed head to toe in black lying inside the back door, face down. He had two bullet wounds in his back and there were two bullet holes in the wall next to him. Without a doubt he was trying to escape.

'He might be the man who broke in here,' Nathan said.

'The problem is, this was not self-defence,' Jarrod said, seriously.

Sian wasn't registering what he was saying.

'He was trying to get out,' he added.

Still Sian couldn't grasp what he was trying to say. All she could see was this man stretched out on her floor, a man she didn't invite in.

'You can't just go shooting people willy nilly, even if they do break in to your home,' Jarrod said, while sending a text.

Sian opened her mouth, yet words weren't coming to her.

Moments later another text came through. 'This photo is closer up. Be prepared, as it may be distressing for you.' He paused, analysing Sian's face. 'Are you ready?'

Sian nodded.

He showed her the pic. Even though the dead man's eyes were closed, she still immediately recognised the short, neat hair, the David Bowie cheek bones and strong jaw. Sian stood glued to the floor.

'Do you know this person?' Constable Jarrod asked.

Sian nodded.

'Do you know his name?'

She nodded, clearing her throat. 'His name...' her voice came out as a croaky whisper. She cleared her throat again. 'His name is Brendon Durie.'

FORTY

The Sergeant

Several loud hammer strikes, and the trapdoor was thrown open. Light streamed down into the blackened cellar, and Sarah and Louise shielded their eyes. A ladder was found in the shed, and lowered down. The yard and house were littered with armed police. Superintendent Barry Graham was to the side, arms folded across his bullet-proof vest. He was looking cross. Or was it dismay? Louise always found him hard to read.

'How did you get yourself into this mess?' were the first words that dropped from his mouth when Louise approached him.

'Kerryn Gillespie,' she said, swiftly.

Her words lingered in the air for a few moments, then, 'We thought he was down there with you,' Barry said.

'He's working with Brendon Durie. Whacked me over the head, and chucked me down into that pit.'

Barry swore under his breath, and then called over his radio that an escaped perp was on the loose, and likely to be armed and dangerous. He paused for a moment before saying, "His name is Constable Kerryn Gillespie, from the Lakesford Police Department. I repeat Kerryn Gillespie.'

The attending officers exchanged glances as the call came through.

'How could you not have known?' the Superintendant asked, gritting his teeth. 'The Commissioner is going to have a word or two to say about this.'

Louise had nothing to say. She always got an icky vibe from Kerryn, but she just assumed he had a crush on her. He never did anything to raise alarm bells. He was unkempt, often turned up late for work, but always followed his orders, even though it seemed like he couldn't be bothered at times. Louise assumed that was because he was lazy and unfit. Let's not forget he should be higher up the ladder by now, and he possibly held a grudge. She should've checked. She should've checked that Kerryn actually called the Woodville Police Department.

A female police officer wrapped a blanket around Sarah's shoulders, and guided her away from the crime scene to a patrol car parked out the front.

'Are you alright?' Barry asked.

Louise sighed irritably. 'No. Time was wasted down there. Brendon Durie-'

'-Yeah, we know about him,' he said. 'Found with two bullet holes in his back in Sian Tanner's house, in Woodville.'

'Dead?'

'Yes.' He scanned her face for a reaction, but she remained stony faced. On the inside she was shouting for joy. But, then...

'The perp?'

He shook his head. 'We don't know, yet.'

'The only suspect they have is Sian Tanner, who claims to have been hiding out at her neighbours' place when the incident took place.'

'And the weapon?'

'It hasn't been found. The bullets taken out of the walls show it to be a handgun, possibly a Glock 17. They're chasing up licences for this particular model.'

'Any witnesses?'

'None. Sian Tanner says she saw a black sedan drive up to her house, she said she heard four gunshots, then the car drove erratically back down the street again.'

'I'm sorry sir, but I just can't believe it was Sian Tanner.'

'They've had no witnesses saying they saw a black sedan driving erratically away from her house. The rural road she lives down has only three houses on it, all several metres apart from each other. Her closest neighbours weren't home, and the people who live in the third house said they never saw this car. I'm afraid it doesn't look good for Sian Tanner.'

'But surely sir, this is self-defence?'

'The victim was shot in the back, twice.'

'For breaking and entering?'

He shrugged. 'So far, there's been no proof that he broke in.'

Louise let out a small howl of frustration. 'There was a restraining order against Brendon Durie. He was not allowed to be within three kilometres of Sian Tanner. He broke that court order.'

'Unless she let him in.'

'Sir, there's no way Sian Tanner would have let Brendon Durie into her home. I know her. I know what he did to her. This is a man who had a bloody underground cellar built, so he could torture his victims. I'm telling you now sir, she did not let him into her home.'

'There's no point getting all uptight about it!' he said, sternly. 'You know the law in New Zealand. You can't attack someone even if they *do* break into your home. The correct line of action is to call the police. That's what we're here for.'

'I doubt she had a phone,' Louise said softly.

'We're done here,' SI Barry said. 'You need to get yourself cleaned up. I'll arrange for you to speak to a therapist.'

'I don't need a therapist.'

'That was an order,' he said, as he walked towards the open trapdoor. Forensics, dressed in their white, disposable suits crawled all over it taking samples, and shining their torches down into the dank cellar.

'Sir!' she called after him. 'Who called it in?'

He stopped and turned slightly, 'An anonymous caller, a female. We suspect a neighbour.'

Britney. Hopefully she took Louise's advice, and returned to her parents.

FORTY ONE

Sian Tanner was released, once they discovered Constable Kerryn Gillespie's body with a suicide note pinned to his jersey. He had confessed to shooting Brendon Durie twice in the back, using his police issue Glock 17. It was also the Glock 17 he used to shoot himself in the head. He was found in a stolen car, parked on the side of a secluded road, on the outskirts of Wellington. Inside the car's glovebox was an electronic plane ticket to Hong Kong, bought online the week before. The car was a black sedan.

The note gave no clues as to why he killed Brendon Durie; they had a good working relationship, but perhaps that had gone just a step too far. It seemed that Kerryn's loyalty toward Brendon Durie had finally caught up with him.

Louise volunteered to take Sian from custody in Wellington back to her home in Woodville. The journey was a two hour drive and they were silent for most of the way. She had visited Alice Granger a couple of days before to inform her that Brendon Durie was dead, and that Sian Tanner would be released. Alice was in custody until her case goes to trial for her role in the killing of Damon Ridge, and was still quite sour about it. As far as she was concerned, she did nothing wrong. Damon Ridge was a lowlife, who did not deserve to breathe the same air as his victims.

For a woman who was always elegant and tidy, it was quite a shock for Louise to see Alice Granger, age 61, without make-up, sloppily dressed, black lines under her eyes. For a tiny moment, Louise wondered if she did the right thing arresting her friend. She could have turned a blind eye; it wouldn't be the first time an officer has done that. But it was too late now.

Unsurprisingly, Alice already knew about Brendon's death. It was all over the news, but she didn't know that Sian was the only suspect until of course, Kerryn's body was discovered two days later.

'The wicked web we weave,' Alice muttered, without smiling.

'Did you have anything to do with Brendon's death?' Louise asked.

Alice shrugged. 'How could I? I was in here.' She failed to make eye contact with Louise.

'You could've made a phone call.' Louise suggested.

'To who?'

'Your hitman.'

'But I didn't, and I couldn't.'

'Why? Because I had the cell you used to call him on? You may have memorised his number for all I know.'

'I could have, but I didn't.'

'You had every reason to want him dead.'

Alice fell silent. To Louise it looked like she was debating in her mind what she wanted to say. She licked her dry, cracked lips and said, 'I wanted him dead, alright. He kidnapped and tortured my daughter. But I still had nothing to do with his death.'

Louise couldn't read her.

Alice leaned back in the plastic chair, and folded her arms. 'Don't you already have a confession from that dead police officer? Can't you just let it lie?'

'He was on his way to Wellington airport,' Louise said, watching Alice's face closely. 'He had a plane ticket in his car, bought a week before. He could've made it, too.'

'If he didn't stop off at Woodville to kill Brendon Durie? I guess he had a change of heart,' Alice said, coldly.

'I guess.'

The timeline meant that Kerryn would've had minimal time to drive to Woodville, to shoot Brendon Durie. Shoot the man who was supposedly his friend. When Gillespie's cell phone was checked, they found communication from him to Durie, updating him on what was going on; *threw the bitch down the well and Britney getting nervous. What do I do about it?* There was no reply to that message. But Brendon sent an unrelated message later that read, *I've watched her from afar for too long. Today's the day. I am in her house.* Gillespie replied to that message with, *Have fun.* Gillespie knew where to find Brendon. He knew where the house was, because Louise had told him when she found out. *The house at the end of Tucker's Road in Woodville.*

Louise hunted Britney down. It was fairly easy since she was a workmate of Brendon's at Hillocks. She was hiding at her parents' home in a modest home in Townsville, a suburb in central Lakesford. She confessed that she was the one who called in the crime. Kerryn had threatened to kill her if she ratted on him, and tried to convince her that Louise was a dirty cop who was determined have Brendon put away forever. Then he made a show of arresting and cuffing her in front of Brendon's neighbours. Instead of taking her to the police station, he took her to an abandoned warehouse, and waited for instructions from Brendon. None came.

While he was taking a piss out the back of the building, Britney escaped, nabbing her cell back before running. Still with her hands in cuffs, she ran down the road and hid out the back of a 'tiny homes' building site, from where she called her father. Once he got her home, he used his metal cutters to cut the cuffs. She pretended it was a silly game she and Brendon had played. He went very quiet and seemed embarrassed, asking no questions.

Britney still hadn't received any communication from Brendon, and was now starting to worry about him, too. It was approximately five hours from the moment Louise was thrown down into the cellar, until Britney called 111. If she'd rung sooner, the outcome may have been completely different.

If everything Britney said was accurate, Gillespie would have been in the vicinity of Woodville, when she called the police. The black sedan that Sian Tanner had seen drive to her house while she hid at her neighbour's, was the same model sitting in the warehouse. It was reported stolen days before.

But the stolen car seemed to be part of Gillespie's plan. Steal the car, drive to Woodville. Find Durie and shoot him. The suicide may have been an afterthought, when he realised what he'd done. He had a plane ticket to Hong Kong. He could've made it. There was a delay in the police being called to Sian's house. She had no phone and couldn't get inside her neighbour's house, so she waited until they got home, and then Nathan called the police.

For Sergeant Louise Ratahi at the Lakesford Police Department, too many things didn't add up. The suicide note left on Gillespie had no blood splatters upon it. The only possible way that could happen was if the note had been pinned to Gillespie's chest after he shot himself. Also, the way his legs were spread, his left leg was stretched over to the passenger side, which made it look like his body had been moved there, either when he was unconscious or dead. There were also fragments of fabrics that weren't from his clothing. Due to the fact that the car was stolen, it was difficult to say how many people had been inside the car.

But no-one else seemed bothered by the irregularities, none of her colleagues wanted to pursue it more closely. A rotten constable was the murderer of a man who came from a well-known, rugby-playing family. The Lakesford Police Department wanted nothing more than to forget it. But the press hounded them, asking why the police hadn't noticed a murderer was right under their noses. And why was there not more assistance for those with mental health issues within the Police Force? Little came to the fore about Brendon Durie's seedy past. As far as the press was concerned he was the victim, and the LPD were the real perpetrators.

As Louise pulled up outside Rosie's place, Sian seemed forlorn. Sian's house was still cordoned off. Even though the body had been taken away, forensics was still there searching for hair, saliva, blood samples, anything that indicated that Kerryn Gillespie had been there. So far, they hadn't found an ounce of evidence. That of course, didn't mean that he wasn't there, it just meant he was fast and clean, which didn't really fit his given persona.

Rosie gave Sian a big, warm hug when they got inside the house. Louise had offered to take her back to Lakesford to stay with friends, or her mother, but Sian declined, saying that her life had moved on and she had unfinished business in Woodville.

'Which is?' Louise asked.

'I'm trying to figure out what happened to Ben Stokes.'

'I'm not familiar with him,' Louise said.

'I don't expect you to be. He disappeared in 1956. He walked into the forest, and was never seen again. He was only sixteen.'

'The bush can be like that. It happens all the time; trampers and hunters going missing in the hills. The rescue helicopter is called to find them.'

'It's been good for me to have a project to work on to take my mind off what happened back in Lakesford.'

'Look, if you need to talk about Brendon Durie's death, I'm always here.'

'I was offered a therapist, but I think I've had enough therapy to last a lifetime. Besides, I'm not upset that he was killed. I'm glad he's gone. I'm just shocked that it was done in my home, by a police officer. I saw his photograph on the news. He was the officer that arrested me for speeding, when I wasn't. He put me in his unmarked car and took me to that warehouse where *he* was waiting. Funny, looking back I thought he was a fake cop, when he was actually real. You can't trust anyone these days.'

'You can trust most people, Sian. Ninety nine percent of the world's population are good,' Louise said.

'Is that an accurate statistic?' Sian asked.

Louise laughed. 'No, but you get what I'm saying?'

Sian gazed out the car window. Miles and miles of green paddocks dotted with white sheep. Now and again there'd be a house floating on an ocean of green, but always hills that rise up large and daunting, signifying a land of earthquakes and volcanoes.

'I think I know where he's buried.'

'Who?' Louise's mind was still on Brendon Durie.

'Ben Stokes. I think I found his grave.'

'Grave? So someone buried him?'

'There's a plaque laid and an oak tree planted for him in town. It says he vanished without a trace. But someone knew otherwise. I need someone to help me dig it up.'

'Sure,' Louise said, apprehensively. 'Where is it?'

'In the forest.'

FORTY TWO

After lunch, Louise and Sian grabbed a garden trowel and a shovel from Rosie and Nathan, and entered the forest. Straight away Sian turned towards the river and kept moving until something familiar appeared. All the time she looked skyward for the yellow ribbon tied to the limb of a totara tree. At one point Louise muttered that they were going around in circles, but Sian was determined. It took a good couple of hours, but Sian finally found the spot, pointing upwards at the ribbon, still there even after all this time.

Sian used the garden trowel to scrape away the top soil, and Louise started to dig. With every plunge of the spade into the black earth, Sian was hopeful, while Louise had doubts. A shining cuckoo called in the trees above. Sian glanced upwards to catch sight of it. It wouldn't be long before it would fly back to the Solomon Islands. Such a long journey, just to lay its eggs in the tiny warbler's nest. She listened to the tail end of the cuckoo's call to indicate whether or not it would rain. The river nearby chatted as it moved rapidly towards the Pacific Ocean. Louise suddenly stopped digging and wiped her brow.

'I think I've found something.' She crouched down, and pointed to what looked like a bone. She snapped off a large fern leaf and brushed the dirt away. There were more bones. Sian covered her mouth, stifling a gasp. Benny Sorenson had been right all along.

Louise moved about in the forest until she could get reception, then called the Woodville Police Department to send the forensics team, currently working at Sian Tanner's house, into the forest. 'We've found possible human remains.'

FORTY THREE

The Contract Killer

Marilyn Eagle sat on the edge of the bed that she had shared with her husband for thirty eight years. She had stood by and endured the worse of it all, the years he was in Serbia, Iraq and then later in Afghanistan. He said he was getting too old for it all. But it wasn't the combat he was fed up with; it was the sitting, waiting for hours on end in the dry heat or the dry cold, until the assigned target was to appear. It was also the fact he missed his best friend, his wife, who always waited eagerly for him to return.

Marilyn noticed a spot of blood on her shoe and found a tissue to wipe it off. It had been a long day and she was exhausted. Even though she had achieved everything she set out to do, it still didn't quite fill the gaping hole within her soul. He was dead, and no amount of revenge would change that.

She was quite a catch when they met. Completely above his class, and 8 years older, but she liked to rebel against her father's wishes, and Ken was only too happy to comply. He left the SAS at the ripe old age of 49 and got a job selling insurance. They viewed it as just a fill-in career until he retired at 65. But Marilyn could see the fire dying in his eyes. He missed the excitement and travel, and when the opportunity came calling one day, she thought that this was exactly what Ken needed.

After years of moonlighting as a very successful hitman, he got hit himself. Marilyn never saw this coming. They were always careful about everything; who they took on as clients - many they turned down - staying completely anonymous, and never creating a paper trail. But they messed up. There was something they overlooked and they were paying a steep price.

He was dead. The awful memory of the phone call from the surgeon who removed the bullet, circled torturously in her mind. The confusion in his voice said it all. Ken was in ICU and improving by the hour. He came out of the coma, was talking and could sit up, although walking was difficult. Then overnight, he died in his sleep. His potassium levels were exceedingly high and the hospital authorities had begun an investigation into his death, as had the police, into his shooting. This was not good news for Marilyn. This merely shone a bright light onto his alternative career.

He was believed to have been shot with a Glock 17. Ken told Marilyn, when the ICU staff were distracted in a conversation about the All Blacks, that he was hoodwinked. There was a second man there, and it was that man who shot him. 'They duped the duper,' he joked.

Marilyn didn't think it was a laughing matter. 'Did you get a look at him?' she asked softly, suppressing the fury that was rising in her chest.

He shook his head. 'He came from behind and it was dark. Durie must have caught on that the meeting was going to be a hit.'

'Do you think that woman had something to do with it?' she asked, bitterly.

'No. She wanted him dead. She paid the deposit.' He closed his eyes and turned away from her. 'I messed up. I messed up big time.'

'No!' she barked, the nurses turning to see what she was snapping at him about. 'This was not your fault.' She breathed out her tension, saying, 'Let me fix this.' She rose from her chair, kissed him on the cheek, and left.

And now Birdie was dead, and someone has to pay. After the conversation she had with Alice Granger at the lagoon, she came to the conclusion that Alice wasn't involved in her husband's shooting, but she was frightened. Durie had her by the balls, so to speak. But that's Alice's problem. Marilyn's problem right now was to find where Brendon Durie was, and kill him. If her beloved husband is dead, then Durie doesn't deserve to live.

Her small schnauzer, Misty, trotted into the bedroom as if she knew her mistress was sad. She jumped up onto the bed and nuzzled her hand, then nestled down onto her lap.

The exhaustion weighed upon her like a storm cloud. She looked at the clock on the wall. 1.17 am. It was a job well done.

She had gone to Brendon Durie's house yesterday morning, just as a cop was leaving with a young blonde in handcuffs. The girl would be no older than 18, Durie's taste no doubt. But where was Brendon Durie? She got out of the car, ran to the house and peered through the window. The house seemed empty, no movement and no sound. She raced back to her car, searching the road for the police car. She assumed it would be on its way to the station. Instead, she found it heading in the opposite direction, to the industrial side of town, where the loading docks are.

This had just got interesting.

The cop pulled up outside an abandoned warehouse, climbed out of the car, unlocked then dragged up the garage door. He then drove inside and pulled the door back down.

She waited impatiently for thirty minutes down the road. It bothered her that this cop was inside with that girl. Was it a fake arrest, just so he could have his way with her? Then it occurred to her: was this the second man involved in her husband's shooting? If so, then Brendon Durie had someone working on the inside this whole time. 'Genius!' she said, shaking her head.

Marilyn then caught sight of the blonde girl, still cuffed, running out of the warehouse and onto the building site next door. 'Good, she's escaped. Now, let's focus on the cop.'

He still hadn't come out, but Marilyn thought this was a good opportunity to pay him a visit. She could play dumb. She was good at that. She could pretend that she saw the handcuffed girl run out of the warehouse, and just wanted to check that there were no casualties. Not that the girl looked like she could hurt a fly, handcuffed or not.

Leaving her car parked down the road, she ran across the road to the warehouse. The windows had been blacked out with paint, so she couldn't see in, which pricked her suspicions. Inside was the echoing sound of a coughing engine, a car having trouble starting. It wasn't the cop car, she knew that much.

Marilyn ran around to the back of the warehouse, where she had seen the girl emerge from. The door was open, and she peered cautiously inside the large spacious building. The police car was inside towards the front of the building; the second car was next to it, a black sedan. It was low to the ground, one of those stylised cars with mag wheels that hooligans like to drive. She watched as the cop clicked the hood open, getting out of the car to check the engine. He was looking panicked, probably desperate to get away before the blonde escapee dobbed him in.

What caught her attention though, was the large zoo cage to her right, with a naked woman hanging upside-down inside it, her hair and hands sweeping the ground as she slowly swung. She was facing away, either unconscious or dead. The fat cop ignored the swinging woman, which angered Marilyn even more. She had no choice. She had to take action.

She ran back to her car and drove it up to the side of the building, took Ken's assault weapon – an AK47, out of the boot of the car along with a gym bag of essentials, and strolled casually in.

Marilyn dropped the gym bag loudly onto the concrete floor to grab his attention, and then called out, 'Pardon me,' pointing the weapon at the cop. 'I think we need to have a little chat.'

The expression on his face was a mix of puzzlement and fear. A posh sixty year old wearing a soft pink track-suit, and holding an AK47 in her white gloved hands, doesn't happen every day, even in his line of work.

As she drew closer to him, she quickly inspected the hanging woman. Her skin was shiny, flawless like plastic. She *was* plastic, a mannequin. Moving on.

'Where is Brendon Durie?' she asked, pointing the rifle at his head.

He cringed. 'Have you worked one of those before?'

'No. But there's a first for everything. Luckily for me you're a wide target. Now, where is Brendon Durie?'

He remained silent. She aimed for his shoulder and pulled the trigger, but the bullet missed and hit the warehouse garage door, making a hell of a sound.

'Whoa!' she cried in delight. 'That felt great! Again I ask you, where is Brendon Durie?'

Kerryn was trembling now, but still he remained silent.

'Did you kill my husband?' she asked.

He shrugged.

'My husband was a hitman, hired to kill Brendon Durie. The hit was to take place at the lake. Were you there?'

The expression of realisation on the cop's face said it all.

'I think we need to take a little drive,' she said, taking a step towards him.

'He's in Woodville,' he suddenly admitted.

'And you killed my husband?'

'I was...it was Brendon.'

'I know all about Brendon Durie. Get this car started. We're going to pay him a visit.'

FORTY FOUR

The Contract Killer

Kerryn, under pressure because of a loaded weapon pointed at his face, managed to get the black sedan humming. Directed by Marilyn from the back seat, they began their journey to Woodville. She had already checked the glove box and the boot for weapons, finding only a handgun. Her husband taught her well. *Keep yourself safe first. Always!*

'Is this a Glock 17?' Marilyn asked, holding the handgun in her gloved hand, while the rifle lay across her lap.

'Yes. Standard police issue,' he said, swallowing a lump in his throat. 'How did you know that?'

'It's the weapon that killed my husband. It's also the weapon that will kill Brendon Durie.'

'What do you mean?' he asked.

'Keep driving.' She had had it all planned out in her head from the start, but life can throw curve balls, and stumbling across Kerryn Gillespie was one of them.

The journey to Woodville was mostly silent, apart from when Marilyn decided to tell Kerryn about how she met her husband, knowing that he won't survive to tell anyone else about it. Once they got to the edge of Woodville Township, which was in the middle of nowhere with nothing but paddocks for miles, she told him to drive down a back road. She then pulled out a refill pad, and told him to write his suicide note.

'Don't fret. It's just a back-up plan in case you try to do a runner, and I have to shoot you. I have no intention of killing you, don't worry,' she lied.

He took the pen in his shaking hand, and she told him what to write. Then she told him to fold it up neatly and place it in the glove box. He reluctantly did as he was told.

'What were you planning on doing to the girl?' Marilyn asked.

'Nothing,' he said. Marilyn dug the point of the Glock into the back of his neck. 'Alright! I was waiting for instruction from Brendon,' he yelled.

'Is he your boss, or something?'

'Sort of.'

'A side line business is it? Torturing women?'

'I never do any of that. It's Brendon. He has unusual tastes.'

'Is that what you call it? Unusual tastes?' Alice Granger wanted him dead for that very reason. Marilyn wanted him dead for an entirely different reason. *Two birds with one stone*, as they say. 'Why is he in Woodville?'

'Because of a girl, his ex.'

'Revenge, or a happy reunion?'

'Revenge,' he said.

'It looks like we're going to quash his plans. What's her name?'

'Sian Tanner.'

'Where does she live?'

'I don't know the exact address.'

Marilyn then held the Glock to Kerryn's head and pulled the trigger. It was swift and there was quite a bit of blood. She had no use for him anymore. Quite frankly, he was exceedingly annoying and he desperately needed a shower, especially now. She was surprised at how little that hurt her. She felt nothing. Perhaps it's because she had nothing to lose, and nothing left in her life to live for. She let out a squawk of laughter and surprised herself with its volume and intensity. Then she calmed down and thought about her next plan of action. It was to find Brendon Durie.

No! Ken's voice came into her mind. *First, get yourself cleaned up.*

She looked down at the blood splatters covering her soft pink tracksuit. 'Oh! Yes, of course.'

Her gym bag, also soft pink, was sitting on the seat next to her. Inside was every possible thing she could think of. Two changes of clothes, matches, lighter fluid, bottle of vodka for cleaning purposes and mental health assistance, her cell phone - the homepage is a pic of Ken holding Misty the dog - her two most favourite people in the world - a black balaclava, and her shocking pink handbag that contained all her credit cards, ID etc. It was a tad heavier than she had planned, but she cannot complete the task unprepared.

Marilyn dragged another tracksuit from the gym bag, this time a white one, and another pair of gloves. She covered the bloodied pink tracksuit and gloves with lighter fluid and set them alight, then tossed them into the ditch. She waited until it had completely disintegrated before running around to the driver's side, where fat Kerryn the cop sat with his head blown apart. Then she unbuckled Kerryn's belt and using her feet pushed him over to the passenger seat. That was not easy, and she realised that she should've kept her pink tracksuit on, because she has now bloodied up the clean one.

Marilyn sat down in the driver's seat and went online on her phone to find photographs of Brendon Durie back in his rugby playing days, and now in his role as CEO of Hillocks, a large dairy company.

'Handsome enough,' she muttered as a car flew past. The first car she had seen in miles. She started up the engine and took one more look at Kerryn slouched over in the passenger seat. 'You can't stay like that, you'll scare everyone,' she said to the dead body.

Then he beeped. A cell phone sound. She reached into his bloody pocket and dragged it out. A message from BD that read, *I watched her from afar for too long. Today's the day. I am in her house.*

Marilyn wondered if she should call the police. The image of the mannequin hanging in the cage haunted her. *Did he do that to her?*

She scrolled through previous messages. Many messages were Kerryn asking for instruction and Brendon giving it. Payment for various exercises was discussed as well. The latest message from Kerryn read that he had pushed the bitch down the well, and what should he do with Britney? There was no reply. Brendon was probably far too busy stalking Sian Tanner. *Creep.*

Then she read the conversation between the cop and Brendon about the Granger woman. Brendon had a hunch that the meeting with Alice was a set-up. He knew her history. He knew she liked to hire hitmen, and he wouldn't be surprised if the same was planned for him. He was asking Kerryn to back him up and be prepared to take a shot if needed. Kerryn agreed. Deal done, Birdie is dead.

Rage reared its ugly head again. *Focus*, she heard Ken's voice in her mind. *Focus on the task at hand.*

Last house, at the end of Tucker's Road, Woodville. A message sent from Kerryn to Brendon, two days' before the conversation about Alice Granger. 'Got you!' she smiled.

She text back Brendon, *Have fun.* 'Dead man!' Then found Tucker's Road on online maps. With adrenaline pumping through her veins, she sped off down the road towards Woodville Township. Going by the map, Sian Tanner's house was on the other side near the Manawatu River. But because her passenger was a mess, she had to avoid any prying eyes, which meant avoiding driving through the town. If Ken was here he'd hide the cop's body in the boot, but she didn't have the strength for that.

In her roundabout way, she managed to get to Tucker's Road and drove slowly and inconspicuously down it. It was an unsealed, rural road with only three houses on it. It was now early afternoon. The sun was shining and the sky blue. Children will be at school and adults will be at work. What are the chances that she'll be seen? Slim to none.

The road was long and straight, and at the very end she could see the dark greenery of a forest that stretched for miles along the flat, and then over a hill in the distance. As she drew closer to the forest, she felt an icy shiver run down her back. It was the first time since she began this journey that she had felt a little apprehensive. She wasn't afraid to die. That wasn't it. It was something else.

Marilyn came to the last house at the end of the road, grabbed the Glock 17 with the cop's fingerprints all over it, and slid it into her pink handbag. She got out of the car and knocked on Sian Tanner's front door. There was someone moving inside, she just hoped like heck it wasn't Sian Tanner.

After waiting a few seconds, she went around to the back of the house hoping to find another door, and as luck would have it, the back door was wide open. As she stepped boldly inside the house, a tall, handsome man stood in the kitchen holding a knife.

'Brendon Durie?' she asked, pulling the Glock 17 from her handbag and pointing it at him.

FORTY FIVE

The Contract Killer

S till holding the knife in one hand, Brendon raised his hands into the air; his expression was a mix of amusement and pleasure. 'You've got the wrong person. But I'd love to play a game with you. You look like my type of woman.'

'My name is Marilyn Eagle, the wife of Ken Eagle, also known as Birdie.'

He licked his lips and shrugged. Those names meant nothing to him and why would they?

'You killed my husband.'

'I don't kill people.' That was an honest statement. He doesn't kill people; he only tortures them, and if he wants someone dead he gets his sidekick to kill them. 'Why don't you put that gun down, Marilyn?'

She stepped towards him as he stepped back. They did this dance several more times. He was getting aroused, and that made her sick to her stomach.

'Where's the girl?' she asked, then heard Ken's voice in her head. *You're taking too long. Do it! Shoot and run! Shoot and run!* She was about to pull the trigger when he lunged at her. The Glock dropped to the floor with a thud. He grabbed her by the hair and bent her over the table. The bedroom door upstairs slammed shut. They were not alone. Brendon became distracted. He thought he had seen someone run out of the house, after he had let himself in and was making himself at home in the living room. The back door was unlocked, Sian Tanner had become careless. Didn't he teach her anything? Footsteps ran across the floor upstairs. He grinned. She was still there ready for the picking.

When he turned back, Marilyn had the gun in her hand again and was standing in the living room. He rolled his eyes. 'You don't have the guts,' he said.

'Heard from the cop lately?'

He laughed. The old lady was messing with him.

She pulled the trigger and the bullet hit the kitchen cupboard. He turned and ran towards the back door. She fired three more shots, two of them striking him in the back. He fell to the floor and lay still.

LEAVE! Ken yelled in her mind.

The rest was a blur. Marilyn sped away, stopping at a secluded roadside to cover the dead cop with her tracksuit jacket. Then she drove in the direction of Wellington, finding a location that was both within walking distance of a small town, but isolated enough so the cop wouldn't be found for a while. This was helped by the fact that she had driven the car into a ditch, so it wasn't easily seen from the road. Not only that, the car looked stolen and abandoned. That type of car often got swiped, only to be found again several miles away, without the tyres and radio. So it was no surprise to her when he was found, two days after she dumped him there.

So Marilyn Eagle, wife of contract killer Ken Eagle, walked to the small town carrying her soft pink gym bag. She was offered rides by passersby, but she wasn't in the mood to chat to strangers. She had done her homework on the car, cleaning up any sign of evidence that she had been in it, as well as moving the fat cop back into the driver's seat and placing the gun in his limp hand, leaving the suicide note on the passenger seat. While she was looking through the glove box, she had found a plane ticket to Hong Kong and that only played into her plans.

FORTY SIX

One Month Later

Sian placed her bag of clothes on the sofa and looked around her home. The place felt different. There had been a number of people coming and going over the past four weeks and perhaps that was what she was sensing.

While she was staying with Rosie and Nathan, she had decided that she would do up Mayfields and sell it. It came with a decent acreage, enough for someone to extend the house and set up a hobby farm. Or perhaps a property investor would be interested in building three or four new homes on the land, since many people are moving out of the cities. She will miss the house, though. She will miss Aunt May's memory and McCrae's Forest, the haunting bird calls, the rustling of leaves and the mysteries buried within.

The place by the back door where Brendon Durie's body had lain, showed no signs that someone had died there, least of all her enemy. The blood splatters had been cleaned up, but the bullet holes remained. The bullet holes were proof that he was dead, proof that he will never hurt her again. She felt a weight of fear rise from her. For the first time in years she breathed out and relaxed. Everything was going to be okay from now onwards. From now onwards no-one can hurt her ever again.

Upstairs, the bedroom floor and bed had stray leaves and bugs scattered about, blown in through the open window. Nothing had changed here. It still felt like Aunt May's bedroom, not hers.

She felt a crackling of glass beneath her shoes. The moving photograph had fallen off the wall, the glass frame had shattered. She picked up the photograph. It was empty. The old couple that Sian assumed was May's parents had vanished, as had the young man. All that remained was the studio background that was there in the very beginning, before the background changed to forest and Ben Stokes emerged from the shadows.

Sian placed the photograph on the bed, a debate going on in her mind. *Did that really happen?* She had to admit that she was a bit of an emotional mess when she had come here to hide. Perhaps what she witnessed in this photograph was nothing but her mind and eyes playing tricks. It's quite possible. High stress does strange things to one's senses.

During her time away from her house, Sian visited her therapist in prison. Alice was still awaiting trial for hiring a hitman to kill a man called Damon Ridge. There was apparently footage of the hitman doing the job, with Alice Granger watching on. The hit man was never found and Alice said that she only knew him by his alias, Birdie. The trail went dead. Sian never knew Damon Ridge, but going by what she was told, the world is better off without him.

As to be expected, the Durie Family were up in arms over Brendon's death, and were devastated that the person who took his life didn't suffer for it. Of course in their eyes, Brendon Durie was a fine upstanding citizen who didn't deserved to be murdered, especially by some jealous cop. Strangely, none of his family knew that he had still kept in touch with Gillespie. They thought Brendon had outgrown that loser years ago.

'Hello!' a man called out, knocking on the open front door.

Sian ran down the stairs to greet Sergeant Lee from the Woodville Police Department. He had in his hands a basket loaded with food; homemade preserves, cheese scones, breads, cake and slices, and elderberry cordial.

'A gift from some of the locals, to welcome you home,' he said, placing the basket on the dining table.

Sian was chuffed. A stray tear ran down her cheek. She didn't think anyone really cared. In fact after the shooting, when life went on and Sian went back to work at the library, she had felt people were judging her, perhaps accusing her, even after Kerryn Gillespie's confession note. So this was a lovely surprise.

Lee said, 'So I thought I'd also update you on the bones found in the forest, since you were doing your own little investigation.'

Sian held her breath. The bones had been on the back of her mind throughout the entire ordeal that had taken place at her house. She was dying to go into McCrae's forest to take a look, but was warned against it. It's been the one thing keeping her overactive mind busy. The one thing she owed Benny Sorenson.

'The bones are definitely human, an adolescent male. The time of death fits in with Ben Stokes' disappearance.'

Sian couldn't hold her breath any longer, she breathed out in a gush.

Lee continued, 'Sergeant Ratahi said that a friend told you where the grave was.'

'Benny Sorenson.'

He raised his eyebrows. 'What, from the dead?'

'No. I vaguely remember, back when we were kids, Benny talking about Ben Stokes' grave. He took me there once. It took me some time to find it again. But the yellow ribbon hanging from the branch was the giveaway.'

'Yeah, Ratahi pointed that out.'

'Could Forensics tell how Ben Stokes died?' Sian asked.

'He died from a fractured skull, by a blunt object. They suspect the head of a spade or shovel.'

'Could it have been an accident?'

'Not likely. How did Benny Sorenson know there was a body in there?'

The burning question! Sian swallowed hard. 'Benny said he saw the murderer a couple of times. He said the person wore a green raincoat, and kept the hood over their head so he couldn't see their face. He said they wore gumboots too, the Redline brand. He said he saw the hooded person at the grave apologising for shortening Ben's life.'

Lee was listening intensely. 'How long ago are we talking?'

Sian paused, taking her mind back. 'I guess we were eleven or twelve. So fifteen or sixteen years ago.'

Lee dropped his eyes to the floor, analysing the information. Then he said, 'It was his father who was head of police here then. Then of course, he was stood down after Benny died because he began drinking too much. I think he was devastated by his death, felt responsible for it.'

'Sam Sorenson said Benny died because his father smashed him over the head.'

Lee rolled his eyes. 'I'd take what Sam Sorenson says with a grain of salt. His death was an accident, plain and simple.' Then his eyes flickered about the room as a sudden thought occurred to him. 'So did Benny Sorenson say whether it was a male or female that visited the grave?'

'No. Like I said, their head was covered.'

'But he said he heard them speak?'

'Yeah.' Sian realising where he was heading.

'I wonder if Benny did know who it was, but was too afraid to say.'

'I wonder.' Sian tried to go back in her mind to that day when they visited the grave. She tried to read young Benny's face. Was he covering something up? Did he know the truth but was too scared to say? Did it have something to do with his father?

Interrupting Sian's train of thought, Sergeant Lee said, 'There was another thing. His body was clothed. There are still fragments of the fabrics. But there were particles of a fabric that didn't fit with a sixteen year old boy's choice of clothing.'

'What was that?' Sian asked.

'A woman's white lace handkerchief. Not the type of article a boy would have in his possession when he went out fishing or duck shooting. That's why I was asking whether the Sorenson boy could tell if it was a male or female.'

The walls suddenly closed in on Sian. She could feel her cheeks burning as a trickle of sweat ran down the back of her neck. The lace handkerchief, the green raincoat, the yellow ribbon. Benny boy wasn't scared for himself, he was scared for Sian. He knew all along who had stood at the shallow grave and apologised. He knew whose voice cried out in the forest, and whose green raincoat covered their head in shame. He knew who the murderer was from the moment he saw her standing there under the yellow ribbon tied to the branch of the totara tree. Sian can only assume now that the reason Benny Sorensen suddenly wanted nothing more to do with her and told her never to come back to Woodville, had nothing to do with his hormones or his sudden dislike of girls. It was because the murderer had found him out. This compromised Sian's safety more than ever.

'Are you alright?' Sergeant Lee asked.

She nodded. 'I'm fine. I just need some time to settle back in.'

'Okay. I'll leave you to it.'

FORTY SEVEN

As soon as Sergeant Lee left, Sian raced upstairs. The white lace handkerchief lay on the floor amongst stray leaves and broken glass. She stepped over the glass and flung the wardrobe door open. The green raincoat hung there like the shell of a body. The raincoat she saw every day when she reached in there to drag out her own clothes. Even when Benny Sorenson mentioned the green raincoat and Redline gumboots back when they were kids, it hadn't dawned on her the death of Ben Stokes had anything to do with her aunt.

She inspected the pockets of the raincoat and found bits of garden twine, dirt and dried grass. She got down on her hands and knees and pulled out the shoe boxes containing remnants of fabric and sewing articles. Inside one of the boxes were the ribbons, but no yellow. That's because the yellow ribbon was in the drawer wrapped in a red, woollen scarf. She pulled open the drawer and picked up the reel of yellow ribbon. It was hard to tell if it was the exact same yellow, as the ribbon in the totara tree had faded over the years. But still, it was another piece of evidence against her Great Aunt.

Sian sat on the bed and reflected on the conversations she'd had with both Mavis and Fred. Then she thought about the children's book May wrote, The Boy in the Woods. She ran downstairs and found it on top of a stack of books.

The story was of a boy who was stuck in the woods, but couldn't leave unless someone said the magic words. She paused and gazed up at the fly-spotted ceiling. 'I wonder what the magic words were?'

She read on, the consequence of staying in the forest was that he never aged. He became friends with children, in particular a little boy called James, who grew up before his eyes. Eventually James grew out of playing with the little boy, and moved on to adult things. Then one day he met another little child, a girl called Daisy, who somehow figured out the magic words so he could leave the forest. He grew up like everyone else, which he didn't mind, got a job, married and had a family. It was when he became old and crippled with arthritis, that he returned to the forest to become young again, only for the forest to turn him away. He died that day and was buried under fallen leaves and twigs.

'Just like Ben Stokes,' Sian said out loud. She threw the book back down. 'This story is crap! Why didn't you write what the magic words were?'

Feeling frustrated, she went to the laundry to grab the dust pan and shovel to clean up the broken glass upstairs. Sitting at the door were Great Aunt May's Redline gumboots, a brand so common in New Zealand it's not even worth mentioning them as evidence. She found the dust pan, ran back up stairs, and began to clean up the mess. As she crouched down a gush of wind blew through the open window, and the photograph fell to the floor.

She glanced at it. It had changed.

In the photograph were two young people, teenagers, holding hands like young lovers. The boy she recognised as Ben Stokes, and next to him a fresh faced girl, as happy as can be, her Great Aunt May.

FORTY EIGHT

No matter how hard Sian tried, she just couldn't get to the bottom of it all. She had come to the conclusion that her Great Aunt May had killed Ben Stokes, she just didn't know why. What did that boy do that was so awful that a teenage girl smacked him over the head with a spade? It had to have been an accident; there was no other reason for it.

She asked Mavis and Fred more questions about May's relationships and whether she was involved romantically with Ben Stokes. Fred said he had no idea, but if they were living across the road from each other, it's possible they may have been involved. Mavis said she had arrived to the area later and never knew Ben Stokes, so she wasn't much use.

She did think there was one more person she could ask. The very last person on the entire planet Sian wanted to speak to. But her line of enquiry had dried up. She had no choice.

She punched her mother's number into her new cell. It rang five times, before a distant weak voice answered the phone.

'Mum! It's me, Sian.'

'Yes, I know who you are, you don't need to shout. I have a terrible migraine.'

So what else is new? 'I was wondering that maybe you'd like to come down for a visit?'

'Oh! I don't think so. It's a four hour drive. I couldn't bear it.'

'Okay, how about I come and visit you?.'

Her mother paused. 'What is this about? Why don't you just tell me now why you want to speak to me?'

'You're my mother-'

'Don't give me that bull-crap. You never cared before.'

That's so untrue! I always cared. I was always there for you. You just didn't like it when I had to put myself first for a change because of that pig Brendon Durie, who you wanted me to stay with, even when I told you what he was doing to me.

'Who is Great Aunt May?'Sian asked, after a long, angry pause.

Her mother stuttered and stumbled on her words. 'Well...we never found out, exactly.'

'If you don't tell me the truth, I will come down there, break into your house to turn all the lights on, turn up the music and be generally a nuisance until you do.'

'Don't be ridiculous,' Bev said.

'Your first given name was Daisy, wasn't it? Like the girl in Aunt May's book, who knew the magic words to release the boy from the forest?'

The line went dead.

'Hello? Mum, it's time you told me the truth.'

'Alright! God my head hurts.' She sighed again. 'Great Aunt May is my biological mother.'

Snap! Sian always wondered. Bev was always so vague about May, yet she didn't mind Sian spending summers at her house. So she must've trusted her. Also Sian and May were so close, like grandchildren are with their grandparents. This did not surprise her.

'When did you find out?'

'When you were about four years old. She found me and wanted to be part of our lives. I was hesitant at first, and then when your grandparents died when you were six, I thought I'd give it a trial.'

She chuckled. 'You two became instant friends. Do you remember meeting May?'

'Yes. I took to her like a duck in water. She was quirky and wonderfully eccentric.'

'Everything that I wasn't,' Bev said bitterly. 'Of course the migraines hampered me, so sending you to May's place was good for all of us. Your brother didn't like it there much. But he's from different stock. He's more like your father.'

'Who was *your* father?'

She spoke, but her voice was so weak, Sian could barely hear. 'Sorry?'

'I asked May once, and only once. She said it was the boy who disappeared,' she said, forcefully.

'Ben Stokes?'

'Yes, I guess.' She breathed out as if a massive weight of shame had rolled off her back. 'They were very young. May was sent away to a Girl's Home to have me and I was put up for adoption. No-one knew a thing.'

'They could have only been fifteen or sixteen.'

'Accidents happen. But back then people were prouder. Incidences like that would've been brushed under the rug, and never spoken of again.'

'You sound unsure,' Sian said, picking up the doubt in her mother's voice.

'I am unsure. May loved that boy, without a doubt. But I don't think it was him who got her pregnant. I have no proof, of course.'

'So why say it?'

'I just remember that she had been preparing for the question, knew it was coming, and had rehearsed the answer. She wanted Ben Stokes to be my father, but I don't think he was. They were so young.'

'You think she was raped?'

'I don't know. It's so long ago I don't think you'll ever find out.'

'So who killed Ben Stokes, then?'

'Who killed him?' her voice sounding horrified. 'He disappeared.'

'No. His bones were found recently, buried in the forest. His skull had blunt force trauma to it. Someone killed him.'

The line went dead again. 'My father?'

It just occurred to Sian why her mother has been so weak for so long. Her adoptive parents were hard working people who didn't know how to show affection, or saw little point in it. The only time young Bev got any attention from her mother was when she was ill. The habit grew into a lifestyle.

'Of course I wouldn't know that,' she snapped. 'If you ask me, it was probably the person who got her pregnant, or his father.'

FORTY NINE

Sian sat next to Benny Sorenson's grave in the small Woodville cemetery. His headstone read that he loved life and will be missed by his brothers, sisters, mother and father. This was the first time she had visited Benny since she'd returned to Woodville, and thought it was time to ease that pang of guilt that stayed with her wherever she went.

She had much to update him on - that the likelihood that Aunt May did kill Ben was minimal to none. She explained to him that he was right. It was Aunt May who stood crying over the grave of her boyfriend Ben, but there's no way that it was she who killed him. When Benny Sorenson heard her say that she's sorry to shorten his life, it may have been because she told someone about being pregnant, and maybe that person killed Ben Stokes.

That didn't quite explain why Benny angrily told Sian never to return to Woodville, when they were fourteen. Perhaps at that point Benny did have a drinking problem like his father, and Sian's rose coloured glasses were too thick to see the truth. She did notice that he was changing as they grew older, but then so was she.

Due to insistence from the Woodville community on the discovery of Ben Stokes' murdered body, a private investigator had been hired by both the Woodville and Wellington Police Departments to find out who killed him. So far it's leaning towards Ben Stokes' father, amplified by the fact that Fred Anderson said all along that there was something weird about him. But both Mr and Mrs Stokes were long since dead, and so it looked like no-one was going to pay for the crime.

The PI also asked Sian and Bev to give DNA samples to see if they were a match to samples taken from Ben Stokes' bones. Bev refused unsurprisingly, but Sian's results came back a strong likelihood that they were related. Sian was at first ecstatic, until the thought occurred to her that Ben's father could also be the one who got May pregnant.

That, they may never know.

FIFTY

The Contract Killer

Marilyn laid the AK47 across her lap. It has been three painfully awful months since Ken had died, and the thought of living a day longer in an empty house filled with all those memories only made her morose. Ken Eagle was not only her husband, but he was also her best friend. When she came home that day from shooting both the fat cop and the woman-beater, she felt completely at a loss. It had been an exceedingly long day and she was terribly exhausted. The automatic reaction was to tell Ken all about it, but when she came home to a deadly silent, cold house she felt depressed, and if it wasn't for Misty she would've ended her life then and there.

She had no-one to discuss her marvellous achievements with. The fact that she planned it all out... well...the plan changed a few times through the day, but still. She devised the suicide brilliantly, and then to make it look like the fat cop killed the woman-beater too. She's a complete genius! A marvel! Ken's alternative career was their delicious little secret. She'd accomplished much in one day and she knew that he would be as proud as punch.

But he's not here. His side of the bed is empty and cold. The old, worn armchair that Marilyn had threatened for years to donate to the Salvation Army, sat soulless in the corner of the living room, his bum imprint still in the cushion, and black marks on the fabric from newspaper print that rubbed off his hands.

She couldn't possibly live another day without him by her side. She left Misty in the good care of her neighbours with her favourite toy, and bag of treats. Today was the day. She raised the rifle to point under her chin. It was awkward, but as she was about to pull the trigger a chime sounded out. It was a sound she had not heard in weeks. Birdie's cell phone. She found it in his jacket pocket in the wardrobe.

She opened the text, it read, *I need someone gone. I was given your number.*

Who?

Mack Durie. I'm prepared to pay top price.

'Another Durie,' she said, then Googled his name into her cell. A ton of information came up of him being a well-known sports commentator, used to play rugby for Waikato, blah, blah, blah...oh and he used to beat his wife, pushed her down the stairs and then paid gag money to shut her up.

A surge of adrenaline travelled through Marilyn's blood, her heart pumped faster, and her skin prickled at the thought of doing it again. She tossed it over a few times in her mind, whispered 'I'm sorry,' to Ken, and then replied with, *I'll do it.*

GLOSSARY

Totara, Pohutakawa, Rata, Kauri, Kowhai, Kawakawa, Manuka, Kanuka - Trees and shrubs native to New Zealand. They're an ancient variety that do not shed leaves and are either a female or male.

Tuatara - Reptile native to New Zealand. Believed to be the last living dinosaur, and is extremely endangered.

Silvereye - also called Wax-eye or White-eye. Very small nectar drinking bird. Native to New Zealand

Weta - large prehistoric-looking insect, with sharp pincers. Some species grow to be the heaviest in the world. They are basically large, flightless crickets.

Gumboots - rubber boots for wearing outdoors. Also called Wellingtons.

Morepork - small owl, native to New Zealand

Tui - seemingly black, although in the light you can see it is multi coloured, with white tufts of feathers at the throat. In the honeyeater family of birds native to New Zealand and have one of the most diverse singing voices. They are native and fairly common in New Zealand.

Bellbird - olive green in colour, and a little larger than a sparrow. Their song is similar to the tui, except less diverse. They are also nectar drinkers or honeyeaters.

Fantail - bird the size of a finch, with a large fanned out tail. Very friendly, and native to New Zealand.

Shining cuckoo - cuckoo that flies all the way to New Zealand from the Solomon Islands to lay its eggs in the grey warbler's nest. The call can be heard at the beginning of October, signalling springtime.

Grey Warbler - a tiny, grey bird with a huge singing voice.

Taniwha - monster in Maori mythology that lives in deep pools in rivers, in dark caves or in the sea, especially in places where there are dangerous currents or deceptive breakers.

Maori - native people of New Zealand, believed to have travelled from Hawaii.

Kiwi - flightless bird with long, curved beak. A distinctive feature being that its nostrils are at the end of its beak to sniff out worms in the earth. Usually comes in various shades of brown and is endangered, but due to conservation efforts their numbers are steadily growing.

Printed in Great Britain
by Amazon